A REASON TO BELIEVE

A REASON TO LOVE SERIES: BOOK 2

T.K. CHAPIN

Branch Publishing

To claim a FREE Christian Romance visit offer.tkchapin.com

Version: 12.12.2018

ISBN: 9781791599256

Dedicated to my loving wife.
For all the years she has put up with me
And many more to come.

CONTENTS

NOTE FROM THE AUTHOR

God so *loved* the world . . . five words that most, if not all, Christians know by heart. It's simple, yet so complex. I don't believe I'll ever fully understand the unsearchable and unfathomable depths of God's love, but I am thankful for His love nonetheless. This new series, *A Reason To Love*, is a series that focuses on God's love moving through us and unto others. Often, our most difficult times in life are the times God uses to mold and shape us, to make us something new. I know in my own life, I've never enjoyed the difficult times, but I would never trade the growth that came from them. The times when we feel we are being bathed in fire, I believe, are a refinement process the Lord is putting each of us through. He doesn't make bad things happen, but He can and does use them for our own good and His glory.

In this second book, *A Reason To Believe*, we follow the story of Tyler and Olivia. Tyler is a solid man of faith who devotes himself to God in a lot of ways, but he still has a lot to learn. Olivia grew up in the church but never came to the saving knowledge of Jesus Christ. She's a gal with a sketchy past and a longing for someone to truly love her. Tyler's a man whose ideal type of woman he wanted to marry was never someone like Olivia. Can these two find love in each other's arms? Or are they better off apart?

I pray this inspirational Christian romance inspires your faith, warms your soul, and fills you with the hope that is only found in the death, burial, and resurrection of our Lord Jesus Christ. May this story bless you in reading it as much as it has blessed me in writing it.

Sincerely,
    T.K. Chapin

CHAPTER 1

*T*HE SUN WARMED OLIVIA'S CHEEKS as she stood in the garden. She cupped a hand over her eyes to shield the sunlight and to catch a glance at the car driving up the driveway toward her and her husband Bruce's home. It was a blue sedan and she didn't recognize the vehicle. A plume of dust followed the car as it came around the final curve of the dirt road. Close enough to see into the windshield now, she spotted a young blonde woman behind the steering wheel. She didn't recognize her. As the car came the last few feet, Olivia could make out the expression on the woman's face. It wasn't good.

Removing her gardening gloves, Olivia tossed them into the wheelbarrow and headed out of the garden to go meet the stranger. It was high noon and Bruce wouldn't be home for another eight hours. Her pulse climbed and her stomach whooshed as her whole body felt uneasy about her unexpected visitor.

The car came to a stop not more than a few feet from Olivia. The woman jerked the car door open and got out, slamming it behind her. Olivia flinched.

"Are you Mrs. Montgomery?"

"Yes." The stranger knew who she was, but Olivia got the sinking feeling that wasn't a good thing. "Can I help you?"

The woman removed her large oval dark-lensed sunglasses and let out a relieved sigh. Folding the sunglasses, she slipped them into her purse and came the rest of the way over to Olivia. The stranger shook her head in pity, tilting it as she raked a hand through her full-bodied blonde hair. "I'm Lisa—Bruce's girlfriend."

Olivia froze. Disbelief clouded her mind, and she took a step back.

"What?"

"I've been seeing your husband for five years, ma'am."

Olivia shook her head, not able to believe what the woman was saying to her. "No. I don't believe you. You have the wrong man."

"Oh, yeah? He has a little brown mole on his inner left thigh."

Clasping a hand over her mouth, Olivia fought back tears as she gasped. "How could he do this again? How could he do this to me?" She was thinking out loud, ignoring the fact that Lisa was still there. "He barely has enough time for dinner . . ."

The woman walked over to Olivia's rose bushes sticking out from the garden and let her fingers glide across the tops of the red petals. She glanced back at Olivia. "He finds time for what he wants to do."

Heat from her anger started to well up in Olivia, not just toward Bruce but this tramp. "What's the point of telling me all this? And who are you?"

Lisa paused and then turned and came back over to Olivia. "Bruce is too scared to tell you. He fears you'll hit him over the head with one of your cast-iron skillets or something."

2

Olivia would like to do a lot more than that right now. Tears pushed through and she wiped them. "Who are you?"

"I already told you. I'm Lisa. I'm the love of your husband's life. It's time you two broke up so he and I can finally be together without worry."

Tears started down Olivia's cheeks. "But *who* are you? How did you meet my husband?"

She started toward her car, ignoring the questions. Lisa paused before getting in her car. Holding the driver-side door, she peered up into Olivia's eyes. "He met me when he was in the grocery store picking up a sandwich for his lunch, if you really care to know the details."

With that, Lisa got in her car and left. As her taillights faded in the dust behind the car, Olivia dropped to her knees. Her heart ached with a pain that was deep and lasting. Had her husband really been cheating on her for five years? Was it true? Again? Could he have been seeing this woman for so long without her knowing? Her cousin Rachel's words came echoing in her thoughts. She'd warned Olivia on several occasions that all men were the same. They took what they wanted and they didn't care who they hurt in the process. But Bruce had been so different. He had been *special* in the beginning. Olivia kept wanting to tell herself it wasn't real, but the truth fought against her.

WHEN OLIVIA HEARD Bruce's car pull up outside later than expected that evening, she grabbed her cast-iron skillet from the coffee table. She went over and stood by the door, raising it up above her head, just like he had told Lisa she would do. Barbaric? Yes, but whatever Bruce wants, Bruce gets. She was ready to strike her cheating, no-good husband. She listened as he pushed the key into the door's lock, then the doorknob turned. He came walking in. All her anger and determination melted away in an instant. She wanted to swing, to hurt him, to make him feel just a tiny portion of what she was feeling right now, but she couldn't do it. When he turned and looked at her, then the pan, then back at her, she dropped the skillet on the floor and started to cry.

"What is the meaning of this?" Anger and a bit of fear lit in his eyes. He slammed the door behind him. "I work all day to come home to my wife with a skillet in the air, ready to hit me?"

Olivia's throat closed up, her chest knotted, and she couldn't speak a word in that moment. Picking up the skillet, she walked through their living room and headed for the kitchen as he continued to belittle her with horrid comments. She stopped listening and just kept thinking of Lisa's face and how she had been so bold to come out to visit her. *Five years.* The two words echoed through Olivia's mind, slicing and dicing all her good memories with Bruce.

Then, Olivia worked up the courage inside to say it. Stopping, she turned to Bruce. "Lisa came by this afternoon."

He stopped his tirade. He looked remorseful, but little good that did at a time like the present.

"She was very pretty, Bruce. Prettier than the last one."

"Stop."

Olivia walked over to the island in the kitchen and leaned her arms on top of it as she directed her gaze toward him. Her tone of voice stayed level as she spoke. "I don't think she knows about Michelle from a couple of years ago. At least, she didn't act like it. She acted like you two were it for five beautiful years."

"You don't understand, Olivia." His tone was much gentler now, even genuine. He let out a sigh and raked a hand through his hair. "We're in love."

"You're a fool, Bruce. An absolute fool!" She took a breath, then let her nerves calm for a moment. "But then again, I was a fool too, a fool to stay with you after the first affair. Or was it your second, since you cheated on me *and* Lisa with Michelle? I have to hand it to you, Bruce. That must've taken skill, deceiving three women at one time. Or are there more lucky ladies? Why would you ever stop at three?" She paused, sorrow filling her. "What was I thinking? Once a cheater, *always* a cheater." Walking out of the kitchen, Olivia walked down the hallway and into her and Bruce's bedroom. She opened the closet door and pulled out an already packed suitcase she had prepared earlier. Bruce followed her into the bedroom.

"Stay here in the house, Olivia. You can keep it."

Suitcase in hand, she shrugged. "Why would I want the house?"

"Your garden. I know you love it. We should both have something we love. Lisa is like my garden."

"How *dare* you compare that homewrecker to my beautiful garden!"

He grabbed her arm, stopping her. "Look at you. When I found you, you had nothing going on in your life, and I gave you a home and a purpose! You're nothing without me."

"Maybe so, but I'd rather be nothing without you than stay and be nothing with you. You did brighten my life up back in the day, and I will never deny that. It's time I moved on, like you already have. Go be with the woman you *love*. I don't know a whole lot in this life, but I know enough to know I don't deserve this. Goodbye, Bruce." Pulling free of his grip, she walked out of the room and out of his life.

WITH EACH MILE Olivia drove further south and away from Colville, away from Bruce, she felt better. She wondered after the last time he had cheated if he'd do it again. A part of her must've suspected he would, thus the reason she'd held onto the signed divorce papers for three years. After Michelle, she did hold a thread of hope that he wouldn't do it again, that things would work out, but today, it became clear to her that he'd never change. Not only did he do it again, but he had kept this Lisa gal for years. He'd had her through the entire Michelle debacle. Olivia was wrong yet again, just like she was wrong about Ryan, about Seth, and about Champ. So many men, so many mistakes. She knew something was wrong with her and her ability to pick men. There was no denying that truth anymore now. Every man she met and fell in love with ended up letting her down. This one was the worst and the longest investment of her life. She had wasted seven years with Bruce and was now over thirty years old. The thought of dating was preposterous. Some girls just don't get lucky in life, and Olivia was now convinced she was one of those unlucky ones. Wiping hot tears from her cheeks, she pushed a strand of her long, layered brunette hair behind her ear and focused on the road.

As an hour passed, sleep began to gnaw at her, but she resisted the best she could. She needed to reach Spokane, to reach her parents' house for the walk of shame up the pathway to their front door. They hadn't been on speaking terms for years, but she knew they'd take her in without hesitation. Rolling down the window, she let the cool night air flood into the car to wake her up. The chill of the air pressed against her cheeks, bringing up her level of consciousness. She thought of Bruce and her heart ached again. Olivia's dreams and plans for life had gone up like a vapor of water, returning to the place they'd once come, her heart. She wept bitterly. Rolling up the window as the air became too cold, she began to get sleepy again, her eyelids becoming heavier each time she blinked. Olivia longed to get to her destination as soon as possible. Then suddenly, she awoke as her car went off the road and into the darkness. She was driving through a field. She grabbed the steering wheel, trying to gain control, but it was too late. She hit something hard, and the car flipped and rolled, knocking her unconscious.

CHAPTER 2

*S*TARING UP AT THE CEILING as Tyler sat on his couch in the apartment above his bowling alley, he tried to count the tiles as he waited for his brother, Jonathan, to come out from the bathroom. He had his brother over for their weekly business meeting to discuss an important matter in regard to *Willow Design,* the company they had started shortly after Jonathan's wife, Marie, had passed away years ago. God was blessing the business and they were looking at several properties in Spokane to lease office space. Life was good, but for Tyler, he still felt an ever-increasing longing in his heart for a wife and a family.

Emerging from the restroom, Jonathan shut the door behind him and walked toward Tyler.

"Kylie and I are taking Rose and Peter to Silverwood tomorrow. You should come with us. It'd be fun."

Tyler's lips curved into a smile. "That sounds nice, but I'll let you and your family enjoy this one, Brother. Plus, I have a reservation at *The Inn at the Lake* for tonight."

Jonathan's eyebrows rose and he sat on the couch beside

Tyler. "You're going out to Diamond Lake? Really? I didn't think you were a 'relax at the lake' type of guy."

A light laugh escaped Tyler's lips. "You're right. I'm not. But I recognize the need to change that, so I'm taking some time off to clear my head." Pulling out a pamphlet from his pocket, he handed it to Jonathan. "There's some good fishing out there and I haven't fished in a long time. I probably won't be available until next Tuesday or so. If there's an emergency, you can look up the inn and call me. I'm not sure about cell reception out there."

"You going to see Chet while you're out there?" Chet was an old friend of Tyler's he had met at *Wendy's* when Tyler was working his first job as a burger flipper. They hadn't spoken in about two years, and Tyler wasn't sure if Chet would welcome him in if he showed up at the cabin.

He shrugged. "I don't know. I'll see how things go."

Seeming hesitant, Jonathan didn't speak for a moment, then he set down the pamphlet on the coffee table and turned to Tyler. "What's eating your soul, Brother? You've been different for months."

His brother could see right through him, but it was no surprise to Tyler. He and Jonathan were close. They shared every good and bad thing with one another, and running a business side-by-side had only intensified their closeness. Tyler rose from the couch as his brother's words penetrated through his chest and struck right where it hurt the most, his heart.

"I know this might sound dumb to you, Jonathan." He stopped and turned toward him. "But I want a wife, a family, a life outside of myself and the business. Really, I want what you have. I see the way you are with Rose, Peter, and Kylie. I've been craving that life a little more each day that goes by."

"Ask God for it. If it's in His will, He will do it."

A sardonic laugh worked its way out of Tyler's lips as he crossed the living room floor and over to his bookcase. He picked up a picture frame that held Jonathan's family photo. "*God's will*. Do you ever wonder if maybe God's will doesn't match our own? Like what if He doesn't want me to have a wife? To have kids and all that. Maybe it's not in the cards for me. I know God's will is most important and what I should strive for. I just don't know if His will matches my own on this. I'm not sure how I'll feel giving up that dream if that's what He wants me to do."

Jonathan was quiet for a long moment. Then, he stood up and walked over to Tyler and rested a hand on his shoulder. "Those desires you have for a family are God-given, Brother. Trust in His timing."

"You know how impatient I am." He turned to his brother. "I've been waiting on God to do this and it's just not happening. My desires for it are intensifying, as well as my discontentment."

"*Trust* God, Brother. Listen, I'm starving and Kylie will have dinner ready in twenty. I'd better start heading out." Jonathan walked over to the table and started loading his laptop. As Tyler watched his brother collect his things, he thought about that day in the restaurant when they were eating and they happened to meet Kylie. She ended up becoming Jonathan's wife, and now they had a beautiful life together. It came out of nowhere, but God wasn't surprised. It had shown Tyler that God does work things together for good, but that had been two years ago now, and his own wife hadn't come.

Tyler approached his brother. "Thanks for always being there for me. You're a good brother."

Winding up the laptop power cord, Jonathan stopped and looked at Tyler. "You were there for me after I lost Marie.

When the world turned its back on me, you never did, and I'll never forget it. Have a fun, relaxing time at the lake, Bro."

A COUPLE OF HOURS LATER, after Tyler had finished up the last bit of work he needed to do so he could relax on his trip to the lake, he went into his bedroom to pack a duffel bag. As he did, he could hear noise from the bowling alley below his bedroom floor boards. It was starting to get late, and on Friday, that meant cosmic bowling and large crowds. He had meant to move out from the apartment above the bowling alley a while back, but he still hadn't pulled the trigger. Every time he thought about moving, he'd feel anxiety and stress, resulting in finding excuses not to do it. The mere thought of packing everything he owned in a moving truck made him uneasy.

Once his bag was packed for his trip, he headed out the door and down the narrow stairway to exit the bowling alley. As he pushed open the door and arrived out on the sidewalk, he peered down each direction of the road. There were people walking up and down the sidewalks on both sides of the road. It was Friday night and it was downtown Spokane. The city was alive and bustling with activity. In his younger days, he'd be joining in on the fun, hitting every little bar up and down the boulevard, but not anymore. He'd left that life behind him a long time ago.

Crossing the sidewalk to his car, he opened the trunk and tossed his bag in, then went around and got into the car. Turning the key over, he headed for Diamond Lake. He had told the inn he'd be arriving late because of work, probably by ten o'clock.

While slowing his car down in the right turn lane on Highway 395 to turn onto West Dennison-Chattaroy Road, he spotted the faint glow of taillights in a field further north.

His heart skipped a beat as fear gripped him in the worst kind of way, and he wasted no time. He turned off his blinker and floored the gas pedal, speeding further down Highway 395, and then whipped his car around in the middle of the highway. He pulled off to the side of the road and jumped from his car, his heart hammering in his chest. There was hardly any traffic at that time of night, and he wondered how long the car had been lying there upside down. He called 9-1-1 to report the wreck and hung up as the voice on the phone asked more questions. Tyler sprinted through the knee-high grassy field and to the car.

"Hello! Can you hear me? Anyone there?" His words came out loud and commanding. Walking along the back side of the car, he pressed his hand against the car and moved to the driver side. A fire ignited toward the front end of the under-carriage of the car. If someone was still in the car, he had to move quickly. He got down in the darkness and grass and tried to see inside. Using the flashlight on his phone, he peered in through the broken driver side window.

A woman hung upside down in the car, unresponsive. His heart feared she was dead.

"Ma'am!" he shouted. "Can you hear me?"

Her eyes opened slightly, life flickering in them. She didn't respond but let out an aching groan. Blood was smeared across her face, and she let out a cry before losing consciousness again. He was relieved, but he knew he had to get her out of there in case the car was to explode. Ripping off his button-up blue shirt, he used the shirt to push the shards of glass in the window out of the way and then placed the cloth over the rigid glass shards left so they wouldn't hurt her on the way out. Partially maneuvering himself into the car, he strained his arm to reach her seat belt buckle, praying it wasn't jammed in the collision. Luck-ily, it clicked open. She fell, but he caught her in his arms.

Then, he shimmied himself and her out through the window.

Panting as he exhausted every ounce of energy from his muscles, Tyler pulled the unconscious woman through the tall grass toward the road and away from the car. Hearing the paramedics getting closer, but still off in the distance, he caught his breath and then tried to get the woman to respond to him.

"Ma'am, are you awake? Can you hear me?"

Tears started to stream down her face, mixing with the blood smears on her face. Her eyes opened suddenly and went wide. Her voice cracked and she pushed out, "What happened?"

Thankful she was responsive, relief flooded him as he smiled and wiped blood and sweat from his brow. "You were in a wreck, but you're going to be okay. You're safe now. What's your name?"

"Olivia. Olivia Montgomery. I'm scared." She tried to sit up. Easing her back down, Tyler looked her over and noticed her hands were bloodied and a gruesome sight. He turned away, not wanting her to see his reaction and get scared.

The car exploded in the distance without warning, startling both of them. Tyler flinched, knowing that a few moments slower and they'd both be dead. Sending a prayer to God with thankfulness, Tyler bent over Olivia and shielded her in case some of the debris were to fall on her. None hit either of them, and he relaxed and peered into her sea-blue eyes once more.

"Olivia, the paramedics will be here soon. Try not to move and don't worry. I'm not going anywhere."

Seeing her eyes begin to close, he came close to her face and held her cheeks between his palms. Tapping his hands on her cheeks, he stared into her eyes.

"Look at me, Olivia. Stay with me. Stay awake!"

Her eyes opened and they held one another's gazes.

When the ambulance finally arrived, the paramedics went straight to work on the woman and Tyler watched them intently. He worried about how bad her injuries were, especially her hands. The paramedics communicated what they were doing to help her and commented on his timing as far as rescuing her. The man went as far as to call Tyler Olivia's guardian angel, coming when he did. He denied it and attributed it to an act of God and His divine timing.

As they loaded her into the ambulance a short while later, a police officer stopped Tyler and had a few extra questions about his statement. Then, after he was done with the questions, the officer looked at Tyler for a moment, most likely noticing the concern in his face.

"Try not to worry about her, sir. We've called her husband and he's on his way down from Colville. She also has some family in Spokane. Everything is going to be okay, and she'll have her family with her soon."

Tyler paused. *Husband?* His insides shrank. Why'd he feel so uncomfortable with the thought of her having a husband? He pondered it for a moment and then the ugly truth came forth from his heart. *You thought saving her life could turn out to be the beginning of your beautiful love story. She would be eternally grateful, and you would live happily ever after.*

He beat himself up internally as he returned to his car to leave and for the rest of his drive to the inn. *You selfish, selfish man.* How could he be so self-centered to think he could benefit from the horrific situation at hand? He knew he was in the wrong, especially as the adrenaline from the rescue left him. Tyler knew he didn't pull over at the wreck to get a date out of it. He pulled over to help whoever was in that car regardless of their beauty or gender, but that fact did little to settle the uneasy feeling he had. He felt uncomfortable with the reality of his own selfishness that he had felt when he heard she was married. Though all the guilt weighed on him heavily, he couldn't get the image of her face out of his mind. Despite all those scrapes, despite all the blood, and despite the fact that she was married . . . Tyler found her breathtakingly beautiful.

CHAPTER 3

FLUTTERING HER EYES OPEN, OLIVIA didn't move her head, but she surveyed the ceiling above her and what she could see out of the corners of her eyes. Between what she saw and the sounds of machines beeping nearby, it didn't take long for her to realize she was in a hospital room. She tried to move parts of her body, but pain shot through every area that she attempted to move. She relaxed and quickly fell back to sleep.

Sometime later, she awoke again. Finally able to turn her head, she peered out the open blinds in the hospital room window and saw Bruce standing on the other side, talking with a nurse. He ran his hand through his hair and shook his head. She ached, not just physically but emotionally as she watched her husband. She knew that even if Bruce was at the hospital right now, he'd be gone soon. He didn't care about her. She'd never felt so alone, so isolated as she did right there in that moment. Soon, the conversation between Bruce and the nurse concluded and he came into the room, shutting the door behind him.

"Oh, you're awake." He sounded more annoyed than

relieved to hear himself say it. He took a few steps closer to the bed, surveying Olivia with a look of pity. His voice was void of care and already gone from the hospital. "You really got yourself banged up. A few cracked ribs and two badly broken hands and wrists. You have a bunch of nerve damage in the right hand and they had to operate on you. Do you have any idea how worried you made people?"

With a pained effort, she pushed out a question. "What happened, exactly?"

"You were in a wreck on your way to Spokane. I assume on your way to your parents'?"

She closed her eyes, a sudden pain rippling through her shoulder blades. Fragments of the wreck skipped through her mind like a charred rolodex retrieved from a fire. There was a person there, a man. She remembered his arms around her as he pulled her through the grass, the blades of grass pressing against her face.

"Who got me out of the car?"

"What do you mean?"

A single tear escaped her eye, and she couldn't hold the image anymore as the pain became too much to bear in her hands and ribs. Olivia looked at her husband and longed for his touch even now, after all he had done. She clung to the thought of him just brushing a finger against her skin to make her feel okay in this painful moment, but he never did. She started to cry, her words breaking apart. "I hurt so badly, Bruce. Why'd this have to happen? What did I do to deserve it?"

He glanced at his cell phone and nodded. "You're a fighter. You'll get through this just like you get through everything life throws at you, Olivia. Your parents will be here tomorrow. They are over in Montana right now and couldn't get a flight in until the AM."

When Bruce turned around and walked away from her

hospital bed, Olivia's throat tightened and her chest contracted, tears spilling down her face despite her best attempts to fight them. She never thought Bruce could hurt her more than he already had, but he'd managed to do so without even so much as a goodbye. She had given him all of herself, and even now, with her whole body in pain after being in a wreck, he still didn't have even an ounce of care in his body for her. Did he ever care?

An hour passed after Bruce left, and a doctor arrived in the room.

"Mrs. Montgomery, correct?" He flipped papers on the clipboard in his hands as he stared at the papers.

"Yes." The sound of being called by *his* name made her skin crawl.

"With you unresponsive, we ran some basic tests before surgery for some answers before we proceeded. Are you aware you're pregnant? The HCG levels would put you early on, maybe two months, if I had to guess. With no spotting or cramping and it being so early on, I just wanted to assure you your fetus should be fine, but you should schedule an ultrasound with your OB as soon as possible for peace of mind."

"What? That must be incorrect because I am not pregnant." Fear panged her heart.

"I promise you, false positives do not happen with blood tests. Congratulations to you and your husband."

Hot tears welled in her eyes at the news of the pregnancy. *No. Please, no.*

OLIVIA'S PARENTS, Dan and Kora, came on the first flight back to Spokane and arrived at the hospital by nine o'clock the next day. Though she and her parents hadn't been on speaking terms in almost three years due to their different beliefs—her choice, not theirs—they didn't hesitate for a moment when they got the call. They loved Olivia and would truly do anything for her. She couldn't help but feel relief wash over her as they both entered the room. Tears streamed down her cheeks as all the anger in her heart from their last conversation melted away, leaving only love toward them for being there for her no matter what choices in life she had made.

Showering her with kisses and affection, her parents spoke nothing but words of encouragement and love to her in her time of need. As the minutes turned into hours, questioning gazes shot around the room from both of them. Olivia knew exactly what they were wondering before a word was even uttered about the matter.

"Where's Bruce?" her father finally asked. Olivia didn't respond to her father's inquiry. She couldn't. The heartache kept her lips tightly zipped.

Her mother wasted no time jumping into the conversation. "He's probably at work, right? We all know he's far too busy to take some time off, even if his wife has been in an accident."

Though her mother was absolutely right about how she had always suspected the worst about Bruce, it didn't make her right about how she went about discussing Olivia's husband in such a cold way. It wasn't very Jesus-like of her. Her mother didn't even know the half of it, not a clue about Lisa or Michelle. Olivia didn't dare share Bruce's sins with the two of them while she was married. She didn't want to give them more reasons for hating the man than they already possessed. *I guess hiding the truth is all over now,* she thought to herself, knowing she and Bruce would never be together again. Mustering strength from deep in her soul, the same strength she had relied on to find the courage to finally leave Bruce, she looked at each of her parents.

"I left him."

Both of her parents looked genuinely shocked and glanced at one another.

Olivia flinched from a surge of pain as it burned in her right hand. She adjusted in her hospital bed, trying to make herself more comfortable with not only the physical pain she was enduring, but the emotional pain as well. Once she got the pain managed to a tolerable level, she spoke again. "I was on my way to Spokane to your house when the wreck happened. I was coming home."

A doctor walked in and went over the details of the injuries with Olivia's parents, then turned to Olivia.

"You're ready to be discharged."

Her dad came over and touched her shoulder. "We're going to grab some coffee before we leave. We will be right back."

"Okay, Dad."

Dan and Kora left to go get coffee from the cafeteria on-site. The doctor stayed in the room. After they were out of the room and well on their way down the hall, the doctor came closer to the bed and to her side.

"You're going to be okay. A nurse will come in shortly and give you the at-home care papers along with the prescriptions you need to pick up from the pharmacy."

"Great. Thank you. Hey, there was a person last night who pulled me out of the car. Do you have information on who he was?"

His lips curved into a frown. "I'm afraid I don't have that kind of information, but maybe the police do?"

"Okay. I just want to thank him. I'll try them. Thanks for everything."

"You're welcome. Be sure to follow up in a week at my office, and get an appointment with an OB."

As he left the hospital room, Olivia glanced out the window of her room and thought of the shadowy figure from last night. Pressing her eyes shut, she thought of the stranger. The fragments of the memory she held were like those of a shattered mirror. A piece here, a piece there, with no clear understanding of exactly who was there or what had happened. All she could focus on was the warmth she felt as he carried her when she could not walk.

CHAPTER 4

*S*ITTING AT A TABLE ON the patio just outside the lower-level living room of *The Inn at the Lake,* Tyler sipped on his mug of coffee and read his Bible. He was reading in the book of John that particular morning. While he read, his thoughts kept drifting to last night and how he had rescued that woman from the burning car. Unable to concentrate any longer, he returned the slip of paper marking his spot in the Bible and closed it. Peering down at his hands, he fixed his eyes on the scrapes and scratches he had gotten from what had transpired. Then, Olivia's sea-blue eyes invaded his thoughts, causing his heart to ache, knowing how frightened she had been.

Lifting his eyes to the morning sky, he closed them tightly and held out his arms. He poured himself out in prayer. "Lord, I am in Your hands. My life is clay and You are the Potter. Lead me in the direction I should go and I will trust You." He paused, thinking about the strength he'd felt surge through his muscles to heave the woman out of the burning car and drag her away from it, all happening moments before the explosion.

He continued his prayer. "I know it was Your strength that enabled me to do what I did last night. You saved her, not me. You are the one with the power, the strength, and You deserve all the glory, here and now, and through eternity." Then, tears welled in his eyes as his heart clung to Olivia's sea-blue eyes in his mind. He clung to her beauty as he held her image in his thoughts. His voice broke apart as his selfishness bubbled within him. "Remove my yearning to go find her, to see her, to want to be with her. I know she's married, Lord. I know Your will would never entangle me with a married woman."

A little while later, at eight o'clock, the rest of the house was awake and Tyler found his way upstairs to the dining area for breakfast. Greeted by Charlie, the husband of Serenah, whom he had met last night at the door, he quickly fell into conversation about the events of the night prior. He went into great detail but made sure to give credit to God.

"It was a God thing for sure." Tyler raked a hand through his hair. "We could've both died in my attempts to save her."

"But you didn't." Charlie took a long drink from his coffee and set it back down on the table beside his plate of half-eaten eggs and toast. "God works in miraculous ways, Tyler. When I think of God at work in our lives, I think of the ants. They are always on the move, always working, and God is no different. Sometimes, it takes time to see what God is doing, but He is always up to something in our lives."

Just then, little Emma, Charlie and Serenah's daughter, came skipping through the dining room and went straight outside through the open French doors that led out to the patio. Tyler peered over and watched her as she pulled three small ponies from her sparkling pink purse and set them on the patio's railing just outside the door. Emma reminded Tyler a lot of his brother's little girl, Rose. In a few years' time, she'd be just as old as this girl.

24

Turning his attention back to his conversation with Charlie, he shifted his thoughts away. "I read in the pamphlet that there was good fishing to be done on this lake. Where would I rent a fishing pole?"

Charlie tipped his chin toward the lake. "There's a shed down by the dock that has a few poles and tackle boxes. You can get a box of worms up the road at the gas station."

Serenah walked into the dining area from the kitchen and chimed in. "We had a guest catch a huge trout right off the dock last month. If you want to go out and fish, you can use one of the canoes down by the water too. Whatever you want to do."

He thought of years ago when his Uncle Jack took him out on Bear Lake for a fishing trip. It was merely four months before his uncle passed away, and that last memory with him held a special part in Tyler's heart. They had bonded over worms and silence in a cheap metal boat. Tyler looked over at Serenah.

"Thank you. I'll be here for a couple of days so I'll probably do both. Where's a good place to eat for the meals I don't get here in the morning?"

Charlie adjusted in his seat and pulled out his wallet. Opening it up, he handed Tyler a couple of coupons for a place called *Dixie's Diner*. "Best burger in the state."

Playfully slapping him on the arm, Serenah rested her hand on her husband's shoulder as she smiled. "He's just saying that because we have a vested interest. We own the diner."

Tyler smiled and pocketed the coupons. "Thank you, and Serenah? The breakfast was amazing. You were right about that Amish butter adding flavor. You know, this inn is quite the awesome place to stay. So peaceful and calm and quiet. It's a delight so far."

"Aw, I'm glad. We hope you enjoy your stay, Tyler."

Serenah took his empty plate and left back toward the kitchen. Charlie stood up and shook hands with Tyler.

"It was nice meeting you. I'll see you this evening for songs by the fire pit down by the lake?"

"Count me in."

Leaving the dining area, Tyler returned downstairs to his room to get his wallet.

AFTER HIS TRIP to the gas station to get bait, Tyler headed down to the shed by the lake to find a fishing pole. Upon opening the shed doors, an earthen musky smell wafted through the dark and cramped space. He could see inside the shed and saw gardening tools and a wheelbarrow, and then, there in the corner beside the old wooden shelving, sat three fishing poles and two tackle boxes. Maneuvering his way inside, he stepped over a flower pot, a couple of bags of fertilizer, and then finally arrived at the fishing equipment. Lifting a fishing pole, he inspected it. The handle was in great shape, the spool functional, and each guide was in good shape. There was even a weight already attached to the fishing line. The only thing missing was a hook. Propping the pole up against the shed's wall, he opened the tackle box and used his phone's flashlight to search for hooks. He found a package of hooks. Closing the tackle box, he latched it shut and took it, along with the pole, out from the shed.

"Hi, Tyler." An angelic voice startled him from behind.

Turning around, he immediately recognized the woman from the wreck last night. He stumbled and dropped the pole in his hand, his heart immediately beating faster than it had in a long time. Bending down, he picked it up and stood upright, trying to slow his breathing down at her sudden appearance.

26

"Olivia." He tried to sound calm and collected, which was anything but how he was feeling at the moment.

"You know my name?" Tilting her head to the side, she looked at him with a curious expression on her face.

"Yes, you told me last night. How did you find me here?" Seeing her hands wrapped, an arm in a sling, and proof of the wreckage all over her body, Tyler shook his head. "Wait, why aren't you at the hospital?"

"I'm on my way home now. I just had to find you and say thank you. I called the police and they gave me your name, so I looked you up and found your business number, and your outgoing voicemail said you were here. You know, you shouldn't give so much information on your whereabouts."

His heart beat even faster. She looked more beautiful than he had recalled her looking in the low lighting of the night. She crooked her head to the side, adding a little bit of playful attitude to her comment. Snapping out of his thinking, he glanced over her shoulder. The thought that her husband must be waiting for her made him refocus. "You're probably right, but at least it did some good. After all, you found me. Anyway, you're welcome for rescuing you, but the truth is that it was all God. He just used me as a tool to help you in a time of need."

She looked dismayed by the mention of God. "*God?* How could you even mention God? If He existed, He was the one who left me there to die in a field until you came along."

With that one sentence from her lips, Tyler would have suspected his attraction and desires for her would be gone, but they didn't go away so easily. "He works in mysterious ways, Olivia. Your husband up there waiting for you? Maybe you should be going."

"What? I'm actually in the process of a divorce, not that it's any of your business." What looked to be confusion littered her face as she continued to stare at him.

"Oh." Tyler felt his insides leap with joy at the mention of a divorce. He blushed inwardly at his excitement over such a matter. He knew divorce wasn't something to be happy about. He felt ashamed of himself and prayed for forgiveness for the increasing selfishness he felt around this woman. He peered into Olivia's sea-blue eyes a moment later. They held glints of sadness he hadn't seen before. "I'm sorry to hear that. Divorce is ugly."

A light laugh escaped her lips and she turned her head. "Don't be sorry for me. He just wasn't the one."

"The one?"

"Yeah, you know, the one who would make me happy and treat me right forever and always." Her gaze shifted over her shoulder, then back at Tyler. "Hey, I need to get going. My husband may not be here, but my parents are waiting. Again, thank you. The police said the car exploded and I wouldn't have made it out without you."

As she walked away from him, he was moved in a way that he didn't like. He felt an intense desire for her to stay there with him. The feeling was similar to last night when they were loading her in the ambulance. He started to be suspect of his feelings about this woman. Maybe they had been brought on by the sheer fact that they had met when both of their lives hung in the balance. Tyler didn't understand exactly what was going on inside him or why he'd be attracted to someone who loathed the idea of God, but he was, and not only that, but she brought out a selfishness in him he did not like seeing.

When she walked away that day from Tyler at the inn, she didn't leave without leaving something behind inside Tyler. It was a pebble-sized rock of discomfort lodged in the very depths of his soul. The discomfort was brought on by his desires and his selfishness to want to be with her, despite her hatred of God. It drove him mad knowing that such a beautiful woman was saved from death's grip by God and yet was filled with the darkest of darkness. She had spoken evil of Tyler's Savior, and it was like rottenness to his bones, yet he still felt an attraction toward the woman. Why? Why didn't God let his attraction fade away at the very moment she'd voiced her disdain for his Creator?

After she left, he walked away from the spot where he was standing and tried to push the thoughts of her away from his mind. He traveled the rest of the way down to the dock and strolled across the planks. Coming to the end of the dock, he placed the tackle box down and sat down beside it. He grabbed the end of the fishing line and propped open the tackle box. Pausing for a moment before he grabbed the package of hooks, he bowed his head. *Thank you, Lord, for all that You do. I don't know why You saved her or why You used me to do it, but You do know why. I pray that Your will be done in her life and that she finds You, Lord. Amen.*

CHAPTER 5

A WHIRLWIND OF THOUGHTS SPUN together in Olivia's mind on the way up the hillside next to the inn toward her parents' car. She hadn't expected Tyler to be so attractive or so misguided. *Mama and Dad would be thrilled to hear he believes in their God,* she thought with a sting of indignation in her heart. She just wanted to thank the man, and he had to go and give all the credit to *God.* If God really existed like everyone around her seemed to think, He wouldn't have let her be hurt so often and so frequently by the men in her life and He surely wouldn't let her almost die in a car wreck last night. What kind of loving God would do such a thing? *Or maybe that was punishment for my sins,* she thought grimly for a second before brushing the thought far away from her.

Her mother held open the car door for her and she climbed into the back seat. Olivia peered down at her wrapped hands, and as the car backed out of the driveway, she shifted her thoughts away from Tyler and to her injuries. She knew she wouldn't be using her hands anytime soon. Hot tears filled her eyes as she stared out the window and

31

rested her wrapped hands against her belly where her child was growing. If there was a God out there like Tyler and her parents thought there was, He sure was cruel.

After a few minutes, her father caught her gaze in the rearview mirror and struck up a conversation.

"Once you're healed up, my buddy Gus at the car lot has a job for you as a receptionist."

She smiled. "That'd be great. Thanks, Dad."

"How'd it go with Tyler?"

Her heart jumped when Tyler's face flashed in her mind. He was handsome, strongly built, and obviously, a white knight, the way he ran toward her wrecked car. She didn't want to give her parents the satisfaction of knowing he was a Godly man, for she feared they would push her to stay in touch with him moving forward. She didn't want that. So, she steered the subject elsewhere, to one that she couldn't avoid forever even if she tried. She knew it'd drop the Tyler talk straightaway.

"I'm pregnant."

The cares for Tyler vanished as she had predicted, and her father pulled the car over to the side of the highway leading back to Spokane. Trembling, he opened his car door and got out, slamming the door behind him. She watched as he started to travel down the shoulder of the road. He was distraught and flailing his arms about wildly. Her mother turned in her seat to look at Olivia, a pity-ridden expression on her face that made Olivia feel worse than she already did.

"Don't mind your father. He'll be happy in time. A new life is always a celebration, but sometimes, the circumstances can just be . . . unfortunate. You understand?"

Heart aching, hand resting on her belly, and tears rolling down her cheeks, Olivia nodded.

Kora turned to face forward in the car. Neither of Olivia's parents had to say much to her to communicate all the disappointment and sadness the news had brought to them. Sure, her mother tried to comfort her in that moment, but it did little to ease the hurt Olivia felt on a deep level. Then again, a lot about her parents hurt.

It'd be difficult to raise a child on her own and without the child's father's daily involvement, but she could manage it, couldn't she? Doubts began to blossom in Olivia's mind, in her heart. How would she feed the child? Provide a home for the child? She knew her parents' love would last mere weeks before it ran cold and she was sent packing out the door again. Then what? Her gaze found her hands, her broken and destroyed hands that were of no real use now. Fear rippled through her whole being like a storm crashing on a shoreline. *What am I going to do?* The thought sent a terrified sensation to the core of her being.

At her parents' house, after settling into her old bedroom from her childhood that had since been converted into a guest bedroom, she called her mother.

"Mom?" Her mother came in. "Could you call Rach for me and hand me the phone?" Rachel was the one who'd warned her not just about Bruce, but about all men and how they were the same. Rachel was more of a best friend than a cousin, and it had been years since they last spoke—again, because of her relationship with Bruce.

"Sure, honey." Picking up the old-school rotary phone, her mother dialed Rachel and then placed the phone on the pillow beside her ear. As her mother left the room, her cousin picked up on the other end of the phone.

"Hey, Rach." Olivia's voice was hesitant, wondering if Rachel would be mad at her for going so long without communication.

"Olivia! I was just talking about you the other day and how we went skinny dipping in Suncrest at Long Lake in November! Do you remember that?"

Her heart smiled with relief that all seemed to be forgiven as the memory brought back a chill from head to toe. "Cold day that day. We lost the keys in the snow and couldn't find them for like twenty minutes!"

"It was *five* minutes max, Olivia. You're such a drama queen. Nothing ever changes. Anywho, what's up? It's been like what, six years since we've chatted?"

Olivia's heart warmed. "Yes. Too long, *way* too long. We need to hang."

"Come on over."

Olivia's gaze landed on her bedroom door and she thought of her parents. They were down the hall in the living room. Dad was probably reading his Bible by the fireplace and Mom was likely knitting a new sweater while she listened to him read the Bible aloud and rocked ever so slightly in the rocking chair. She started to think about how she could ask for a ride, but then reality surfaced as her hands began to ache, and she wept.

"What's wrong?"

Olivia's words broke apart as she pieced reality together for her cousin. "I don't have a car anymore, and my hands . . . my hands are busted up really badly."

"Oh, my goodness! *Why*? Wait." Silence for a moment, then Rachel came back on the line. "I was wondering why you were calling from your parents' phone number. What happened with Bruce? What's going on, exactly?"

"Long story, but I'll tell you all about it—" Her hands throbbed and she glanced over at the night stand and at the pill bottle. "I have to go. Come over when you can, and I'll fill you in on the details. Okay?"

"I'll be over tonight. Promise. Eight o'clock."

Rachel hung up the phone, and the phone handset rang with a deafening dial tone in Olivia's ear.

"Mom." At her call, her mother hurried quickly in

through the door and over to the bed. Lifting the phone from the pillow, she hung it up on the night stand.

"Need anything else?"

"Medicine. It hurts."

"Where?"

"My hands mostly, but everywhere else too."

Her mother grabbed the prescription bottle and tapped a couple of pills out into her hand, then set the bottle on the nightstand. Then, she helped Olivia sit up. Her mother lifted the glass of water from the nightstand and put the straw to her lips. Olivia took the pills and downed them, then took a drink from the straw.

"Can I get you some food? Are you hungry?"

"Not really."

Coming closer to Olivia, Kora cupped her daughter's face in her hand. "Remember, dear, you're eating for two now, plus eating helps make sure the pain pills don't upset your stomach."

More pain surged through Olivia. This time, it was emotional. She still hadn't called Bruce and broken the news to him about the pregnancy. She honestly didn't want to tell him. She knew it'd only bring out his anger and cause Bruce to assume she wanted to be with him, which wasn't the truth. She didn't want to be with Bruce, even if she was having his baby. She held a measure of worry that Bruce might want to work things out when he finds out she's pregnant, or even worse, that he still doesn't want her. She couldn't win emotionally with either outcome.

Her mother soon left her bedroom and she sank beneath the safety of the covers. Her chest heaving and her heart hurting, Olivia desperately wanted all the pain and anxiety to just go away. If only she could slip out of her broken shell of a body and go be someone else for a moment, live someone else's life . . . maybe then, at least for a moment, things wouldn't be so bad.

RACHEL SHOWED AT OLIVIA'S PARENTS' at eight o'clock that evening. She didn't come through the bedroom door, but instead to the bedroom window with a quick series of knocks. Olivia jolted and then got out of her bed. Going over to the window, she motioned at her to enter, and Rachel pulled the window up and open.

"What on earth?" Olivia laughed. "The front door works perfectly fine, Rach!"

Rachel didn't laugh but looked Olivia over from head to toe. "You look terrible."

"Thanks."

Shaking her head, she climbed in through the window and immediately wrapped her arms around Olivia and held her close for a moment.

"I'm so sorry this happened. Tell me everything."

Olivia explained everything from the moment Bruce's mistress came for a visit all the way to the inn, but she left out the pregnancy at that moment. It wasn't quite real enough to Olivia to share yet.

"Wow."

"Can we change the subject? I'm still wondering why you didn't come in through the front door."

Rachel let out a chuckle, loosening the tension in the air. "I wanted it to be like the old days. You remember how many times you sneaked out? Or I sneaked in when you were grounded? There for a while, I'm pretty sure we used the window more than the door."

Olivia recalled her younger days when she was still living at home and under the strict rule of her parents. They grounded her constantly for poor grades, bad attitudes, and any and every other little thing they didn't approve of that she was doing in her life. She felt like she was being constantly punished for her lack of belief in their religion, their God. She never could get them to admit it to her.

"Man . . ." Olivia said with the memories funneling through her thoughts. "We were quite the rebels in those days."

"Speaking of the old days." Rachel pulled her purse off from around her neck and walked over to the bed. Setting it down, she unzipped one of the pockets and retrieved a painted glass pipe. Immediately, Olivia shook her head and pointed to the purse.

"Absolutely not! Get that out of here!"

A blush crawled into Rachel's cheeks, reddening them. "Wow. I'm sorry. I didn't know you weren't into it anymore."

Recognizing she had hurt her cousin's feelings by the reaction, Olivia felt a piercing sting in her heart. She gentled and reached out, lightly touching her casted hand and exposed fingertips on Rachel's arm. "I'm sorry. I just . . . I just can't go backward. Also . . ." Olivia sat down on the bed and her chin dipped for a moment. Lifting her gaze toward Rachel, with tears glistening in her eyes, she shook her head, resigning herself to the fact that this is really happening. "I'm pregnant."

Rachel covered her mouth as her eyes widened. "No way!"

"Yes, way."

"Do your parents know?"

"Yes."

"How are you going to take care of a kid?"

"My dad's friend Gus needs a receptionist at the car lot, so after I heal up, I'm going to work there. Also, I'm enrolling into Carrington College for their dental assisting program."

Rachel was quiet for a long moment as she sat down

beside Olivia on the bed. Her tone was somber. "Sounds like you're going places in life."

"I have to keep moving forward or I'll slip, I know it. You have a job and your own place, Rachel. You're doing well too."

Her cousin's lips curved into a wry smile. "Sure, assistant manager at *Zumiez* is something to strive for in life."

"That store is awesome. You're doing a lot better in life than I am. I'm getting divorced, I'm pregnant, and I have two broken hands I can't use!"

They laughed lightly, then Rachel leaned her head against Olivia's shoulder. "I'm glad I have you not only as a cousin, but as a best friend. And, best of all, you're back in my life."

"I'm glad too, Rach. You've been like the sister I never had, and I've missed you like crazy for all these years. I'm so sorry for that. Now that Bruce is out of the picture, I'll make sure that never happens again!"

CHAPTER 6

CHARLIE AND SERENAH INVITED TYLER to *Church on the Lake* for morning services that Sunday, and he obliged. After breakfast, and after Charlie and Serenah had already left the inn, Tyler headed to his room on the lower level to get ready. As he walked into the room, he looked toward the window facing the lake, spotting a bird just outside the glass. It sat perched on a branch and looked as if it was peering in through the window, right at him.

He walked over and sat down on the small padded bench beneath the window and peered out at the bird. It had a soft blue hue on its topside with a white underbelly. The bird tilted its head, looking as if it was flashing a confused look at Tyler. He laughed lightly and sent up a quick thanks to God. *Thank You for the morning visitor.*

Tyler was beginning to see the beauty in the small things again in his visit to the inn and away from the city. Yesterday, when he was fishing off the dock, an eagle flew overhead and caught his attention. Last night, while he sipped on a cup of hot cocoa and sang worship songs with Charlie and Serenah at the fire pit by the shore, he was overwhelmed by the sense of connection with a fellow brother and sister in Christ. Without work or a television to distract him, Tyler was seeing more and being distracted less. He felt like he was starting to see God's hand in everything and in all things.

While staring out at the bird, it began to sing and he listened. Tyler thought about his home above the bowling alley back in Spokane, the constant sound of crashing pins. He knew right then that he had outgrown that place and it was time to start building a house, building a future. *Maybe Diamond Lake is a good place to build,* he thought as he stood up from the bench and went over to the dresser.

Pulling out a pair of slacks, he laid them out on the bed, then grabbed a pair of socks and his belt. Finally, he went over to the closet and took from it a long-sleeved white button-up shirt. Laying it on the bed with the other items, he went into the bathroom and took a shower.

As the hot water crashed over his head and shoulders, he closed his eyes. Flashes of Olivia's sea-blue eyes invaded his otherwise peaceful thoughts. That pebble of discomfort grew a little more. *C'mon, God. I don't need to worry about her or think about her anymore. There's so much I can focus on here. Help me to focus more on the glory that is Yours.*

He shut the shower off and wrapped a towel around his waist. Wiping the mirror with a hand, he saw his reflection come into view. Salt seasoned his otherwise black hair on the sides of his scalp, making him feel old. Before the gray showed, he'd considered himself young, youthful, and full of life ahead. Once the gray started showing up a few months back, he became far more aware of how quickly time was fading, and his desire to have a family became stronger.

He shaved, gelled his hair, and then got dressed. On his way out to the car in the driveway, he saw pine cones and pine needles lying below the towering pines and he thought of Chet. His old friend had refused to work a real job after his stint at *Wendy's*. Trading in a time-clock for pine needles, he began basket weaving, of all things, specializing specifically in pine-needle baskets. He figured out a way to not only sell the baskets but to market them. *Maybe I will go see him,* Tyler thought as he got into his car.

Finding his way to a seat near the front right side of the sanctuary, Tyler set his Bible down and began to greet the people near him. As he turned around to see who else he could greet, he saw Chet sitting three rows back from him. Tyler's eyes widened upon seeing him in attendance at church. Chet had had a hard heart toward Jesus, the Gospel, and anything to do with God for as long as Tyler had known him, and the fact that he was in attendance on Sunday morning was more than surprising. It was unfathomable. Moving out from the row of seats, Tyler made his way over to his old friend.

Chet lifted his gaze as Tyler closed in. He smiled and rose, moving out from the end of the row to shake Tyler's hand.

"I haven't seen you in ages, old man."

Chet laughed. "It's been a while, kid. What brings you out to Diamond Lake?"

"I'm staying at the inn."

"These people are good folks. I know the pastor and his wife well. I haven't had a chance to stay at the inn, but I attended a Bible study there back a while ago."

"A Bible study?" Tyler couldn't hide his surprise any longer.

Chet lifted a hand and nodded. "I know, it's weird to hear about me in a Bible study, and probably to even see me in a place like this on Sunday. I'm a changed man, and God gets all the credit."

41

"I tried talking to you about Jesus about a million times. What happened?" Tyler became more excited by the moment, realizing Chet was truly saved.

"Yes, you did, and those were seeds that took some time to grow, but they did, and there was a reaping. You see, kid, I met Jesus face-to-face right after I had a short trip to Hell and back."

"Hell? What?" Tyler shrank back. He would never discount someone's experience but knew to tread carefully whenever someone had an experiential trip to Heaven or Hell, for their stories were outside of the God-breathed, inspired Word of God.

"Not literal hell, but I got lost . . ." He paused, unable to continue for a moment as tears welled in his eyes. "I lost Margret last year, then I was diagnosed with pancreatic cancer. My whole world came crumbling down around me, and those words you spoke to me so long ago came back. You read me a verse you had memorized. I still remember it to this day. *Psalm 23:4, 'Even though I walk through the darkest valley, I will fear no evil, for you are with me; your rod and your staff, they comfort me.'* I looked it up in my Bible Margret forced us to keep on our bookcase, and I read it over and over again and wept the whole time. It struck a need so deep down in my soul I couldn't push it away. I was walking in a dark place and felt utterly hopeless as the walls of Hell were all around me. Then, I found Jesus. I came to the church the next morning. It was on a Tuesday at seven o'clock, and that's when I met Charlie. He sat with me and spoke with me and cared for me. He wasn't like the pastors I had been acquainted with in the past."

Tyler was awed by the story and moved with over-whelming joy to hear all that God had done with Chet. Here he had thought Chet was upset with him about a disagreement years ago, but he wasn't. He was busy working on his relationship with the Lord after losing his wife and being diagnosed with cancer. He searched for words, but only one could come out of Tyler's mouth. "Wow."

"Yes, wow. Sadly, I wasn't ready for Jesus when you spoke to me back in the day, but I found my way there." The music struck up on the stage at the front of the church, and people started taking seats. Chet peered over Tyler's shoulder, then back at Tyler. "Come by the cabin after church and we'll catch up. I'll make you a sandwich."

They shook hands again. "I'll be there."

Walking back to the row he had his Bible sitting in, Tyler glanced behind him at Chet once more. He caught a glimpse of him hugging another brother in Christ. *He really found You, Lord. That's amazing.* Tyler joined in the singing, letting his voice carry as joy and peace flooded over his heart. The fact that Chet had found Jesus gave him hope for Olivia and many nonbelievers he had met in his life. His friend had been hard-hearted for years and that shell was cracked open by a combination of life's difficulties and God's power, grace, and mercy.

FOLLOWING THE SERVICE, Tyler mingled with the congregation over coffee and donuts. Chet didn't stay long but left shortly after service. Sitting at a table with Charlie and Serenah, along with a few of their friends, everyone fell into light conversations. Some were speaking about the sermon that Charlie had delivered about being a servant, while others talked about their children and life's latest happenings around Newport. Then one of the guys at the table, Dylan, turned to Tyler.

"That wound on your knuckles looks fresh. Mind if I ask what happened?"

"I don't mind." Explaining how God led him to the scene

of the accident, Olivia, and her visit to the inn, Tyler ended his spiel with a sigh.

"You seem rather disappointed with the situation."

Tyler nodded. "I am. Pray for her. She doesn't believe in Jesus."

"Let's pray right now." Dylan scooted his chair closer to Tyler and bowed his head as he rested a hand on Tyler's shoulder. "Dear Lord, we come to You today lifting Olivia up to You. We ask You to soften her heart and to draw her close to You. God, You are the sustainer of life and it's only through You we can have peace. I also want to ask a special prayer over my brother in Christ, Tyler. May Your wisdom and truth be ever-present on his heart and in his mind. Amen."

Lifting his gaze to Dylan, Tyler nodded. "Thanks, man."

"You're welcome."

Excusing himself from the table a short time later, Tyler said his goodbyes and drove over to the far western side of the lake where Chet's cabin was located. Nothing but a dirt road, open acreage, and a small bundle of trees were on the property. The cabin was isolated from the rest of the lake's community and Chet loved it that way. As he drove down the bumpy road, he couldn't help but appreciate the fact that it hadn't changed a bit. As he came around the bend in the dirt road that came alongside the patch of trees, he recalled Chet being offered a large sum of money if he'd sell some of his land, but of course, he'd refused. He said that it was handed down to him in the family and he wouldn't let it go easily.

Parking beside the same beat-up Chevrolet pickup truck that Chet had been driving for years, Tyler got out of his car and surveyed the property. A stump used as a chopping block sat beneath a small tin shelter where stacked and chopped wood was piled up for the approaching winter months. Trees dotted the property, a small cluster to the right side of the cabin. Not much farther down the dirt road, Tyler could see Chet's old barn, most likely still full of Chet's stuff. Then the lake, which brought the property into its rightful beauty, was positioned perfectly behind the cabin, only a short walk to the shore line. There on the shore was a fire pit with burned up logs and a camping chair.

As Tyler headed to the front door of the cabin, he peered at the cabin itself, a gorgeous one-level wood cabin with an old chimney and a wraparound porch older than he was. As he came closer, he saw the same old rocking chairs they had on the porch the last time he visited. Sadness invaded Tyler as his gaze landed upon the one that belonged to Margret, Chet's late wife.

Tyler went up the steps onto the porch and knocked on the frame of the green-painted screen door.

Chet opened the door with a wide grin and then pushed open the screen. It creaked on its hinges.

"The coffee is on and sandwiches made. You still like turkey and bacon, right?"

"You betcha." Tyler walked in and noticed a shoe box on the coffee table on his way into the kitchen with Chet. Oscillating fans were in both the living room and kitchen, doing their best to keep the air moving and the sweat off. Finding his prepared sandwich on a plate at the kitchen table, Tyler took a seat.

"This looks great. Thanks for making it."

Chet sat down in a chair at the table. "You're welcome."

"So, tell me what you do with your time now. Still weaving, I take it?"

"Yep. I also do some work at the church. There for a while, when I was in better health, I let the youth come out once a month. Usually the last Friday of the month, I'd have them all over to roast marshmallows. We'd sit around the fire and tell stories, then I would teach them out of the Bible. We had a good time. I figure it's something, and that's a whole lot better than nothing. You know, I don't regret much in my life, Tyler, but I do regret not finding the Lord sooner. I don't think my life would've been easier if I found Jesus earlier, but I know I could've had Him with me and done a whole lot more for Him."

Moved with compassion and also guilt over his own lack of involvement with his church, Crosspoint, in Spokane, Tyler nodded as he finished a bite of sandwich. "That reminds me of the sermon today. It was a gut check for me. I feel dumb for how little I thought about serving before today. I'm so focused on my work and what I have going on that I was blinded to it."

"You still have a lot of years ahead of you, kid. A full life to serve Jesus."

His words reminded Tyler of the cancer he had briefly mentioned at the church. "Tell me more about the cancer, if you're willing."

The smile that followed on Chet's lips confused Tyler. Then he spoke and it all started to make sense. "Doctors gave me two months and that was about nine months ago. I reckon I won't be here much longer, and then I'll hopefully be joining Margret in Heaven."

"I didn't know Margret was a believer."

"I don't know if she was either. I look at it this way. I wasn't there in those final moments of her time on earth. She went when I was out to town for groceries. I know she knew about Jesus. She could've had a conversation with God right before she went." Chet was quiet for a long moment. "I guess I'll figure it out when I get there. I have hope, though."

Wiping his mouth with a napkin, Tyler turned his head toward the living room. "Hope is good. What's in the box?"

"Oh, just pictures from the past of Margret and me. Some old memories of when we had those kids come live with us for a while." He paused again for a long moment. "Sometimes, I wonder what life would've been like for the two of us if we had found the Lord earlier. I also wonder what things could've been like if we could've had our own children. I know Margret always felt bad that she couldn't give me kids, but truly, I didn't care. I had her, and that's all I needed."

Tyler longed for a love like the one that Chet spoke of; then unwillingly, Olivia came to his thoughts.

In the attempts to get his mind off Olivia, Tyler refocused his mind to the conversation. "Going down the road of *what-ifs* and *what could've beens* is a dangerous and bumpier road than your dirt driveway."

He let out a chuckle. "I know. Come on, finish up your sandwich and I'll show you what I looked like forty years ago when I was your age."

CHAPTER 7

*W*HEN THE SUN ROSE ON Monday morning, Olivia Montgomery was still in pain from her wreck. Despite the discomfort, she had a drive deep within her to move forward quickly with her divorce. Her father was able to retrieve the luggage from her wrecked car on Saturday after making a few phone calls to the wrecking yard. There, tucked in the front flap of her charred suitcase, were her divorce papers, still signed and ready. Her father was already gone by the time she made it out to the kitchen for breakfast that morning, but her mother was there and cooking at the stove.

"I've already called and made you an OB-GYN appointment. It's at eleven o'clock this morning." Her mother's words came as Olivia sat down at the kitchen table for breakfast. Her mother made her a plate of eggs, sausage, and hash browns.

"Thank you. I was just lying in bed wondering about that." Olivia focused her attention on the fork on the plate in front of her. She had been in this battle for three days now, the battle to feed herself and not rely on her mother to lift each bite to her lips. Every meal was a painful reminder of how broken she was, how dependent she was on her parents. She felt like a child again and it was driving her into the depths of despair. She sat at the table for a long moment, then her mother came to her side and gently placed a hand on her shoulder.

Her mother's words were full of grace and love. "It's okay to need help, Olivia."

"I want to try, Mom." Reaching out her arm that wasn't in a sling, she brought the casted hand down to the plate and used her thumb to pick up the fork, pressing it against her casted palm. Pushing the fork down into the eggs, it slipped out immediately and the metal clanked against the plate. Her eyes welled with tears and she peered up at her mother's face. "Why did this have to happen to me?"

Her mother grabbed the fork and sat down in a chair beside her. Pushing a strand of Olivia's hair out of her eyes, she placed it behind her ear and gently brushed her fingers against her daughter's cheek. "I don't know why it happened, Olivia, but I do know I am here for you, and your father is too. We're all going to get through this. You only have to wear the cast for six weeks and then you can start physical therapy. Only six weeks. Think about that, dear."

A pang of anxiety radiated through Olivia's entire being. It had only been three days. How could she go six weeks? She could feel her sadness starting to weigh heavier and heavier on her soul, dragging her down into the murky depths, back to the familiar place of despair. Feeling vulnerable, she opened up to her mother.

"Last night, I dreamed of my garden." Her tears were now mingled with a smile on her lips as she recalled the beautiful dream. As she thought of the dream, the depression loosened its grip on her and she could feel it subside. "The tomatoes were finally ripe and I picked one and bit into it."

"Was it juicy?" Her mother gave her a bite of eggs and a slice of sausage with it.

She chewed and swallowed, then responded, smiling as she did. "Yes, the juiciest tomato I had ever had. They were big too." Her thoughts faded from the dream, and suddenly, she was back in her parents' kitchen and at their table. Her gaze fell to her busted hands. "I don't know if I'll ever have another garden of my own."

"Someday, you will. Think about your future garden, or about that dream every time you feel down. You have to focus on the good, dear."

"I'll try."

AFTER FILING the divorce papers at the courthouse, her mother drove her to the OB-GYN appointment where they found out she was two months along. Afterward, they took a trip to Walmart to pick up prenatal vitamins and groceries. Olivia decided to split off from her mother in the store and went into the baby section. As she looked at infant boy and girl clothing, a memory bubbled to the surface of her mind of the last time she had strolled through a baby section in a store. It had been a year and a half ago, after she and Bruce had been on good terms for a while, or at least in her mind, they were. That day, she had found an infant girl's sunflower dress. She loved it so much that she bought it. That evening, when she attempted to show it to Bruce, he freaked, saying it wasn't smart to buy clothing for children when she wasn't even pregnant. The haunting memory made sense now, since she knew that he was still with Lisa. *A pregnant wife doesn't mix well with having a girlfriend.*

Resting her hand on her two-month pregnant belly, she fought back the tears. Her heart ached bitterly, thinking of Bruce and the truth about Lisa.

"There you are. Look what I found on clearance for seventy-five percent off!"

Olivia turned around to find her mother holding a car seat. Reality that a child was coming into the world became more real at the OB-GYN appointment, and even more real now at seeing a car seat in front of her. Steeling her nerves, she nodded.

"I love you, Mom."

Her mother tilted her head and smiled at her. "I love you too, dear. Come on, let's get you home to eat and rest. You look tired."

Her mother placed the car seat in the front of the shopping cart and then put an arm around Olivia and brought her out of the baby section.

As her mother loaded the items from the store into the trunk of the car, Olivia stood beside her and caught glances into the bags. Smoothies, some of Olivia's favorite foods, a gallon of chocolate milk, and so on. Every item had purpose, had meaning, and came from a loving place in her mother's heart. She was starting to see her mom in a new light, one that she was blind to years ago.

"You're a good mom." Olivia had never spoken those words to her mom before. She immediately felt awkward for saying it. "Sorry, I just—"

Her mom interrupted her by hugging her. "Thank you."

Her mother put the cart away in the cart return nearby and Olivia got into the car. As her mom got into the driver's seat, Olivia turned toward her.

"You really didn't know you were a good mom?"

She shrugged before turning the key over. Then, she looked over at Olivia. "It's always nice to hear someone appreciate what you do. You know? And can I be honest for a moment?"

"I prefer that you be that way in every moment." Olivia smiled, and her mom laughed.

Then, her mother lightly began to shed a few tears, and she tried to keep up with wiping them as they fell. Her voice broke apart as she spoke. "It's been so nice having you around the house. I know these circumstances aren't the best, but to take care of my little girl again has been so nice. It gives me a purpose. I thought after you cut off communication with us the last time, we wouldn't see you again. I felt like I did something wrong and I didn't know what I had done."

Seeing her mother moved to tears caused Olivia to cry too. Her heart opened. "Honestly, it's been hard to be home, but I love seeing you and Dad. As for cutting off communication . . . I know it's not something you want to hear, but I just don't believe what you and Dad believe. And truly, I've always felt you two viewed me differently for it and pushed me away in the process."

"Honey, we just want you to be happy, and it's the way we are happy. We find so much joy and peace and love in the Lord Jesus Christ. Think about it. Don't you want what's best for your child growing inside your tummy?"

"I do."

"Okay, then if you had something in your life that brought you immense joy, love, purpose, happiness, and peace, wouldn't you share that with your child and want the same for them?"

Something in Olivia's heart and mind clicked for the first time in her life in regard to her parents and their faith in God. She nodded. "I would."

Her mother smiled, then patted her daughter's leg lightly. "There, then you at least understand to a degree now. We love you no matter what you choose to believe, who you choose to love, or what you choose to do. Our love doesn't stop based on something you do or don't do."

Pulling into the driveway back at home a short while later, Olivia noticed Rachel's car in the driveway. She turned to her mom.

"Care if I get out of the house for a while with Rach?"

"Not at all. Maybe you can get Rachel to help me get the stuff into the house before you go?"

"Sure, Mom."

Entering the house, Olivia found Rachel asleep on the couch and the television set blaring. Surveying the living room, she spotted the remote tucked between Rachel and the couch and snatched it up quickly. She set the remote on the coffee table and used her thumb to press the *Volume Down* button repeatedly.

"Hey, I was watching that," Rachel said with a yawn as she sat up on the couch.

"Yeah, sure, on max volume and asleep? I'm not even sure how you were asleep with it that loud."

She stood up. "Have you been to *Zumiez*? The music is cranked all the time in there. I'm part deaf now."

They both laughed.

"Hey, can you help my mom with the groceries and then we can go?"

"Yes."

After the groceries were inside, Olivia found her mother in the kitchen putting the groceries away in the pantry. She tapped her shoulder.

"We're going to go."

Placing a box of rice into the pantry, she turned and looked at the two of them. "Okay. Olivia, you sure you don't need to take some medicine before you head out?"

"No, I'll be fine until I get home, I think. It's only been four hours. They last sixish."

"Okay. Have a good time. Take care of her please, Rachel."

"Will do, Aunt Kora."

As Olivia left out the front door with Rachel, she was reminded of her newfound appreciation of her mother. Their cry in the car earlier lingered in her heart and was cutting away at the old hard layers of anger and indignation she had been holding onto for years. Her mother, for the first time in Olivia's life, seemed to be more of a real person instead of a tyrannical dictator. She held onto that joy as she left to go spend time with Rachel.

CHAPTER 8

*U*PON ENTERING HIS FLAT ABOVE the bowling alley on Wednesday afternoon, Tyler took one look around his abode and knew the time had truly come. It was time to sell. He loved his home, and he didn't mind the bowling alley that brought in a few extra dollars each month either, but he knew after spending the last four days at Diamond Lake that it was time for a change in his living arrangements. He crossed over the threshold of his apartment and shut the door behind him. He went promptly to the laundry room across from his bedroom and tossed his dirty clothes into the washer. Recounting his time with Chet and all the fishing he had gotten in, not to mention the amazing pastor and his wife who ran the inn and church, Tyler was thankful for all God had done with his time away at the lake. Thinking more about where he would build his house, he held onto the idea of building his house right there on Diamond Lake. Chet had even offered a piece of his land to build on.

He closed the washing machine lid and went out, flipping off the light switch and closing the door behind him.

Walking into the kitchen, he went over to the counter and thumbed through his mail. He had given Vinny, the manager of the bowling alley, a key to let himself into his home to water his plants and drop off mail while he was gone. Arriving at the end of the stack of mail, he found an over-sized large envelope. Opening it, he found concept art from a client. The client was no artist, but it was enough of a rough idea that it would help Jonathan with the preliminaries. After looking it over, he set it down on the counter with the rest of the mail and then walked over to his newest plant, a ficus. It was only a couple of weeks old, and it was growing into something beautiful already. Lightly rubbing a leaf between his fingers, he smiled and thought, *I won't let myself get so busy again that I can't appreciate the smaller things in life, Lord. Teach me to always stay thankful.*

A knock came a moment later. *Who could that be?* He pondered on his way to answer it.

It was a man he thought looked familiar but couldn't place in his mind. Tall and burly, he looked like he could send Tyler, a fairly fit man, straight to the floor with a single punch. He was carrying an olive-green satchel over his shoulder. Tyler became uncomfortable and raised an eyebrow. "Yes? Can I help you, sir?"

The man's voice matched his manly appearance well, deep and rich in tone. "Yes, I'm from Crosspoint Community Church. I'm associate Pastor Carson. Can I come in?"

"Okay." Side-stepping to let him come in, Tyler was still confused. "What are you doing here? Did I do something?"

Pastor Carson raised a hand and a soft smile curled on his lips. "There's no problem, Tyler. We just like to check in with members when they haven't been seen around church in a while. I tried stopping by yesterday, but Vinny, your manager down there in the bowling alley, said you wouldn't be back until today. He's a nice guy, by the way."

"Yeah, he is." Tyler's defenses calmed and he led the pastor into the living room area to sit down on the couch. He offered him a drink and he took a bottle of water. They discussed his recent trip out to Diamond Lake, and then the pastor probed further into Tyler's life, and ultimately, his heart.

"Our records show you haven't been to church in over a month."

Tyler felt embarrassed for his lack of attendance and adjusted in his seat as he grew increasingly uncomfortable. "You really go the extra mile in keeping tabs on people, eh?"

He shrugged, still smiling. "Pastor West sees us all as the flock, and he's trying to help the body of Christ. We also have to keep him accountable and minister to him. We're all in this together, and we know the difficulties that life has to offer."

"Can I be honest?" Tyler hesitated until the pastor nodded. "I don't see how my church attendance has anything to do with my walk with Christ."

"I understand the defensiveness you're feeling right now, Tyler. Let me ask you this. Do you believe the Bible is one hundred percent true and accurate and is the inspired Word of God?"

"Yes, I do."

"Then, you accept the Gospels?"

"Yes."

"Okay. All through the gospels, people's walks of faith are an ongoing community project. We are blind to our own shortcomings and will make concession after concession for ourselves even for things that are blatantly sinful and wrong. When we have close brothers and sisters in Christ who can come along with us and speak truth to us in love and honesty, we are able to see that sin we are blind to. This isn't just about you Tyler. It's about me, it's about Pastor West, and it's about everybody in the body of Christ. You see, Jesus Christ is the head, and the rest of us are the body. Galatians 6 tells us to bear one another's burdens, 1 Corinthians 1 tells us to live in harmony, and Ephesians 4:15-16 tells us to speak truth in love to help others grow. I can keep going if you need me to?"

Tyler shook his head, smiling as conviction was already slaying him in the moment. "That's okay. I get it. This past Sunday, while I was out at Diamond Lake, I was actually convicted about my lack of serving at church. I want to be involved, and I do want to attend more."

"Serving is a great way to get plugged in. What do you think you'd like to do?"

Tyler was quiet for a long moment as he pondered the question. Nothing came to mind outside of *anything*. "Anything, really. I just really have a desire to serve. You know what I mean?"

"Good answer." Pastor Carson jotted a note down on his notepad. "We have a few volunteer openings on Sundays, Wednesdays, and even a few other behind-the-scenes types of gigs. I'll meet with the other pastors and discuss it. Tell me, what do you do for work? What are you skilled in?"

"I run the business side of an architecture company with my brother. I'm good at speaking with clients and negotiating." Tyler laughed. "Not sure how that comes in handy at church. Oh, wait, I do enjoy sports and working out, so if there is any desire for something like that, I can lead it."

"How do you feel about young people? Like youth group stuff?"

Tyler paused, hesitation on his heart and mind. "Well, yeah, I guess so. I was thinking adults."

"Adults tend to do a softball team during the spring and summer, but other than that, the youth are the ones who tend to need activities. You don't seem confident about the youth. Is there any issue?"

Steeling his nerves and pushing away the selfishness inside him that made him hesitant about working with kids when he wasn't blessed with any of his own, he shook his head. "I'm okay with youth."

"Great." The pastor combed through his satchel and the folders inside. Retrieving a stapled form, he handed it to Tyler. "Fill this out and get it turned in tonight at church or next Sunday, whenever you come next."

"What is this?"

"Just a questionnaire about your faith and also a background check. We have to protect ourselves, the children, and you." Rising to his feet, Pastor Carson smiled warmly as he looked into Tyler's eyes. "Give whatever you end up doing some time and let the Lord lead you through it. I promise you, sometimes, it will be difficult, but just showing up is over half the battle. You show up, and the Lord's Spirit will do the rest."

Tyler was comforted and encouraged by the pastor's words and kindness. As he walked with the pastor over to the door to show him out, he nodded with confidence. "I think it'll be an adventure no matter what. Thank you so much for coming by. It really means a lot."

THAT EVENING, Tyler drove over to Jonathan and Kylie's house to drop off the concept sketches that had come in the mail. Upon being let into his brother's house, he handed him the envelope. His brother pulled the sketches out and glanced at them.

"You sign the lease for our new business office, Jonathan?"

"Yes."

"We need to get the mail switched over to the office."

"I'll get on it. Did you have a good time at the lake? You seem relaxed," Jonathan mentioned as he glanced up at Tyler.

"It was just what my soul needed." Tyler recalled the burning car and the pretty woman and was immediately regretful he hadn't called Jonathan about it after it happened. But Tyler didn't want to worry him while he was off having family time on Saturday at Silverwood. He could've called on Sunday, but he was at Chet's house until late. Now it was Wednesday evening, and he was back in town and his brother still didn't know. Lowering his voice, Tyler looked at Jonathan's eyes while they were still down on the sketches.

"I have to get to church soon if I want to make it in time, but I need to tell you something first, Brother."

Noticing the shift in tone, Jonathan grew serious and shoved the sketches back into the envelope and led him toward the stairs. Stopping at the base of the steps, Jonathan leaned a hand on the banister and hollered gently toward the kitchen. "Hey, Love?"

"Yes?" Kylie's voice came ringing through from the kitchen.

"Tyler and I will be upstairs in my office for a few minutes. You have Rose and Peter in there with you?"

"Yes. Rose is helping me with dinner, which will be done in about twenty minutes. Peter is playing with his cars on the floor."

"Great. See you in a bit."

Climbing the stairs, the two of them then walked the hallway to Tyler's office. As they came into the room, Tyler fixed his eyes on Jonathan as he crossed the room and sat down behind his desk.

"I helped a lady out of a burning car right before it exploded."

Jonathan's eyes widened and he leaned forward as the shock registered on his face. "When did this happen?"

"Friday night."

His brother's voice lightened and he leaned back in his chair. "Days ago. You didn't call? Are you okay?"

Tyler rubbed his neck as he shrugged. "I didn't want to worry you, and I am fine, obviously."

"Is that what the gash on your hand is about?" Jonathan glanced at Tyler's left hand.

"Yeah, I'm really sorry I didn't call. I'm fine, and she's okay. Well, she will be okay." Tyler's heart panged as his mind held Olivia's image there. He still couldn't shake his desire for her, nor could he dislodge that pebble of discomfort every time she came up in his thoughts.

"You seem conflicted, Brother."

Tyler raised his eyebrows. "I am. She came and found me at the inn the next day to thank me, and I gave the credit to God in regard to His saving her." Tyler's eyes welled and he had to fight back the emotional response he was having as he thought about Olivia's hatred toward God. "She was so hateful, Brother. Bent out of shape at the mention of God."

"*Tyler.*" Jonathan seemed to know something he didn't know, and Tyler took a step closer to the desk, his face pensive.

"What?"

"She's wounded." Jonathan clasped his hands together. "God's up to something in that gal."

Wanting to get off the subject, Tyler redirected. "Speaking of God's work, guess who was at the church out at Diamond Lake?"

Jonathan shrugged. "Who?"

"Chet!"

Jonathan's mouth fell open, his smile growing as he spoke. "No, he wasn't."

Tyler became excited and sat down in the chair in front of the desk. "Yes, he was! He was there and singing, and wow . . . he is a completely different guy." Talking about Chet and telling Jonathan all about their visit at the cabin reminded Tyler about his plans to sell the bowling alley and build out on the lake. With a deep breath, he spoke the words he felt deeply now. "I'm ready to sell."

With that, his brother knew *exactly* what he was saying by those four words. "This is it, huh?"

With absolute confidence, Tyler nodded. "This is it."

$\mathcal{S}$EVEN MONTHS LATER, THE SPRING thaw did more than just melt the snow and ice. It gave birth to new beginnings and new hope. Olivia's baby girl, Molly, was a March baby and would soon be entering the world, and everybody Olivia loved and knew was excited alongside her. She had been hard at work for the last six months on her dental assisting certification in the evenings, a few times each week. During the day, she was working at the dealership of her dad's friend, Gus, as a receptionist. Though her hands and body had healed, there were still pains that would surface from time to time in her right hand.

Pausing at her post behind the reception desk, Olivia closed her eyes tightly and rubbed the palm of her hand that was hurting.

"You okay?" Jasper, one of the car salesmen, asked as he waited on the other side for her to finish inputting the data for the paperwork of a new customer.

"Yeah, give me just a minute." Her pain had mostly vanished in the last couple of months, and it discouraged her greatly when it came on so violently just a couple of days ago. She fought tears as she tried to massage the pain away in the moment. It wasn't helping. She stood up from her chair. "I'll be right back."

Exiting from behind reception, she went to the ladies' restroom and flipped on the light upon entering. Approaching the sink and mirror, she saw the tears welling in her eyes. Olivia looked boldly at herself. "Come on. You can do this! You're fine." For a moment, the pain subsided and relief washed over her, but then on her way to leave, another zing of excruciating pain tore through her hand like a sharp blade ripping through her flesh. Pressing the hand that didn't hurt against the wall, she braced herself and took some deep breaths, trying to focus on anything but the pain. After a moment, the pain left again. Standing upright, she rested a hand on her nine-month-pregnant belly as she thought of Molly. *How am I going to take care of you when I'm in this much pain?* Worry pressed in on her, taunting her and telling her she couldn't do it on her own. Olivia had just moved into an apartment a couple of weeks ago, and she was finally seeing herself as independent again when this happened.

A long moment passed, and she wiped the pain-ridden tears from her cheeks. Walking out of the bathroom and back over to her receptionist desk, Jasper dug for answers once more.

"Is it the baby? You having contractions or something?"

She had indeed been having off and on contractions this last week, but they turned out to be Braxton-Hicks.

"I'm fine now, Jasper. Let me get this finished up for you."

After work a few hours later, she went over to Rachel's apartment. She let herself in and found Rachel down the hall in the bedroom. The door was wide open and she walked in. On the bed was a pile of dresses, skirts, and blouses, and over with her nose in the closet was a distraught cousin, her back to her. She hadn't even heard Olivia enter the room.

"Rach?"

Startled, Rachel whipped around. "Oh, hey, you. I didn't hear you come in."

Rachel moved quickly to the spot between the bed and Olivia, blocking the view of the mess. A blush crawled into her cheeks.

Olivia laughed. "Why are you embarrassed?"

She shrugged and glanced to her side, looking at the pile of clothing. "It looks like a bull tore through my closet. I'm trying to find something nice for tonight."

"You have a date?" Olivia couldn't hide her surprise.

Her lips curled into a smile as she tilted her head and rocked her body. "*Maybe . . .*"

"Is it that Drew guy from the jewelry store in the mall?"

"Oh, heavens no. That guy is a total player. It's not him. Someone else."

"Who is it?"

She shooed a hand. "Don't worry about it. What's up? What brings you to my humble abode on this fine Thursday evening?"

"I need more." Olivia's face grew somber as the light-hearted tone shifted to a more serious one.

Rachel was quiet for a long moment. Then, without saying anything, she began to put the clothing back into the closet, piece by piece. Olivia felt embarrassed, upset that she wasn't saying anything.

"Can you get them or not?" Olivia's voice reeked of annoyance and lacked the appreciation she knew she should show.

Another long moment passed, only increasing the anxiety in Olivia.

Finally, Rachel stopped and looked at her. "I can, but . . . I just gave you some the other day. Like ten."

"I don't need a judge. I need more relief from this pain. I can't even do my job, Rach. Do you understand how bad this affects me? I have to be able to work to take care of my kid."

"Yeah, and what about Molly?"

A set of daggers tore through Olivia's heart immediately at the mention of her daughter. "Thanks for the concern, but the doctors said the pills were only harmful if used long-term, plus, they gave me some in my early pregnancy, remember? I even went online and asked a few nurse hotlines to make sure I'm being safe. Listen, the truth is I've been off them for months and months. It's barely been two days ago that I started using them again. I tried my doctor, but they blew me off and said to take Ibuprofen and Tylenol. Why do you have to make me feel like an addict just like they did?"

"Sorry." She shrugged. "I just worry about you and Molly." Olivia's eyes burned with tears and she fought them back as Rachel went over to her dresser and opened the top drawer. She moved slowly, as if she was debating on whether to give them to Olivia. This only further hurt Olivia and drove her to a deeper anger and resentment toward her cousin.

"Listen, she'll be here anytime. I promise you, this isn't a problem."

"Okay." Rachel came over and handed her the bottle.

Taking the bottle from her hand, Olivia forced a smile. "Thanks."

When she turned to leave, she regretted her harshness immediately. She stopped her steps and walked over to Rachel and pulled her in for a hug. "I'm sorry. These hormones are making me out of control, and the added pain isn't helping matters either." She started to cry, then continued. "Rachel, I love you and you know that."

Rachel's eyes glossed over with tears. "I'm sorry too! I shouldn't be so worried. I love you."

Olivia let go of her and left her bedroom. As she walked out to her car in the driveway, a contraction came on strong. She stopped as she opened the car door and leaned against the vehicle. Unable to speak, to think, she waited for it to pass. After it was over, she got into the car and drove to her apartment.

LATER AFTER DINNER, her mother came by the apartment to bring over a Noah's Ark mobile to hang above the crib in the baby's room. Ever since the wreck happened, Olivia and her mother had grown closer in their relationship, and Olivia had lowered her defenses. When she was still with Bruce, she wouldn't have allowed something like a Noah's Ark mobile above her child's crib, but now things were different. She wasn't so adamantly against anything and everything her parents stood for, though she still didn't believe. If they wanted to take Molly to church one day, that was fine with Olivia as long as she was able to tell her daughter there were more beliefs out there than just that one religion.

"It's cute." Olivia watched the mobile rotate as a tinkling song played. She envisioned for a moment what it would be like to lay her baby girl down in the crib. There was so much love in her heart for her unborn girl, she couldn't imagine what it would be like when she finally came out.

Her mother agreed and turned to her. "I forgot to tell you, a letter came from Bruce. It's still at my house. Maybe you can pick it up when you come over for dinner on Saturday?"

"Okay, cool. I already know what it is. He called and told me he sent a check to help out with diapers and other needs for Molly."

Her mother raised her eyebrows. "Wow. He's really been good about this whole thing."

"Yeah. The whole thing is kind of strange. He's been more understanding and kind toward me since we've been divorced than he was most of the time we were married." That fact hurt Olivia, but she knew there wasn't much she could do about it. At least he was providing for Molly with a check in the mail every month. Her mother placed her arm around Olivia, and it drove the pain deeper in her heart to know her mother could sense her pain.

"It's going to be okay for you and Molly. Your life is on track and you are working hard to provide for your little angel. Your father and I are so proud of all that you've been doing with your life."

"Thanks. Did you send out the thank you notes?" Her mother had gotten her ladies' Bible study group to throw Olivia a surprise baby shower a few weeks ago. They showered her with gifts from a place of love in their hearts. A high chair, car seat, stroller, Diaper Genie, and more. The ladies had truly gone above and beyond to love on her during this time. Olivia felt nervous at first about the baby shower, fearing it'd turn into a Bible study and intervention about her lack of faith, but it never went that direction. Instead, it was all about her new baby coming into the world. She felt beyond loved and cared for by the group of ladies who were but strangers to her.

"Yes, I sent them out yesterday."

"Thank you."

Resting her good hand on the crib that her father had built, Olivia was overwhelmed with love. Her parents had surprised her these last seven months and had shown her love that was beyond comprehension. "You and Dad have been so kind to me. Thank you for everything. I feel lucky."

Placing a hand on her daughter's shoulder, her mother

gently spoke. "You're not lucky, my daughter, you're blessed. God is pursuing you and showering you with His love using His believers."

Olivia didn't snap at her. She had grown to respect her mother's beliefs. She smiled and changed the subject.

"Would you like some tea?"

"I'd love that."

Leaving the nursery with her mother, Olivia paused and glanced around the pink and yellow decorated room. She smiled. In her heart, though she'd never admit it, she said, *maybe there is a God.* Turning off the light, she shut the door and proceeded down the hallway to prepare tea for her mother and herself.

Joining her mother on the couch, she handed her a cup of tea.

"Your father is so cute. He has a duffel bag all ready to go for when the call comes to go to the hospital. Complete with a change of clothes for all three of us, snacks, sodas, and even cell phone chargers. He even bought you Chap Stick because he read somewhere that's the number-one thing people wished they had and forgot during delivery. He didn't want to miss a thing and wants you as comfortable as possible while you bring our granddaughter into the world. I think he's more excited about Molly coming than I am!" She laughed, taking a sip from her cup.

It warmed Olivia's heart to hear her mother's words about her father. She had worried early on that he was against her being pregnant because of how he had reacted when he found out. But all those worries had since melted away, and it was most confirmed when he found out the sex of the baby. He came home from work that day with balloons, cake, and a banner, all in pink. He was gleeful to have another girl in the family, and it helped Olivia realize just how joy-filled he truly was, even if he didn't show it *all* the time. As her and her mother's cups of tea emptied, it was time for her mom to go home.

"Well, I'd better get home. You still have me on speed dial, right?"

"Of course. You'll be the first one I call. I need a ride, after all."

"You sure you're not going to stop working before you have the baby?"

Olivia laughed. "I'm sure. I can still drive my car and work, so I'm okay." She thought of her hand pains but decided not to tell her mother. She didn't want to worry her or burden her with the knowledge of it. When she did go to the doctor, she told her mother it was for a check-up, shielding her from the truth. Her mother was too kind and would be overly concerned if she knew about the pain, and she didn't need the extra worry. It was hard enough on her when Olivia had left their home to go live on her own with the pregnancy so close to being full-term. She decided she wouldn't tell her parents about the hand pain coming back, not now, and not ever.

CHAPTER 10

MEETING WITH A YOUNG NEWLYWED couple to show them the bowling alley in April, Tyler was running low on his hopes of selling. He had been trying to sell the property for eight months now, and while there were a few offers for the place, they were all laughable in his mind. He was starting to come to grips with the fact that he might never sell and would just have to keep it and rent out the apartment. While showing the couple the place, Tyler was distracted in thought, thinking about his date tomorrow night with Daisy, a fellow volunteer from Crosspoint he had met when he started volunteering with the youth group.

"We'll take it." The woman's comment didn't penetrate Tyler's skull right away. He had become numb through the walk-through tours. She stepped away from her husband and got in Tyler's field of vision. "Sir? We'll take it."

Shaking his head, Tyler raised his eyebrows. "What? Really? For the asking price?"

The man stepped forward, beaming with a smile just as

big as his wife's. "Yes! It's a steal of a deal with the income we'll make from the bowling alley."

"*Finally.*" Tyler let out a relieved sigh. "Someone who understands this is an income property, not just an apartment for sale."

It hadn't happened until this moment, and it did so by total surprise, but Tyler suddenly felt nervous to lose his home. He surveyed the bowling alley's lanes on the other side of the couple, and all the lanes were full of people. He had spent some good years here, and in weeks, it'd be gone if everything worked out.

"I'm going to miss this place. Did you know this right here was my thinking spot?" Tyler pointed out a high-backed bar stool and a small table nearby. Then, he leaned under the table and pointed to it. "My name is even on it!"

The couple laughed and the man took a step toward him. "You can come back and bowl for free anytime you want, or to sit." The man nodded toward the concessions. "You can have all the beer you want too."

"I don't drink, but thanks. I'll come by for sure."

That afternoon, the Feldmans sent in their offer and Tyler accepted. Now, it was just a matter of time in escrow.

Wanting to celebrate, he took a bottle of sparkling cider and two champagne glasses out with him to Chet's cabin, just a little bit up the dirt road from his own patch of land where his house was being built. He ended up taking Chet up on his offer to buy a part of his land and build on it, an offer he felt confident was the right move.

Knocking on the screen door, he didn't wait but instead just walked in with the bottle and glasses in hand.

"Guess who sold their bowling alley?"

Smiling as he came across the threshold into the cabin, he saw Chet asleep on the couch with his Bible in his lap. Warmed to see his friend had fallen asleep reading the Word of God, Tyler walked over to the couch and sat down beside him.

"Buddy, I finally did it. I sold that bowling alley. Honestly, I was starting to wonder if it'd ever sell. What I'm thinking is I'll just move all my furniture and whatnot into that barn, if there's some room out there. Then, when I'm finally move-in ready here in a couple of months, I'll just move it all on over. So, basically, I need to take you up on that other offer to live with you until my house is fully ready."

Tyler leaned forward on the couch and set the glasses down on the coffee table, then poured the sparkling cider.

"I know it's a lot to ask, Chet. But to be fair, you did offer, and I'm over here a lot anyway, so it makes sense."

When Chet didn't respond again, Tyler became concerned. "Chet?"

He reached out and moved his shoulder lightly to wake him.

There was no response and his skin felt cold.

Chills ran the length of Tyler's spine and he jumped away from the couch. He covered his mouth and fought tears back. "Chet. No."

He peered up at the ceiling and cried out to God. "Why'd you take him right now, God?"

Tyler's chest tightened and his breathing shallowed. Slipping his cell phone out of his pocket, he dialed 9-1-1 as he kept stealing glances at his friend. As the operator answered and he had to respond to the question of 'Reason for calling,' his heart shattered into a million pieces.

"My friend. He passed away."

TYLER'S BROTHER was kind enough to come out to the cabin that evening to help deal with all that needed to be done when someone passed away. Jonathan had lost his wife and had been through it all before. He, too, knew Chet, but he wasn't as close to him as Tyler had become, especially over the last several months. It brought Tyler a great deal of relief to have someone there dealing with the funeral arrangements and so forth with him.

After Jonathan hung up with the funeral parlor in the living room, he joined Tyler at the kitchen table and sat down. He was quiet for a long moment, just watching as Tyler combed through the documents they had found in the desk near his bed.

"I couldn't imagine being the last one left of all your family." Tyler's words came as he shook his head and read over the directions on how to shut down operations of Chet's website.

Jonathan responded, "I think at that point, you're kind of ready for Heaven if you have a family of believers."

Tyler's heart went cold with a deep chill. He knew that other than Chet, his family hadn't been believers. A desire to change the topic to something lighter pushed against him, and he shuffled the papers to the one that dealt with his will. "He left his money to the church, then the cabin and land to me."

"Wow." Jonathan's eyebrows lifted. "You must've made some mark on the man."

Tyler shook his head. "I was just his friend. I remember people thinking it was odd back in the day when we were hanging out all the time. Such an age gap between Chet and me, but honestly, I loved this man like a brother." He shook his head again. "I can't believe he's gone now. I'm sad but I know he's better off in Heaven. He was in a lot of pain, and God knew Chet would pass away today. The Lord wasn't surprised like I was."

"That's very true. He is with his Lord and Savior now. So,

what now? You have a cabin and a house on the same property?"

Tyler started to laugh. When it didn't subside right away but rolled into an uncontrollable laugh, Jonathan joined in, laughing uncontrollably. They stood up and tried to calm themselves, but if more than a moment passed without laughing, one would bust out into laughter again. There was no explanation for the fit of laughter other than a gift from God. Finally calming down about five minutes later, they wiped their tears.

"I don't even understand why that was so funny," Tyler said, wiping his eyes as his abs were inflamed from laughing so long.

Jonathan shook his head. "I don't know either."

Tyler rested a hand on his hip and then placed his other on the back of the kitchen chair.

"I don't know what I'll do with the cabin. For now, I'll live in it. Once my house is built, it'll sit. Maybe the youth group can use it for a weekend or something? I don't know."

"That's a good idea."

A few hours later, Jonathan was getting ready to leave, but before he did, he and Tyler prayed in the living room. Jonathan rested a hand on Tyler's shoulder as they both bowed their heads.

"Lord, we come to you today for Tyler's close friend, Chet. We pray that he is enjoying Heaven. Please help Tyler's heart be comforted during this time of loss. We know Chet is with You now. His body is no longer under the curse and he is pain-free. We pray that You guide and protect us and lead us in the way we should go in our lives. We pray these things in Your precious and holy name, Jesus. Amen."

"Thanks, Brother." Tyler wiped a stray tear and patted Jonathan on the back and walked him to the door. After Jonathan left, Tyler decided to stay the night.

He sprawled himself out on the recliner in the living room and started in on a stack of photos from Chet's life. Each one he looked at, he'd set on a pile on his chest. Some, he had already seen when he had visited Chet that Sunday when he was out visiting Diamond Lake last summer. Then, toward the end of the pile, he saw photos he didn't recognize. Seeing an old black-and-white photo of a young man in a service uniform, he flipped it over. In blue ink, it read, **Chet '55.**

Tyler thought about it for a moment, then realized he'd most likely been in the Vietnam War. He flipped the photo over to look again at the picture of Chet. He was young and clean-shaven, with a whole life ahead of him. He thought it was interesting that Chet had never mentioned his past war experience. Then, leaning in closer, he saw a Purple Heart medal on his service jacket.

Conviction filled Tyler as he recalled his saving of that woman last summer. He had bragged to Chet about it. He had bragged about it to practically everyone he came across. He hadn't been quiet about it like Chet had been about receiving a Purple Heart, and Chet had been in a war, the closest place to Hell on earth a person can get. Admiration for Chet's life overtook Tyler, and he prayed right there for courage to be such a man as Chet.

SLEEP evaded Tyler later that evening in the recliner. He didn't want to go back to Spokane, not right now, and he also didn't want to sleep in a dead man's bed or on the couch where he had breathed his final breath. In the hopes of finding inspiration to sleep, he drove into the town of Newport to walk around the quiet streets.

He pulled alongside a curb and got out. Shoving his hands into his coat pockets, he started to walk beneath the street lamps that dotted the path of the sidewalk. His breath was visible, and the cold April night's air lashed against his coat, penetrating and chilling his skin. Not long into his walk around town, a slow-moving car pulled up beside him, still moving as the driver's-side window came down.

A woman's voice came from the shadow. "Alex?"

Tyler couldn't see the woman, so he turned fully toward the car.

"Alex?" she again asked.

"Um, no?" He was confused not only because someone had mistaken him for someone else, but that it was happening at one o'clock in the morning. "What are you doing out so late looking for someone?"

"What are you doing out so late walking around Newport?"

He laughed. "Touché. I'm clearing my head to get some perspective. You?"

"Alex is a . . . friend."

"A friend?" He shook his head and peered over as he and the car came beneath a street lamp. He glanced over to get a better look at the woman. His heart stopped and his steps did too. It was the woman from the car wreck in August. "Olivia? Is that you?"

She looked at Tyler and then blinked as it appeared to click in her mind. She rolled the window up and punched the gas pedal.

Chasing after the car, he entered the street and tried to wave her down as he ran, his heart pounding as confusion swirled in his mind.

Out of breath, he finally stopped. He panted for air as he watched her car's taillights vanish around a corner. She was gone.

CHAPTER 11

*H*EART RACING AND CAR WHEELS squealing around the corner, Olivia glanced in her rearview mirror to make sure Tyler hadn't followed after her in his car. Her hands and fingers trembled as she gripped the steering wheel. She hadn't expected to see him ever again after that day at the inn, let alone eight months later at one o'clock in the morning. Embarrassment and shame rippled through her whole being. Not only had she loaded her one-month-old baby into her car in the dead of the night to go get pills, but she'd also seen the man who'd saved her life and repeatedly visited her in her dreams.

Driving straight to Rachel's house, she quickly got out of the car and pulled Molly's car seat out from the back seat. She hurried up the steps and into the house. Rachel paused her movie in the living room and stared at Olivia, wide-eyed.

"What's up?"

Olivia set Molly's car seat down on the floor and covered it with a blanket she brought from the car. Then, she walked into the kitchen, Rachel following behind her. Once in the kitchen, she kept her voice low. "He was nowhere in Newport!"

Rachel raised her hands in defense. "Whoa, there . . . no need to bite my head off."

"I brought Molly with me, Rach! I just needed something for the pain quickly. Typing out my recent paper for school must have really irritated my hand. It hurts so much! So, I go in search for some relief, and I ended up running into *Tyler*."

She lifted an eyebrow. "Tyler? Haven't heard that name in a while. Wow. He was in Newport?"

"Yes, he was, and I was mortified! I had my newborn baby in my back seat, and I was out looking for drugs in the middle of the night like an addict!"

"Hey, now, you're not an addict. You don't overdose, you go months without taking pills, and you don't take more than recommended. But I don't know why you're talking to me like I forced you to go out there. I told you he wasn't home and was probably walking to his friend Steve's house. I didn't say you had to go find him." Rachel walked over to the pantry in her kitchen and pulled out a box of cheese crackers. Popping a handful into her mouth, she shook her head. "Nobody made you do it, and nobody made you take Molly. You could've waited until after you dropped her off with your mom tomorrow, before you went to work."

Her cousin's words pierced through her like a javelin through the heart. Her cousin was right. It was all her own fault. Her eyes welled, and she grabbed her bad hand. Rubbing the palm, she tried to deaden the pain. "I couldn't sleep. I can't keep living like this. It's getting worse every day!"

Rachel came closer and offered the box. Olivia declined. Rachel tossed another handful in her mouth. "Have you tried your doctor again?"

She laughed. "Do you know how difficult it is to get

prescription painkillers these days? They treat you like an addict on your first visit in. In other words, yes, I've tried, and I have failed miserably. I've even gone to a pain specialist. They were even ruder than my normal doctor." Olivia went over to the kitchen table and sat down in a chair. Resting her head against her good hand, she felt all hope draining from her. "I feel so stuck and confused and worried. I can't lose my job, and I only have five more months before I get my dental assisting certificate. But what good will that do if my hand is messed up?"

"You need a miracle of God."

She laughed. "Yeah. I gave up on God a long time ago, Rach. The things I've done? If there is a God out there, this is purely retribution for all the wrong I've done." Olivia's gaze went across the kitchen and to the open archway that led into the living room. She thought of Molly and the fact that she had taken her to Newport with her tonight. "I'm a bad mom. I took my newborn out in the middle of the night, and you're right. Nobody made me do it."

"Hey, now." Rachel came over and placed a hand on her shoulder. Her touch did little to ease the overwhelming sadness lapping against her heart. She didn't know what to do anymore or how to function. She felt like she was heading down a road in the middle of nowhere and it was leading her into darkness. "You're a human being and you want to dull that pain because it helps you sleep so you can get up and go to work in the morning. If you go to work, you can keep providing for Molly. See? It's not *that* bad. You were trying to do what you felt was best."

Olivia nodded in agreement, but she knew it wasn't fully true. She had other options. She'd just been selfish and wanted the instant gratification of relief. Taking the box of cheese crackers off the kitchen table, Olivia reached in and grabbed a handful. Retrieving her hand, she popped them into her mouth. After she swallowed, she turned to her cousin. "Didn't Aunt Tina have bad pain after her horseback riding accident years ago?"

"Yep. I think she did acupuncture and it helped her. Maybe you can try that?"

"Yeah, maybe I can." Hearing Molly make a fussy noise in the other room, Olivia took it as her cue to leave. Rising from the table, she hugged Rachel. "I'm sorry for freaking out on you. I was freaked when I saw Tyler, and then not finding Alex, and . . . I'm sorry."

"It's okay. I'll call Alex and see what happened. I'll come find you tomorrow with a bottle."

"Thanks."

Leaving through the living room, she picked Molly up and went out to her car to leave.

MOLLY WAS awake by the time she arrived home, and she knew it'd take some rocking to get her to fall back asleep after her bottle. Each moment Molly was still awake was like a twist on the knife Olivia felt in her heart. It was her fault her daughter wasn't home tonight and in the comfort of her own bed. In the moonlight streaming in through the nursery window in her apartment, Olivia wept silently for her mistreatment of her own child. As she peered down at her baby girl's soft pink face, she thought of Molly's future. *I know you'd be better off with someone else right now. You deserve the best, and the best is not what I am.* Hugging Molly a bit closer to her, Olivia felt an increasing pain in her soul as the truth of her bad parenting was brought to the front of her mind.

By three o'clock, a half hour after getting home, Molly was finally asleep. Olivia rose up from the rocking chair and laid her gently into the crib. She saw the Noah's Ark mobile hanging above the crib and thought of her mother. She thought about how disappointed she would be if she knew who she had become lately, someone who was hunting for drugs on the street with her baby in the back seat. Her heart ached even more, thinking about her mom telling her how proud she was of her just a short time ago. Leaving the crib, Olivia walked out of the nursery and quietly shut the door behind her.

Venturing down the hallway to her bedroom, she went in and got her pajamas back on, then climbed beneath the warm sheets and comforter. She had about four hours of sleep left before she'd have to get up, and with the pain still present, she knew it'd be a fight all the way through the day.

STARING at the red LED lights on the alarm clock as it struck seven and the alarm sounded, it felt as if a part of Olivia died in that very moment. The thought of a full day of work at the dealership brought an agony that ran deep in her bones. Not just physically, but mentally as she tried to focus on work while having the pain shoot through her hand. Pushing the covers off, she climbed out of bed and went and got ready.

On the drive over to drop Molly off at her mother and father's house, she thought again of last night. Not the fact that she hadn't gotten any pills, but that she had seen Tyler. She had been focused on herself, her pain, her embarrassment, and she didn't stop to consider what he was doing out at one o'clock, walking around the town of Newport. She began to regret driving off from him so fast. He had tried to reach out to her. *Maybe he had been going through something too?* The thought lined up with his comment about being out at that time to clear his head. She felt bad. Thinking about him stirred a long-forgotten desire inside her.

Tyler had crossed Olivia's thoughts off and on since the

night he saved her life. She'd never forget the warmth of him holding her as he pulled her to safety. And what did she do? She had been incredibly rude to him on the day at the inn when she went to thank him. She was angsty toward God and let it dictate how she spoke to him. She'd thought for a moment about looking him up again since then, but her pregnant belly and busy schedule kept her from ever going through with it.

Arriving at her parents' house, she took Molly inside and handed her mother the diaper bag.

"She just ate at the house. There's a can of formula in the diaper bag. I know you ran out yesterday."

"Yes, thank you. Have a great day at work, Olivia."

"Thanks."

As Olivia looked into her mother's eyes, she saw love, approval, and pride for who Olivia had become. It stung to know that her mother only saw what Olivia wanted her to see. It was who she was becoming that she knew her mother couldn't tolerate. The one in chronic pain, the one self-medicating and playing with a fire she'd once played with in her youth. Growing uncomfortable and on the edge of being late for work, she kissed her daughter's forehead goodbye and left to go to work.

CHAPTER 12

ONSUMED WITH GRIEF BUT DISTRACTED by thoughts of Olivia, Tyler sat across from Daisy at the restaurant in silence. He had barely touched his steak and potatoes and said only a few words most of the evening. He could sense that Daisy was growing more uncomfortable with him by the moment, but he couldn't bring himself to think of anything but Olivia. He couldn't stop seeing her sea-blue eyes in his mind, and his desire burned inside him, wanting to see her again.

"*Tyler?*"

Peering up from his plate and into Daisy's eyes, Tyler raised his eyebrows. "Yeah?"

"I asked you if you've had any more offers on the bowling alley."

"Oh, yes, I just sold it. Just waiting for escrow to close." His tone was flat, void of emotion.

"What is wrong with you? That's great news, and you act like you just told me you bought gas at a gas station."

Tyler adjusted in his seat and felt the weight of her words penetrate his conscience. He was remorseful over his behavior. "I know I'm not much for conversation tonight. I have a lot on my mind. I just lost a good friend, and his funeral is in two days, and . . ." He hesitated to tell her, but because they were friends already at church, he decided to spill the truth. He smiled and said, "I also saw someone I hadn't seen in a long time."

"There's that smile. Must be someone special?" She forked a piece of her salad and took a bite as she waited for him to talk. She must've seen right through Tyler.

"I saved her life last year—that's how we met—and honestly, I was drawn to her from the moment I laid eyes on her. It took a while to get her out of my mind, and now that I saw her again . . ."

"Now you can't stop thinking about her. I get it."

He blushed and shook his head, letting out a sigh. "She's everything wrong for me, Daisy. That's what I don't get. She hates God and was incredibly rude the last two times I've seen her, the only times I've seen her. Honestly, I don't understand why I can't stop thinking of her. I think it's her eyes. They're unique."

Daisy didn't say anything but continued eating her salad.

"My goodness, I'm making this the worst date in the world, aren't I?"

She laughed and shook her head, dabbing a napkin on her lips. "It's fine, Tyler. Truly, I like you as a friend at church and we tried this out. You know? No hard feelings."

"Wait, I don't even know her. We can't just write us off because of one date."

She was quiet for a long moment, then she set her fork down. Clasping her hands together, she smiled warmly at Tyler. "Listen, I'm thirty years old. I don't have a lot of time to court people, and I can see the look in your eyes when you talk about this girl. She's special to you, even if you don't fully understand it yet. I want that look when a man thinks about me, and you're not going to be able to give me that."

"I have a look in my eyes? What's that mean?" He laughed nervously, not sure what to think.

"Yes, you do."

After that point in the date, Tyler didn't see any use in dragging out the rest of the night. He had plans to take her to Riverfront Park to walk the paths and to stroll down to the carousel, but he lacked any drive to do so after Daisy was so determined that his heart was elsewhere. So, after dinner at the restaurant, they parted ways. Tyler was on the side of town where his brother lived, so he stopped in to say hello.

As they played pool in the basement, Tyler opened up about the date with Daisy and what she had said about Olivia.

Leaning on his pool stick, Jonathan appeared to process all that Tyler had said.

"She could be right. Your heart might already be leading you straight to Olivia, but I don't think it's something that came from her abrupt kindness at the lake or last night in Newport."

Tyler let out a hearty laugh. "You sure it wasn't how pleasant she's been toward me?"

They both laughed.

Smiling, Jonathan shook his head. "No, I think this might be something else. Something to do with God. Don't quote me or take my words to heart. It's just one man's opinion. Think about it. She doesn't care for God, yet you still have feelings for her. She's incredibly rude, but still, you are drawn to her. Unless it's purely lust, there's something else going on here. Lust has never been a controlling factor for you before, so I don't think that's it."

Processing his brother's words, Tyler wondered if there

was, indeed, something more. "I won't lie about the lust. It's there, but there's more, I know it. Maybe I should go to her?"

"Do you know where she lives? Works? Anything?"

"No." Recalling the night of the accident, he could hear her saying her name perfectly in his mind. *Olivia Montgomery.* "Wait, I know her last name. Montgomery. But she was getting a divorce, so that could've changed."

"I'm sure you can find something online. Especially if you have a last name."

"That's true." Tyler took his turn and sank the eight ball, finishing the game. "You really need to practice more if you're going to have a pool table in your house."

Jonathan laughed on his way to hang the pool stick on the wall. "Sure, I'll get right on that."

WHEN TYLER ARRIVED to his flat above the bowling alley, he wasted no time searching online for Olivia. The plan to look her up was lodged in his brain ever since his brother had suggested it earlier in the evening. He had to find this woman and go to her to have a real conversation, once and for all. Once he did talk to her, he wasn't sure what would happen after that.

Tyler opened a browser and started to Google her, typing in different locations around and in Spokane combined with her name. Finding a Facebook profile, he clicked the link and there was a picture of a tomato plant. Scrolling through the public posts, he found a picture of her. Upon seeing those sea-blue eyes, his heart jumped in his chest. *That's her!* But now what? Seeing that the last public post was three years ago, his insides knotted. Either she'd made her profile private from that point on or she didn't use the account anymore. He hoped for the best and sent her a message.

He went back to Google and did some more searching to

see if he could find anything with the name he had. He found one online obituary, which was for a seventy-eight-year-old woman, and a couple of other dead ends. Then, he found a possible lead. It was a local news station article on a car lot. He skimmed the article that detailed a winter storm that had destroyed multiple cars. Then toward the end of the article, he found her name. ***Olivia Montgomery of Gus's Auto Sales says that they have discounted all the damaged vehicles to low prices to clear them out, and the deep discounts won't last long.***

Bingo! But wait. Is she still married to that man? The thought pushed through his mind, and fear began to entangle him. If she still had the same last name, there was a chance she was still married. Maybe that's why she had sped off the other night in such a hurry. Maybe that's why she was so rude to him previously. Maybe she was still with the man she said she was divorcing and didn't want to look like a fool. Sitting back in his computer chair, Tyler raised his hands behind his head and held them there as he pondered the possibilities. Then, after a few moments of debate, he resolved to go to the car lot. *What's the worst that can happen?* he asked himself. *She says that she is married and asks me to leave?* It was a risk he was willing to take.

THE NEXT MORNING, he called his brother to let him know he'd be late into the office and the reason why. Then, he headed to the car lot to see Olivia. His heart was pounding, and he thought for a moment that something was physically wrong with him. His nervousness almost made him stop the pursuit. He even turned around twice before turning around again and again to go to the dealership. He felt more like a school-aged boy trying to get the courage to ask out a cute girl than a grown man with a successful architectural firm who had confidence for decades when it came to women.

Realizing he hadn't prayed even once since his devotional time in the Word earlier that morning, Tyler pulled off the road and into an empty parking lot to pray. He bowed his head and rested his forehead on the steering wheel in front of him. *Lord, I don't know what I'm doing, but I hope I'm not wrong about this. You know my heart and You know I seek to do Your will. Make it clear when I see her what Your will is for my life. I pray that You stay with me and help calm these nerves I have right now. Amen.*

CHAPTER 13

*O*N THE DAYS IN WHICH Olivia experienced pain, she would slice up the day mentally into four slots of time, each one being two hours in length, with a lunch hour smack-dab in the middle. This was the only way she was able to mentally make it through a work day. In doing this, she always had something to look forward to, and it kept her sanity intact. Halfway into her first block of time this particular day, she was not only fighting tears from pain but from want of sleep that she so desperately craved with all her being. Inputting numbers into the big never-ending spreadsheet as the hours ticked by, she heard her phone vibrate in her purse nearby.

She reached into the purse and checked it. It was a text from Rachel.

Rachel: Sorry again about not coming through yesterday. I'm trying. Love you lots.

She replied, telling her cousin it was okay, and then slipped her phone back into the purse. The car lot's front doors opened, drawing her attention.

Jerking her body, she sat straight as a board as the one

person she never thought she'd see again walked through the door.

She was breathless as he arrived at the receptionist desk. "Tyler."

"Hey, um . . ." His eyes glanced at her neighboring co-worker, Jasper. "Can we talk in private?"

Her heart pounded so hard in her ears that she could barely hear him over it. The sleepiness and pain she had been experiencing all morning had melted away, and her whole being was alert, full of uncontrollable energy. She agreed and stood up, walking with him into a nearby hallway of the dealership that led to the bathrooms. In a hushed voice, she leaned toward him, only a few feet separating them now. "What's up?"

He threw his head back in laughter. "What's up? Are you serious? I saw you two nights ago in Newport."

She blushed. "I was looking for a friend."

"I remember. Did you find him?"

Glancing at her hand and thinking of the pain, she shook her head. "No, I didn't."

"Do you want to go out and grab a bite sometime?"

She leaped at the idea, or at least her heart did until her mind caught up and reminded her of reality. "I have a baby, and I'm going to school right now, and I work full-time."

He raised his hands. "You don't have to give me a list of excuses. If you're not interested, I understand."

When he turned to leave, she jumped across the tile floor and caught his arm. She didn't realize she had even moved until it was over. Then she looked at him, searching his eyes for truth, genuineness. She was terrified of men after what Bruce and all the others had done to her. How could she ever trust a man again? Something inside her egged her on to at least eat food with the man who had saved her life.

"Wait. Don't go, please? I—I owe you at least one date, my

treat. Maybe on one of my lunches, we can go do something? Or this weekend? I don't know . . ."

He moved his arm away from her grip and pulled his black leather jacket sleeve up, looking at his watch. "You have a lunch break at what? Noon? Plan for a couple of hours."

"Yes, I can take it then. Okay."

"Good. That's in three hours. Tell you what. I'll swing by at noon, and I'll be parked right outside. If you come out, I'll take it you want to go on a lunch date. Then we'll take it from there. If you don't come out, don't ever expect to see me again. At least, not on purpose. Also, if you show up, the date will be on me, *my* treat."

"Okay." His confidence sent her heart into flutters, and she knew without a doubt that she would be going on that date, no matter what.

With that, Tyler turned around and left the dealership. As she walked back to her post behind the receptionist desk, she felt confused on how he had managed to find her and light-headed at the thought of a possible relationship. Then, out of nowhere, one of her co-workers, Allison, approached. "Who was *that*?"

"The man who saved my life."

"He's single? Snatch that guy up before he's gone, girl. You don't want to let a man like that roam free."

Olivia laughed lightly, but inside, she knew Tyler was just like the rest of the men she had dealt with in her life. He was interested in her, but not *really* interested. He was no differ-ent. Confident and smooth-talking, muscular, and able to make a girl feel special by a few short sentences and glances. But at the end, once he got to know the real her, he'd hurt her like every other man had done. Turning her attention back to the computer, she tried to re-focus on the work ahead of her and not just the ticking time until noon when he'd be parked outside, waiting for her.

. . .

SHE LOOKED at the clock at the exact second it struck noon and drew herself up out of her seat. Grabbing her coat and purse, she walked over to the front door of the dealership and peered outside. She spotted him and his car. A war raged inside her heart and mind on what to do, if she should go or stay. A quiet voice deep inside floated to the tip of her thoughts. *Go.*

Pushing the door open, she walked out to his car. As she crossed the parking lot over to him, her heart fluttered at seeing him break into a smile. He was attractive, and that meant one thing to her—dangerous. Tyler jumped out of his car and hurried over to the passenger-side door to open it for her.

"Ma'am."

A smile curled on her lips as she got in. *He's good, real good.* Placing her black-sequined purse on her lap, her fingers trembled in her right hand as a wave of pain rippled through the nerves. *Not now, please?* She clasped her other hand over her painful hand and massaged the palm as he got into the driver's seat. He noticed and turned to her.

"You all right?"

"It's just a little pain. I might look healed from that wreck you saved me from, but there's some stuff that never healed."

"Wow, that's horrible that you still have pain. What are they doing to treat it?"

She blinked without a word for a moment. "Nothing. They won't do anything for me anymore." Her eyes welled as a whirlwind of emotional pain whirled around her on the inside. Thoughts of the other night looking for drugs on the streets and her daughter's involvement in the late-night drive flooded her mind. She also thought about the image at work and with her family that she so desperately maintained to make sure nobody knew the truth. It was exhausting. There were so many lies, so much pain, and she had no way out of it.

"There should be some Ibuprofen in the glove box if you need it." Tyler pointed to it.

She opened the glove box. A pistol fell into view and she recoiled.

He laughed. "Sorry. The safety is on, and it's registered, I promise. Behind that."

Glancing over at him, she shook her head. "I can't touch that."

Reaching over, he grabbed the Ibuprofen and handed it to her, then shut the glove box.

As she tapped a few pills out from the bottle and took them, she tried to push the thought of the gun away from her. It made her uneasy. Tyler looked over at her.

"You must be miserable."

It was as if he could see right through her walls and see a part of her soul. Her defensive walls shot up higher and she felt herself closing down. She set the pill bottle down in a cup holder and clasped her arms over her torso as she became nervous. She nodded toward the road out the windshield. "You wanted to eat. Let's go eat."

"Wow, no need to be rude to me."

Olivia looked over at him and tilted her head. "Rude? I don't think it's rude to want to eat on a *lunch* date."

He laughed in a way that made her feel like he had something she didn't have. He had joy. He seemed calm. He raised a hand and shook his head.

"I do apologize for that comment. You're probably uncomfortable with my forwardness about your seeming miserable."

"Yeah, you're right. It did make me uncomfortable. Who

are you to determine who is miserable and who is not? Is that some role your *God* gave you?"

"No, not really. I can just see pain when I look into your eyes. Who knows? Maybe paying attention *is* special in today's age." He put the car in gear and pulled out of the parking lot of the car dealership. He didn't say where they were going, but Olivia grew more comfortable as they drove. She began to not care where they were going to eat with each passing minute. She began to not pay any attention to the clock on her phone either. She had forgotten about the gun in the glovebox also. Olivia was becoming freer with each passing second with Tyler. It didn't make any sense to her, but she wasn't about to question it.

At the restaurant, he pulled a chair out for her, then he took a seat. He prayed over his food before eating and asked more than once if there was anything he could do for her. She felt he was waiting on her just as much as the wait staff was doing for the two of them. It made her a little uncomfortable, but also, in a sense, loved. As their meal wound down and they sipped on their sodas, conversations fell into various topics such as Olivia's child, Molly, her job, her parents, and then finally, her previous failed marriage.

"I can see you really loved Bruce with all your heart, Olivia."

A flicker of pain penetrated her heart. A light nod followed, and then her voice softened. "I poured my everything into that man."

"I can tell that. You know, Olivia, I don't say this often, and I wouldn't have said it about you after the rudeness at the inn or the other night in Newport, but you truly are a beautiful person. You try to give the love you so desperately crave for yourself to every person you care about."

At his words, her heart melted. She felt so understood for the first time in her entire life. Sure, Bruce listened and nodded, and the other guys did too, but none of them truly vocalized their understanding the way Tyler did. She grew more comfortable with Tyler as their time together lengthened. Conversation continued, and then, Tyler told Olivia about a pain treatment his brother's wife had received that had helped.

"Jonathan's wife Marie had acupuncture done, and it worked *amazingly* well. She went from seeking death to being able to relax a whole lot more in life."

"That's the second time someone has mentioned acupuncture. Maybe I should try it."

He took a sip of his cola and nodded. "Maybe God is trying to tell you something by having two people mention it to you?"

Her lips curled into a smile. "I was wondering how far into this lunch date we'd have to get for you to mention *God* again. Too bad I haven't been tracking the time to know how long it's been."

Tyler pulled his phone out of his pocket. "I picked you up at noon and it's two thirty, so two and a half hours?"

Olivia jumped up, knocking the table with her knee and causing Tyler's soda to spill onto his lap. "Oh, my goodness! I'm so sorry! I didn't mean to do that, I just, I'm late back to work."

Wiping his pants off with a napkin, he raised a hand, still smiling as he did. He shook his head. "Wow, I am so sorry about your being late back to work. I should've kept a closer eye on that for you. The pants are no problem. I promise. The pants will be cleaned and forgotten, but this unforgettable moment together will *never* be forgotten."

Her heart smiled at his gentleness. She hadn't ever seen a man who could keep this calm in a situation that was unpleasant. She was used to over-the-top reactions and anger and selfishness, but never understanding the way Tyler was showing right now.

"You sure you're not some kind of Greek god?"

He laughed. "What?"

"You save my life, you are dashing and charming, and you keep yourself cool under pressure. There's something to you I don't get, Mister."

A wry smile surfaced on his lips. "I'm merely a sinful man who chooses to follow Jesus. Come on, I'll take you back to work. I apologize for keeping you longer than intended."

Olivia didn't care for his mention of Jesus, but she left it alone. He had every right to attribute his actions to God, and she wasn't about to try to convince him otherwise. On the drive back over to the car lot, he called his brother, Jonathan, on his car phone's speaker system.

"Hey, Brother. What's the name of Marie's acupuncture guy she saw?"

"Oh, wow. That was a long time ago. Hmm . . . let me take a look around and I'll let you know."

"Thanks, Bro."

Hanging up with Jonathan as they pulled into the dealership, Tyler put the car into park and turned to her. "I'll need your number. You know, so I can let you know who the acupuncturist is."

Olivia glanced down and blushed. "Sneaky way of getting my phone number, eh?"

He laughed.

"I'm just playing. I was going to give it to you anyway. Let me see your phone and I'll put it in there."

Tyler slipped his phone out from his pocket and handed it over. Olivia made the entry in his phone contacts and gave it back. "Thanks for lunch. I had a lovely time."

"We'll have to do it again."

"Soon." Olivia opened the car door and stepped out. She

shut the door and headed back through the doors into work. She might've had pain in her hand today, tiredness in her body, and be in a little hot water with the boss after taking such a long lunch break, but she didn't care about any of it. She had finally met and gone on a date with someone who could possibly be different from all the wrong men she had met and dated before. Thinking of her little girl, Molly, she hoped it wasn't just a hunch but that it was true, that he was everything he was leading her to believe thus far. However, she knew he could be putting on a show, similar to the way she had been doing to those closest to her about her pain.

CHAPTER 14

$\mathcal{A}$RRIVING AT WILLOW DESIGN'S OFFICE in downtown Spokane that afternoon, Tyler had a bounce in his step as he strolled in just past three o'clock. Tossing his jacket across the room to the chairs in the lobby, he promptly went to his brother's office doorway and leaned in with a grin on his face.

"She's fantastic, Jonathan."

Jonathan laughed and pushed himself away from the desk and put his hands behind his head as he leaned back in his office chair. "Yeah? You going to marry her?"

Tyler laughed. "Slow down. I wouldn't go that far at the moment, but she sure is some kind of wonderful. Each second with her was like a slow-moving masterpiece of enjoyment. She has such a kind soul, Brother." Thinking about her sadness and the looming sorrow he sensed radiating from her, his countenance fell. "She is a wonderful person, Jonathan, but sadly . . . she's damaged. She seeks love from horizontal relationships with men that only—"

"Comes from a vertical relationship with God." Jonathan finished his sentence and stood up, coming over to Tyler.

Resting a hand on his shoulder, he smiled. "You're being used by God here, Tyler. You are possibly the only Gospel truth in her life right now."

Uncomfortable with the idea of being the sole representative of Jesus Christ, Tyler shrugged. "I don't know about that."

Removing his hand from Tyler's shoulder, Jonathan held out his arms. "Think about it, Tyler. God places people in our lives to help us, to grow us, and to help point others to Christ. This girl is special and God wants her heart. It was evident when you found her in that abandoned field in the middle of the night, and it is evident now in what's happening."

Me used by God? Tyler smiled at the thought. "I guess I am a pretty good follower."

"Don't become prideful from this, Brother. It's only by God's goodness and unyielding grace that you're involved. Don't touch the glory."

Tyler felt embarrassed and immediately repented to God, then apologized to his brother. "You're right. I'm sorry. Sometimes, it's just so exciting to see the hand of God at work."

"This is true, and it's okay to be excited. We just can't think more highly of ourselves because we're involved." He turned toward his desk and walked over, picking up a yellow sticky note. "Dr. Hall is the acupuncturist she used, by the way. Here's his phone number. Is this for her?"

"Yes, she still has pain from the wreck."

"Dr. Hall does good work. I hope it goes well for her."

Tyler took the sticky note and hugged his brother. "Thanks for being my brother. I couldn't ask for a better one."

. . .

FINDING a few moments later that evening around seven o'clock, Tyler slipped his cell phone out of his pocket and stood up from his desk at work. Walking over to the window, he looked out and down on the city street lit up by cars, street lamps, and business shop windows. He called Olivia. When she answered and he heard that soft and gentle voice come over the phone, his insides turned to mush. He loved her voice. The way she spoke invoked a deep part of him that made his desire for her burn hotter.

"I have the name and number of that acupuncturist for you."

"Oh, yeah?" What sounded like some water swooshing came across the phone line. Then a clank sounded.

"What are you up to?"

"Doing dishes."

"No dishwasher?"

"I have one, but I don't use it a whole lot."

"That's kind of strange. Doesn't it hurt to do them all by hand?"

"Yes, but I have hope that if I use my hands more, it will somehow repair the nerve damage that's there." She was quiet for a moment. "It might be silly, but a girl can hope, can't she?"

"Absolutely."

"Can you text me that name and number? I'll call them tomorrow."

"I could, or I could use it as an excuse to see you."

She was quiet for a moment, then in the most beautiful and sweet voice, she said, "You don't need an excuse to see me, Tyler."

The flame of desire inside Tyler grew at that moment from a candle-wick's flame to a bonfire.

"You still there?"

He nodded. "I'm smiling all over right now. Wait a moment."

Pulling the phone away from his ear, he texted her the phone number and name, then returned to the call.

"Thanks, Tyler. The pain has subsided for now, obviously, since I'm able to do dishes, but I hope this works long-term so it stops altogether."

"I'll be praying it does."

"I know you will be." She was quiet for a moment, then without being prompted, she continued. "I have to put Molly down in a bit. Maybe you can come over once she goes down, around 8:30? I'd love to see you again."

His insides warmed even more, knowing that his feelings were not one-sided at all. Tyler knew that she felt at least some of what he was feeling, and he couldn't have been happier in that moment. "Text me the address and I'll be there."

After he hung up the phone, he sat back down in his office chair, a smile on his face and warmth still in his heart. He didn't know what the night would bring, nor what seeing her for a second time in the same day would mean, but he looked forward to it. Knowing he might end up in temptation and be with a woman who not only was very attractive but was lacking a Biblical moral compass, he decided to spend the next hour in devotional time with the Lord. He grabbed his Bible he kept in the office and picked up in his reading in the second book of Corinthians that he had started a few days back on his lunch break. As he read in chapter six, all the excitement and joy at the evening ahead came to a screeching halt.

Do not be yoked together with unbelievers.
For what do righteousness and wickedness have in common?

Or what fellowship can light have with darkness?
2 Corinthians 6:14

TYLER DIDN'T LIKE what he read. In fact, it angered him so much that he stopped reading and shut his Bible and pushed it away from him on the desk. He sat for a long moment, eyebrows furrowed and arms crossed. He didn't say anything, didn't pray, but just sat brooding over the convicting power of God's Word. The Bible wasn't just a book to Tyler. It wasn't just a bunch of suggestions or guidelines for what you can do if you are a believer. It was the living, breathing Word of God, and each sentence and Word was preciously God-inspired and breathed out as commands for Christian living. He didn't take what the Bible said lightly in the slightest. His thoughts toward the Bible, coupled with the Scripture he had just read, confronted his feelings for Olivia in a very real way.

After he sat in silence for a while, Tyler finally uncrossed his arms and relaxed. Lowering himself out of the chair and to the floor, he folded his hands and rested them on the seat of his chair and bowed his head. *God? Why wouldn't you take my desire away when I saw her at the inn? This isn't a seed in my heart. It's like a virus. A virus that is feasting now, and it's only growing bigger. Help me to understand. Help me! I can't fall in love with a woman who hates You, Lord. I can't do it. Take this temptation I feel inside me away. Please help.* Tyler went on in prayer for close to twenty more minutes, wrestling with God in his heart as he spoke his feelings to the Almighty Savior who was the King of his life. Teary-eyed and broken, Tyler rose up from his knees, but as he did, he felt a presence of calm come over him. Then, a question came to his mind. *What is yoked?*

Driven with passion to understand the Scripture, he sat down in his office chair and began to research on Google what it meant to be yoked. He found commentaries and floods of information on the topic and on the Scripture. He pored over each article, commentary, and Biblical point of view of what the Scripture meant. Tyler reminded himself he wasn't trying to justify anything but merely to understand it better. At the end of it all, just shy of ten minutes till when he needed to leave, he came to a conclusion. The lifestyle of a Christian and the lifestyle of a non-Christian are different, contrary to one another. The yoking together with an unbeliever doesn't work because they run contrary to one another. He also resolved in his heart that he could continue seeing Olivia, because he truly felt he was called to be a light in her life for Christ, but he'd have to be careful and expect turmoil. He was now more aware that not only was temptation at every corner, but at some point, according to the truths of the Bible, they would have to separate if she didn't come to God. It was fundamentally impossible to continue along the same path and live two different and contrary lives, one who hates God and one who loves Him. He knew if he was to pursue a relationship with this woman, it could be a lot of pain and most likely heartache, but he felt the desire to pursue her nevertheless.

SHE ANSWERED the door and welcomed him inside with a hushed voice. As he walked into the apartment, he noticed three moving boxes near a standing lamp in the corner. She noticed his eyes on them.

"I'm still in the process of moving in, kind of. With work and Molly and school on top of it, I haven't gotten everything unpacked."

He raised a hand. "It's no problem. When did you move in?"

"Few months ago. Have a seat on the couch. I was just making us some tea. Wait, do you like tea? I didn't even think to ask."

Tyler let a soft laugh escape from his lips. "Tea is fine if you have sugar."

"I do! I'll be right back."

He sat down on the couch and glanced at the coffee table. There was a *Motherhood* magazine, a tube of diaper rash cream, and a folded newspaper with a crossword puzzle half-done, a pencil beside it. He envisioned what it had to be like to be a single mother in today's world, and he became curious how she held a job, went to school, and took care of a child alone. He didn't grasp how she did it all, but he respected the fact that she somehow did it. As she walked into the living room, he took the cup and container of sugar she handed him.

"You're amazing."

A blush crawled into her cheeks. "Why do you say that?"

"I was just trying to comprehend your life for a moment. A kid, a job, and school work. I don't get how you do it all. I barely have time to manage my work, let alone anything else."

She smiled and then shrugged. "I don't know how it all works, but it does. I do have my parents helping. That helps. I won't lie. It is hard some days, really hard, but I don't see any other way to do it. You know?"

"Yeah, I hear you. Do you have any dental offices you're looking to get employed with when you finish up?"

"I haven't looked around a lot, but I really like my dentist office. Everyone is really kind there and they're understanding with their patients. It's Riverside Dental out in Deer Park."

"Neat."

"Tell me more about your work. You said your brother and you started it together?" Sipping her tea as Tyler stirred in sugar, she smiled at him while waiting for a response.

"Yeah, we started out of our homes and it's grown from there. I run the business side of things and he does the fancy drawings. We have a steady flow of clients now, and we just opened up an office downtown. It was nice to work from home, but it's also nice to leave our work somewhere each night."

As they sipped tea and talked for the next couple of hours, Tyler found that she was scooting closer to him on the couch, raising not only his body temperature and pulse but his appetite for her. Seeing that an eyelash had fallen onto her cheek, he leaned over toward her. "There's an eyelash on your cheek. Hold still."

Gently removing the eyelash, he found himself inches from her beautiful face. His eyes were opened to the dangers of temptation, and he could see and sense his mounting desires. He pulled back and glanced at his phone. "I have an early morning. I'd better get going."

She was quiet for a moment, her desire for a kiss evident in her expression of disappointment. She stood up. "Why didn't you kiss me right then?"

"You're forward, aren't you?"

Olivia shrugged. "I don't mess around, Tyler. Remember? I have a child and I'm really not into games."

He came closer, then cupped her cheek. "Let me ask you something. How many of those horrible men kissed you in the beginning of your relationship with them?"

She pulled away, her cheeks reddened, and she looked down. Her voice quieted. "All of them."

"Exactly." Tyler brought his hand up and pulled her chin with his index finger to make her look at him again. "I'm not like those other men, Olivia. I want to know you, the real you. I want to know your heart before I do something like kissing you."

"But it's just a kiss, Tyler. I know you want to kiss me."

"It's not *just* a kiss. It's a commitment for me. But you're right, I do want to kiss you. But I won't, not yet, not right now. When the time is right, I will." He turned and started for the door. She walked with him. Turning around as he stepped outside, he smiled. "I had a wonderful time tonight, and earlier today at lunch."

"I did too." Her lips curved into a smile. "When can I see you again?"

"I'm going out of town tomorrow after Chet's funeral service in the morning. I'll be gone for about a week on business. How about next Saturday?"

"It's a date, and this time, I'll have my parents watch Molly so we can go out."

"All right. Have a good night."

Walking away as she closed her apartment door, Tyler thanked God and gave Him all the praise for the power He had supplied in self-control not to kiss that beautiful woman. It was God's goodness and God's strength alone that enabled Tyler to resist the urges that fought for control inside his body. He wasn't sure where Olivia and he would go from here, but he had hope above all else to show her God's love, even if that meant they would never be together in the way his heart was already hoping.

CHAPTER 15

THE ACUPUNCTURIST WAS ABLE TO fit her in five days later, on Monday, and Olivia took the morning off from work to go be poked. While she hadn't been in pain when she went in, she did feel less stressed when she left Dr. Hall's office. Walking through the parking lot toward her car, Tyler pressed against her mind. She had been thinking about him ever since that almost-kiss they'd shared last week. He was still out of town, and it took everything in her not to pick up the phone and text him. She wondered if he thought about her the same way she was thinking of him. She wasn't sure if he was, but her longing to see him again was ever-present in her heart.

She got in her car and drove to work. When she entered through the back door of the dealership, she was surprised to see Jasper standing there to greet her with his arms crossed and a silly grin on his face.

"What's going on?" Olivia tried to look past him into the showroom to see if he and Paul were playing another one of their tricks on her, but Paul was busy speaking with a customer on the sales floor.

Jasper raised an eyebrow. "Who's your secret admirer who sent you a bazillion flowers? You have a new guy in your life you haven't told us about?"

Her heart fluttered as she hurried her steps past him and around the corner to the receptionist desk. There, right beside her monitor, was an oversized crystal vase with what had to be a hundred red roses. Her heart melted at the sight and she hurried over to them. Tucked between the brightly colored petals was a note. Plucking the note out of its plastic holder, she hid it as she twisted her body away from Jasper. She liked to keep her private life private, knowing that Jasper and the rest were all close with her boss, Gus, one of her father's close friends. She read the note.

EACH ROSE IS *a moment in which I thought of you. I can't wait to see you again.*

~ Tyler

"So, who's the stalker sending you roses?" Jasper laughed.

Olivia held her chin up, proud to have received such a gift. "He's not a stalker. He's sweet, and we're just friends."

"Red roses don't communicate *friendship*. Just so you know." A moment passed, and Jasper caught sight of a person wandering around looking into cars in the car lot. Olivia turned and saw it was a woman with a fur coat and a nice big black purse. Jasper smiled as his gaze fixed on the woman outside. "I'd better go earn that commission check."

He ran outside as she sat down at her computer. Olivia paused as she set the note down beside her keyboard. She had to fight back tears. She was so happy. Nobody had ever bought her flowers before. As she worked the rest of the day, she not only had less stress from the acupuncture but a warm feeling in her chest as she stole glances at her flowers all throughout the day. Every time a customer commented on them, it made her glow even more.

On her break that afternoon, she sent a text to Tyler thanking him and then called Rachel to tell her about the flowers.

"Why do you get all the guys? I can't seem to find even one! Here you are, out of marriage not even a full year, and you have another one lined up and ready!"

Her insides shifted from joyful to concerned. "Yeah, sure, I can find them all right, but they all turn out to be lame in the end. Look at the bright side, Rachel. You don't have to go through relationship after relationship and heartbreak after heartbreak. You're lucky."

In an accent, she replied, *"Tis better to have loved and lost than never to have loved at all!"* A laugh followed from the two of them, then Rachel continued. "I don't know if I'll ever find a man in this lifetime, but I know if I do, I'll hold onto him."

"Yeah, part of my problem was holding on too long with Bruce. I should've learned after the first time he cheated that he wasn't going to change."

"Or when he made you cut off communication with me!"

"He did have reasons for that, though . . ." Olivia's words trailed off.

Rachel was quiet for a moment before she replied. "I was a bad influence. Yes, I get it. Guess what, chica? I still do those same drugs, and I'm not influencing you."

Olivia didn't like the tension that was building on the phone call. She grew more uncomfortable. She could've mentioned the fact that Rachel had helped her get in touch with Alex out in Diamond Lake and all that for her pills, but she didn't. "I have to get back to work. We'll chat later, okay?"

"All right. I guess I should go out to the sales floor and

pretend to do something for a while." She laughed. "I mean, I need to *manage* the employees. Chat with you later."

As Olivia hung up the call with Rachel, a strange sensation came over her. She suddenly saw Rachel in a very raw and unfiltered way. She saw her as someone who always had something to say and seemed to have a way to relate every conversation to herself. She was always worse off, always at a disadvantage, and always not to blame. Olivia didn't like feeling this way about her cousin who had been there for her through the thick of it back in the day, and even more recently, when she had left Bruce. She pushed the unsavory feelings aside and returned to her desk to finish out the work day.

When Olivia arrived at her parents' house later that day, her father immediately came up to her while she and her mother were in the kitchen feeding Molly.

"Who sent the flowers, Olive?" His tone was soft enough not to alarm her, but she knew it was serious because he had cared so much that he set down his paper in the living room to come in and talk about it shortly after she had arrived at the house. He stood near the counter while she faced him opposite on the other side. Reaching her hands behind her, she gripped the counter as her pulse climbed. She didn't tell Jasper because she didn't want it reaching Gus and her dad, but it had managed to do that even without a name.

"It was the man who saved my life last summer."

"The boy from the inn? Tyson?"

Olivia's mother interjected. Her tone was gentle but firm, and Olivia felt as if her mother was trying to redirect his attention to her. "Tyler. It was Tyler, Dan."

"Whatever his name was, it doesn't matter. What's he doing sending you flowers?"

"Dan."

He held up a hand.

"No, Kora. I want to know." He came away from the counter and got closer to Olivia, only sending her worry soaring. "You have more than yourself to think about now. You can't just bring strange men around my granddaughter. I won't have it."

Olivia was fine until he brought Molly into the conversation. Her anger waxed hot and she shook her head. "First off, she's my daughter before she's your granddaughter. Second off, I'm not as dumb as you think I am. I'm taking precautions and haven't had Molly around him at all. Third, Dad, we're just friends. It's just roses."

"I know how much a hundred roses cost. It's not cheap. This guy is obviously trying to get something."

She couldn't stand by and let Tyler be talked about in a negative light, especially not after he wouldn't even so much as kiss her. "You don't have a clue what you're talking about."

"I don't, do I?" Her father's face reddened and he shook his head. "I know what men are after!"

This madness and sudden anger from her father reminded her so much of her childhood. It hurt. She had to put an end to it, and she knew exactly what would calm him down. Olivia didn't want her parents, more specifically, her dad, to have the satisfaction of knowing it, but she couldn't take another moment of the foolish talk. "He's a Christian, Dad!"

Her father stopped immediately, the tension in his shoulders loosened, and the redness in his cheeks subsided. Both of her parents looked relieved, her mother almost teary-eyed over it.f

"Oh, honey!" her mother said as she crossed the kitchen floor to her, embracing her in a hug. "That's so wonderful to hear."

Pleasing her parents should've felt good, but it didn't. In fact, it made her mad, madder than she'd been in a long time. She had spent years watching her parents hate and disregard every boy or man she brought around the house, and at the mere mention of Tyler's faith, they gushed over him like he's the second coming of their Jesus Christ. They haven't even met him, and boom! They're in love. Hot tears welled in Olivia's eyes and she shook her head.

"What's wrong?" Her father's voice was soft, gentle, and suddenly full of love.

"You two—mostly you, Dad—are the most hypocritical and judgmental people on this planet! You sit there and say you're no different from anyone else and that *everyone* is a sinner, but you do treat people differently all the time! You hated every guy I brought around you two and it was because they didn't believe in God. At the mere mention of this guy being a Christian, you two are loving, supportive, and happy about it. He could be a serial killer, and just the fact that he is a Christian makes it all okay! It's psychotic!"

Her father was quiet for a long moment, her mother too. Then her dad, with tears in his eyes, said, "I'm sorry." He paused, obviously attempting to control his emotions by the way his face grimaced. "You're right, Olive. We do judge, and we have been harsh in the past with people you brought around. The truth is this, though. The fact that Tyler is a Christian says a whole lot about the man. It means, if he's a Biblical Christian, that he acknowledges and loves God above all—which is a big deal in our eyes. That means there's someone above himself whom he is accountable to. Those other men in your life never had that. It also tells your mother and me that he values women, he values life, he values children, and he values family. These are only a few of the facts that being a Christian communicates. So, when you see a big reaction, it's because it is a big deal. Those other people you brought around who didn't believe in God? You know what that communicates? They are their own god and go by their own rules. That's the only thing we knew about them up front was they didn't have God. We know a whole lot more about this guy right away. We don't think he's perfect, but it gives us insight into some of his character."

Olivia blinked the tears from her eyes. Everything her father said made sense. When she was younger, before all the life experience she'd had with rotten men who only worshiped themselves, she would've blown him off. But not now. She knew it was true. People often know when they hear the truth, and she had just heard it firsthand. Walking up to her father, she wrapped her arms around him and hugged him.

"I'm sorry for the way I've been. I know this should've come a long time ago, but thank you. Thank you for taking care of me after the wreck. Thank you for raising me even when I didn't want you to, and thank you most of all for loving me no matter what and no matter how I felt about it."

Her mother came closer and Olivia hugged the both of them. She was overwhelmed with happiness and sadness in that moment. She had been given a new perspective about her parents, a deeper one and one that she could understand. Her heart swelled knowing that she was loved. Then, suddenly, Molly let out a squeal from the baby swing a few feet away. Everyone released from the embrace and laughed.

AT HER APARTMENT THAT NIGHT, after she had put Molly to bed and finished up an assignment, she sat on the couch in her living room and worked on a crossword puzzle. She glanced at her phone on the coffee table, wondering if Tyler would reply to her text she had sneaked in at work hours ago, then went back to filling out fourteen across. A moment later, the phone buzzed and she tossed the folded newspaper and pencil onto the couch cushion beside her. She felt like a kid on Christmas opening a present as she opened the text from Tyler.

Tyler: I'm glad you were happy to get them. I can't wait to see you again. The anticipation alone might kill me.

Olivia: Ha-ha! I'm sure you'll survive. I went to Dr. Hall today. I'm feeling pretty good, though I wasn't in pain when I went.

Tyler: Oh, good! That's great to hear about not being in pain. Listen, I might be flying in a little earlier, like tomorrow, instead of two days from now. Mind if I come see you at work if I get in early? I don't want to intrude if you don't want me to.

Olivia: I insist! The owner and others are lax about visitors coming in unless we have a sale going on because then we get slammed. I might even be able to leave early if you show up early.

Tyler: All the more motivation for me to make it happen!

Sprawling out on the couch with a soft plaid blanket over her lap and a couch pillow behind her neck, Olivia went on texting with Tyler for the next hour or so. They texted about their days apart and the mundane activities that filled them. As the time got later into the evening, Olivia felt her eyelids growing heavier between each response from Tyler. With her phone resting on her chest, she fell asleep.

$\mathcal{A}$S THE WHEELS TOUCHED DOWN at Spokane International Airport at 2:34 PM the next day, Tyler's heart bumped along with the plane as it slowed on the runway. He stared past the passenger beside him and out the small plane's window as he anticipated seeing Olivia once again. He hadn't been able to get her off his mind his entire business trip. Even when he was sitting in business meetings and there was nothing but a few empty glasses and a pitcher of water, he was somehow reminded of her beauty by the simple liquid on the table. The crystal clarity of the water reminded him of how he felt he could see right through Olivia to her vulnerabilities. He didn't take pleasure in the fact that he could see through her, but instead, he felt he was entrusted by God to care for those delicate needs and pains she carried. God was calling Olivia, and Tyler knew he was being used as a tool to help her.

"Sir? The plane is emptying out. Do you mind standing up so we can exit? Or you can just let me by so I can go?" The man next to him was kind in the way he spoke, but it was apparent he was a bit impatient, and for good reason. On the flight, he had told Tyler about how he was being reunited with his long-lost mother he hadn't seen since he was three years old, sixty-four years ago now. The man was in tears as he recounted the years he spent looking for his biological mom so he could not only meet her but thank her for giving him up like she had done. He was grateful for the family he now had because of his mother's selfless choice.

Tyler stood up and placed his hand on the gentleman's shoulder, then shook his hand. "It was nice getting to know you, Ned. I'll keep you and your family in my prayers."

"Thank you."

Exiting the security gates and making his way down the escalator, Tyler was surprised to see Jonathan had come to meet him at the airport. Tyler opened his arms and heart wide to embrace his brother. Jonathan patted his back and then took a step back.

"You did good, Brother. The client couldn't be more pleased with the proposal you pitched them."

Tyler smirked and they fell into step together on their way to pick up Tyler's suitcase at the luggage carousel. "I told you that you didn't need to come with me on the trip, didn't I?"

Smacking his back with warm appreciation, his brother nodded. "You were right."

He let out a sigh and then grabbed his suitcase. "Hearing that never gets old."

"Oh, did you want to leave that?"

"What?" Tyler glanced around on the floor.

"Your pride. Leave it here and don't let the successful visit go to your head."

"Oh, brother!"

They both laughed and headed toward the exit of the airport in good spirits. Walking across the street, they entered the parking garage and headed down the row of cars toward Jonathan's car.

"Thanks again for watering my plants."

"No problem. Your friend Vinny's mom doing better?"

"Yep. The triple-bypass went well and she's resting at home now. How are Kylie and the kiddos?"

Jonathan nodded. "That's good about his mom. They're good. Hey, when's the bowling alley out of escrow? Like three weeks or less, right?"

"Yeah, why?"

"You don't even have a single box packed, Tyler. You'd better get on that."

Tyler came close to his brother and put his arm around him, shaking him lightly. "You're such a good brother, looking out for me and making sure I'm on the right track with *boxes*."

Jonathan laughed and pushed him away. "I am trying to look out for you!"

He laughed. "No, really, Jonathan. I mean, I'm supposed to pack my house up in boxes and move? Uh, wow. I had no idea that's how moving works."

"Okay, enough."

As they slowed their steps and Jonathan popped the trunk of his car, Tyler stopped and looked at him. "I'm just playing with you. I know I need to get stuff moved out, and I also need to make room in Chet's barn for my furniture."

"What about your house?"

Tyler lifted his suitcase and shoved it into the trunk. He closed the trunk and turned to his brother. "I know it's lame that the cheap contractor I hired is taking literally forever on my house, but I can't go backward. It's up to the contractor to get this done, and he's behind. He's going to lose money if he doesn't get his butt in gear because I'm not paying extra. It won't be until it's move-in ready that I can move stuff inside."

"When's the contractor saying it's going to be move-in ready?"

"June."

Jonathan shrugged. "That's only a couple of months from now. At least you have Chet's cabin after you move out of the bowling alley."

"Yeah, I'm not worried."

As Tyler got into the passenger side of his brother's car, he peered out the window and saw a family. A man and a woman with their three kids, he assumed. Seeing them immediately made him think of Olivia as his brother pulled out of the parking stall and headed down the road toward the airport's exit. "I sent a hundred roses to her work."

"Whoa. Weirdo, why'd you do that?"

Tyler laughed. "I like her. She's sweet and kind, and the last time I hung out with her, that night of the lunch date . . ."

"Yeah?" Jonathan glanced over, encouraging him to continue.

"It was revealed to me through our conversation that she has a whole lot of love to give, but she's poured it out to so many different men without getting it back that she's really wounded."

"That's kind of what you were saying before. Sounds like she needs Jesus."

"Absolutely, she does." Tyler let out a heavy sigh, feeling in his heart that it was impossible for her to find Christ. "I don't see how she's going to come over to the light side, so to speak."

Jonathan laughed. "It's not up to you. All you can do is plant seeds, right? The sower tossing seeds. Those seeds are the Word of God. It's up to God to water it and draw her near to Him. That means the pressure is off you, Brother.

Take comfort in that fact and hold onto it. Don't forget Chet and how he found Christ."

Tyler nodded, then was quiet for a long moment as they drove down the road toward the bowling alley. He wanted to see how it would unfold, how she'd finally come to Jesus, but every time he tried to picture it in his mind, it failed. It was as if he wasn't there at all. Distracted by the song that came on the radio, he reached over and cranked it.

"So good to be back in town. I got tired of listening to light classical music in the hotel lobby and in the board rooms."

"I'm glad you're back too, Brother."

ONCE HOME, he tossed his laundry into the washer and quickly checked his mail and plants. Then, he drove down to the dealership to see Olivia. Pulling up into a spot near the doors, he glanced in the mirror and smiled to check his teeth. He was wearing a sports jacket and a pair of jeans when he walked in through the double doors of the dealership a few moments later. Her gaze lifted to his as he walked across the tile floor of the showroom.

When their eyes caught, a crash of warmth lapped against his heart and radiated outward from there. He felt he hadn't seen her in forever, and yet it was just shy of a week.

"You working hard?"

"Depends. How do you define *hard*?"

He laughed and took her hand as she rose from her seat behind the desk. As they fell into step together and headed for the exit, he leaned toward her. "Did the big guy say you could leave?"

"Yep. He said I was free to go since we've been slowing down."

"Nice. I kind of have something for you—well, for *us* —to do."

She tilted her head as she peered into his eyes. "What's that mean?"

"I'm afraid you might not be interested if I tell you, so can we just keep it a surprise?"

Olivia laughed and tossed her hair over her shoulder, revealing her neck. The warmth already in his chest burned hot upon seeing the skin of her neck. His own feelings began to challenge his beliefs about the two of them. He started to wonder if this all was just lust in his heart or if there was something more. At that moment, he prayed to God and asked Him for discernment and guidance. *I need Your Divine help, Lord. Don't let my heart lead me astray from the truth that You tell me. Don't let me fall into temptation with this beautiful woman. Guide my steps, Lord. Please. Your will, not mine.*

Tyler drove out into the country, heading for Diamond Lake. As they left the city and the buildings were replaced with dotted trees in the landscape on both sides of the highway, Olivia stared out the window. "I know where we're going. We're going out to Newport."

"Not quite. Remember that friend I told you about who passed away? Chet?"

"Yes."

"We're going to the cabin that he left me."

"He left you a cabin? Wow, lucky you."

Tyler didn't respond for a long moment. Then, in a sincere and broken tone, he said, "I'd give it up to see him for five more minutes. He was like an older brother to me. I wish I could've said goodbye and told him how much I loved him."

A blush crawled into Olivia's cheeks. "Sorry. I didn't mean to upset you. From what you said of him, I'm sure he knew how you felt."

He raised a hand. "It's okay. I know what you meant. I just

wanted to articulate what he meant to me. You know, Olivia, I wasted a lot of years in my life, even as a Christian, being focused on the wrong things, thinking I had a handle on things when I never really had control of anything."

"You don't think you control anything?"

"Absolutely not."

"What about your successful company with your brother? Not even that?"

He shook his head. "No, all the money and resources and *things* are on loan from God in my mind. It all belongs to Him, ultimately."

Tyler pulled off the road and started their journey down the dusty dirt road toward his house being built, and beyond that, the cabin.

Olivia shook her head as she crossed her arms. "I couldn't imagine feeling like I had no control over anything in my life. I'd go nuts if I thought I didn't play some role in what went on."

"Of course, we play a role in what we decide to do in this life. Ultimately, God has control though. The fact that I'm breathing right now is because I was given breath by God. He was with me when I took my first breath at birth, and He knows when I'll draw my final one too."

"See, I don't like that thinking. I don't like thinking of God as some big daddy in the sky, watching our every move."

"I wouldn't either. I see Him as a loving Father who wants the best for our lives." Tyler pointed out his house being constructed and broke the conversation away from its current bumpy road. "That's mine. Should be done in June. Do you like it?"

Olivia leaned toward her window and smiled. "I love it. The lake as a backdrop is gorgeous, then that wraparound porch. Sweet place. You know what it's missing, though?"

"What?"

"One of those chain-link wooden double-seated swings. Right there on the corner of the wraparound porch. It'd be perfect."

"Hmm. I'll have to keep that in mind."

Coming around a bend in the dirt road, Tyler drove the car around a patch of trees and there the cabin, barn, and lake sat in plain view. Chet's old truck sat parked beside the barn.

"Wow. You have two awesome places to live now? If you get tired of one, you can take a break and walk over to the other." Tyler snickered at her comment. Olivia's eyes went wide and she leaned forward, drinking in the view.

Pulling up past the cabin and a few feet from the barn, Tyler shut off the car and turned to Olivia. "We are going to be working primarily in here. There's a bunch of stuff in there we need to send off to be donated or moved aside and organized in a pretty way. I have to make room for my stuff from my current residence since I have to move soon."

She laughed. "This is quite some date you brought me on, Tyler."

He leaned toward her, knowing she'd lean for him. She came close, but not all the way. He spoke softly. "I know it's lame, but thanks for coming. You don't have to help."

Jerking his body back, he unlatched his seat belt and got out, shutting the car door. Olivia followed suit and exited the vehicle, slamming the door as she did.

"You wait one minute, Mister."

Tyler stopped and turned toward Olivia as she marched up to him. Inches from him, she peered up at him with a set of eyes that could kill.

"What's up?"

"I don't mind helping, but you did that on purpose! I know it. I know this is all new still, but I don't like games, and I am not going to—"

She was so close to him that he lost control. He slipped his hand up behind her neck before she could tell what was happening. His fingers glided up the back of her head and into her hair. Tyler pulled her into him and kissed her deeply. *As good a time as any.* As his lips pressed against hers, the warming heat in his chest exploded and radiated a deep warmth all over his body. Unable to comprehend the depths of his enjoyment, he continued as he didn't want the moment or the sensation to cease. Olivia's hands slid up his sides and forcefully found their way under his shirt. A chilling sensation of pleasure pulsed from her fingertips as they glided over his abs, sides, and then touched his back. Then she started to remove his shirt, lifting it up over his head.

Tyler stopped, and grabbing his shirt in a hurry, he pulled it down.

"What are you doing?" he asked in a husky and frantic voice.

"What?" She took a step back and tilted her head, confusion across her face. "What do you mean?"

"You were taking off my shirt."

"Yeah, I think that's how it works." A smirk appeared, desire evident in her memorable eyes.

Tyler was inflamed. Temptation was on a silver platter in front of him, and out in the middle of nowhere, nobody would ever have to know, but he would. He turned around and started to unlatch the barn door. She approached him, touching his shoulder with a gentle caress. The verse he read that night in his office about being unequally yoked penetrated his thoughts like a searing iron. *What fellowship can light have with darkness?*

"Stop." His voice was firm, his breath short.

"What's wrong, Tyler?"

He turned toward her. "I can't let you touch me one more time like that right now. Okay?"

Slowly lifting her chin, she lifted her eyebrows. "Oh, yeah? And why is that? You worried what God will think?"

"I don't want to dishonor Him . . . or you."

"Okay." She stepped back, holding her hands up.

"Thank you for understanding." Surveying the piles of stuff before them, including a mountain of pine needle woven baskets, Tyler swallowed hard, knowing that it'd take more like weeks, possibly months instead of hours to sort through the lifetime of memories and items his late friend had collected over the years. He started into the piles, leaving behind the lustful thoughts toward Olivia and praying over and over again for God to forgive him and deliver him from the desires of his own heart.

CHAPTER 17

*O*LIVIA'S MIND REPLAYED HER AND Tyler's kiss over and over like a movie you rewind just to relive the perfect moment one more time, even though the replays are never equal to the real thing. Olivia couldn't stop thinking about their kiss most of the afternoon as they worked together to clean his friend's barn. She was tasked with organizing the bags of clothing that were all throughout the left side of the barn. She tossed the ruined clothing in a throwaway pile and the still usable clothing in fresh garbage bags to be donated. Most of the garbage sacks the clothing had been in previously were riddled with holes, some falling apart entirely. The work wasn't easy, and even though there was a chill in the air outside, she and Tyler were able to work up a sweat.

Olivia walked over with another filled black garbage bag for donation and tossed it into the growing mountain. Hurling the bag up top, she stopped and wiped her forehead with her forearm. She slipped her phone out of her pocket and saw her mother had texted her back.

Mom: Molly is good. Don't worry about us. Have fun with Tyler!

"You okay?" Tyler asked as he looked over from where he was standing on the right side of the barn. He set the saw blades he was looking at down on the workbench and came over to her as she slipped the phone back into her pocket. Gently, he grabbed her hand and looked at it. "I didn't even think about your hand!"

"It's fine, Tyler. Truly, I'd tell you if I was having pain. I'm not shy about it." She shook her head, smiling as she did. "I haven't had a single episode since the acupuncturist. Honestly, I thought those acupuncturists were a little nutty for me, but I tried it anyway and I don't regret it."

He let her hand go. "Really?"

The joy in his voice melted her heart. This man seemed genuine in his care for her, and it warmed her whole body. "Yes. I've felt great."

"I'll let Jonathan know. He'll be thrilled to hear it helped another person."

As Tyler walked toward the workbench again, Olivia followed him. "Is his wife still experiencing pain?"

He stopped but didn't turn around for a moment. "No, not anymore. Marie passed away."

Olivia's mind started placing the puzzle pieces together. Maybe Jonathan was responsible for Tyler's faith and it had come about because of his losing his wife? She came closer to him and he turned around. She blurted out her thought process.

"Is her dying why you and he have faith in God?" As the words left her lips, she regretted it. "That sounded bad. So, so very bad. I'm sorry."

Tyler shook his head. He didn't appear offended in the slightest. "No. In fact, Jonathan questioned God for a long time after losing her. It was hard on him." He took a step closer to Olivia, sending her heart rate soaring. "You want to know about my faith, Olivia? Is that what you're asking?"

"No, I just wanted to know if her dying was what brought it about in your family. You know, a lot of people turn to faith because of loved ones passing away. They hope to see them again. It makes sense."

He smiled in a way that made Olivia feel uncomfortable. It was as if he had a big secret she didn't understand or know. He turned and went back to sorting tools and blades out on the workbench. Olivia took one step toward him but then decided against it. She didn't really want to know about his faith. She knew if he spoke too much about it, she'd only hurt him with what she had to say about it.

She turned her eyes to the piles of stuff still yet to be sorted. Her gaze fell on the massive mountain of woven baskets. "You know this place is a bad episode of hoarders, right?"

Tyler laughed and nodded to her over his shoulder.

Returning to the clothing, she grabbed at and yanked a rotted garbage bag that was stuck in a crevice between a mangled bundle of rusted bikes and an old junk car. She dislodged half of it, the contents spilling out onto the barn floor as she held a partial piece of the torn bag. *Great.* She went and grabbed a new garbage bag from the roll a few feet from her and went and started picking up the clothes. Seeing a small girl's outfit, she paused and picked it up. It was a pink dress with white lace and gemstones across the neckline.

"Hey, Tyler?"

"Yeah?" He was clear on the other side of the barn, but their voices carried well.

"Chet didn't have children, did he?"

Tyler maneuvered over to her and peered at the dress in

her hands. She handed it to him, and he smoothed a hand over the dress. "He did for a little while, three of them. He had a late brother who got bad into fighting and the bar scene. He took off on his wife and kids, and the wife ran out afterward too, for a little while, at least. Chet and Margret took on two girls and a boy. This belonged to the smallest girl, Cindy."

"The mom came back though?"

"Yeah, eventually. Ten months later, she showed up sober and employed, with a car and a place of her own. They willingly gave the kids back, even though they were terrified of doing it." He gently handed the dress to Olivia. "It'll fit Molly, right?"

"I think so. You're giving it to me?"

"Yeah, take it. Chet would've given it to you."

She smiled and took it from him. Olivia went and set the folded dress to the side of the barn next to the pile of bags and continued working. As she went through bags of clothing and glanced at various items from this man's life, she had a desire to meet the man. "I would've liked to meet Chet. He sounds like he was a good guy."

"He was one of the good guys." Tyler surveyed the barn with his eyes. "It was a shame he lost Margret. I don't think he ever fully got over it. Who could blame him? I don't think Jonathan got over Marie, and he never will either."

"Wait, he's married now, though, isn't he?"

"Yes, but there's a part of Jonathan's heart that Marie took when she left this planet. Sure, he's found love again, but there's still a piece of his heart missing that has gone to Heaven."

AT EIGHT O'CLOCK THAT EVENING, they closed up the barn and drove the short distance to the cabin to clean themselves from being in the dirty and dust-ridden barn. Olivia washed her hands and arms, and then Tyler came through the doorway of the bathroom. He was covered in oil on his arms and most of his clothing from dealing with car parts and had dirt in both his hair and on his face.

"You're filthy."

He smirked. "You don't look that clean yourself, missy."

Reaching, he plucked a piece of newspaper shredding from Olivia's hair and dropped it, letting it float to the bathroom floor.

"Take a shower." Olivia walked out of the bathroom and shut the door, not only to the bathroom, but also to the door on her itching desires within her.

He hollered from the other side of the door. "Hey, Olivia. You should look around for some food. I know it's kind of strange to search the cupboards because, you know, the guy just kicked the bucket."

"Don't be so brash, Tyler!"

He laughed. "Sorry. Try to find some food around the house if you can. I don't know about you, but I'm famished."

Famished. She laughed and headed to the kitchen. He was right about it feeling odd to pick through a dead man's food supply, but she obliged regardless of the awkwardness of it. Searching in the pantry, she found some rice. In the fridge, a bottle of soy sauce. Then in the freezer, a freezer-burned piece of chicken. She pitched that in the trash near the kitchen's back door. She did some more rummaging and found an unopened bag of tater tots in the back of the freezer and then some sugar-free pudding cups in the fridge on the lower shelf that she hadn't seen on her first peek inside when she found the soy sauce.

Tyler came out from the bathroom and down the hallway. He looked like a new man, being all clean. Upon approaching

Olivia and the kitchen table full of a random assortment of food, he started to chuckle.

"What's so funny? This is what I could find." Her eyes fell on the sugar-free butterscotch pudding cup and a laugh broke through her lips, curving them into a smile.

They took a seat at the table, their light laughter subsiding. Tyler bowed his head and held out a hand, palm-up, for Olivia to grab hold of, but she refused.

"No, thanks. You go ahead."

Olivia started in on her rice and watched as Tyler prayed. She was fascinated that a man so gorgeous and intelligent could be so blind. She hadn't met someone who believed like Tyler did. Not even her own parents were devoted the way Tyler appeared to be. Her parents often missed prayer at meals and rarely put their faith into action. They weren't like Tyler. He seemed to be different. After they ate, he offered to clear the plates and do the dishes since she'd put the food together.

"I'm going to step outside for a few minutes and make a phone call."

He nodded, scooting his arm across the table to pitch the empty pudding cups into the trash can he had at the end of the table. She walked out of the kitchen, through the living room, and out the front door. Stepping out into the crisp cool air and onto the porch, she slipped her phone out and dialed her mother.

"Hey. How's Molly?"

"Still good, Olivia. You still with Tyler?"

"Yeah. I'll be home soon though. I have to work in the morning. I'm sorry I'm being weird about Molly. I just worry."

"That'll never change. We *always* worry about our children." Her mother's words tugged at the memories that Olivia had buried deep below the surface. The drug years, then the Bruce years. Every time she had been in a bad place mentally and making the wrong choices, she'd pushed her mother and father away. Now that she had a child, she felt so much remorse for what she had done earlier in life to her parents. She knew it had to be terribly hard on them all those years.

"You're right, Mother. I'd better get back. Thanks for the update."

She turned and went inside. As she walked in and shut the door, she was surprised to see Tyler was in the living room and in the recliner with a book laid out in his lap.

"What are you reading?"

He peered up at her, then smiled, flashing her the cover. It was the Bible.

"Of course, *the Bible*. I should've recognized it and known we were going to have a Bible study during some part of this date."

He laughed as he shook his head and closed it. He leaned forward and set it down on the coffee table. "If there's a Bible handy and I'm not busy, I read after dinner daily. It's a habit that I enjoy. I wouldn't have done it if you were still in here."

"What magic did you read about in there tonight? Did God tell the Israelites to rape and murder a bunch of innocent people?"

Tyler's lips pursed into a thin line and he frowned as his eyebrows furrowed. "You seem to have a lot of animosity toward God, Olivia. I won't let you speak accusations though. He never commanded anyone to rape anyone, ever. He also never commanded people to murder innocent people. He did, however, use the Israelites to judge nations by wiping them out, so maybe that's why you're confused."

"I'm sorry. I didn't mean to start a whole thing. I really need to work on my mouth." She sat down on the couch next to the recliner.

He let out a short burst of laughter. He said jokingly, "No, not you."

She laughed.

"Well, you about ready to head home?" Tyler put the foot of the recliner down and stood.

"Yeah, I'm getting tired and I still need to get my baby. Oh, dang it. The car lot is locked up. I can't get my car until tomorrow." Sitting back against the couch, she pressed a hand against her forehead. Stress rose within her as her thoughts spun around how she'd get home and how she'd get Molly.

"I will give you a ride. You have a spare car seat?"

She paused, thinking for a moment. "Yes, I do. Well, my mother has a car seat in her car, but then I'll be trapped at my house without a way to drop off Molly at my parents'. You know what? I can just stay at their house tonight and Uber my way to work tomorrow."

"Sounds like a plan. Sorry I didn't think about that before." He reached out a hand to Olivia and she reached out to join him. As she came up and off the couch, he pulled her the rest of the way in, surprising her with another kiss. Relaxing her muscles, she let the warmth of his lips send radiating crashes of tingles from her head down to her toes. Releasing from her lips, he took a step back, smiling as he did. She knew just as much as he did that they were playing too close to the sun. He didn't want that, and she resolved in her heart to respect it, like she knew he was respecting her by choosing it.

He grabbed her hand and they walked to the door and out to his car. As he opened the car door for her, he stopped, then ran inside the cabin. Confused, Olivia continued into the car and buckled her seatbelt. A moment later, Tyler returned outside, the pink dress for Molly in his hand. Olivia's heart melted. *He remembered.* This man was everything right in the world, but she wondered in the far recesses of her mind how long it would last. How long until he grew bored of her or didn't want to put up with her anymore? That faint fear was far back in her mind, but she knew it was there. She felt it every time he looked at her the way that made her insides turn to mush. She felt it every time he touched her, and she felt it most of all when he kissed her.

CHAPTER 18

YLER WIPED HIS SWEATY PALMS on his jeans as he walked beside Olivia to the front door of her parents' house. He hadn't been this nervous since taking Sandra Finks to the prom in high school. He liked Olivia and desired to make a good first impression with her parents. She had mentioned on the car ride to the house that her parents were stout believers of Jesus Christ, and while that should've made him relax, it didn't. Instead, he worried about how he would come across and the questions they might ask him.

Olivia stopped at the door and turned to Tyler. "You seem nervous."

He shrugged. "Maybe a little. After all, these two people are responsible for making you."

She blushed in the low lighting of the porch light. Seeing the red crawl into her cheeks and a smile curve on her lips, Tyler could feel his heart pound and his desire for her grow. He wanted her to feel as special as she was becoming to him. He felt more connected to Olivia in the short span of knowing her than he had with any other girl in his life. The time they spent earlier in the barn working together was nothing short of splendid. Her mere presence cultivated something in him he couldn't explain. He loved every moment he spent with her. He brought a hand forward in front of him and let his hand glide against her cheek. She leaned into it. Peering into her sea-blue eyes, he came closer and kissed her gently on the lips.

"Let's go in."

She nodded and then led him in through the front door. Olivia had called her parents to let them know that he was dropping her off. It was her father's idea for him to come inside and meet the two of them. At first, she objected, but the phone was on speaker and Tyler agreed to go along with the invitation to have dessert.

Walking into the living room, Tyler was greeted by her father, Dan. Her father came closer and spoke quietly. "Hey, you two. Come join us in the dining room. Molly is sleeping just down the hall in the guest room and Kora is serving our ice cream in just a moment."

Tyler followed behind Olivia and her father as they walked through the living room and into the dining room. The room was large and had a long wooden table in its center. They all took seats at the end closest to the kitchen, and soon, Kora brought in the bowls of ice cream along with spoons and toppings. Tyler grabbed the chocolate syrup and drizzled it across the top of his ice cream.

"So, what line of work are you in, Dan?" He handed Olivia the syrup as she motioned with a hand for it when he had finished.

"I'm in banking. It's not a very exciting job, but it pays the bills and I've been doing it since I graduated college."

"Wow. It's great that you've been doing the same thing since you graduated. Pretty rare these days."

Dan nodded, taking a bite of his ice cream.

"What's your degree in?"

"Communications. I know, it's not much, but I didn't really know what I was doing. I just knew I needed a degree. That's how I was raised."

"What about you? I don't believe Olivia has told us much about your company. *Willow Design*, right?"

Finishing a bite of ice cream, Tyler nodded. "My brother is the designer. He's the one with the architectural eye and I handle the customer side."

"Ah, he's not much of a people person, eh? Those creative types tend not to be big on talking."

"Yeah, for the most part. He has his moments, but for the most part, you're correct. He is bubbling with conversation when it's one-on-one with me and him or him and someone he knows, but the second you get a big crowd around him, he shuts down."

Kora interjected. "I have a brother who works at Microsoft and he's like that. He was quiet, shy, and non-social all through his younger years, and he still is a little now, but he's really smart and making the big bucks at Microsoft."

"Where do you go to church?" Dan's question came out of nowhere and tripped Tyler up for a second. A long enough second that Olivia hopped into the conversation.

"Dad! Why on earth would you rush conversation to God? You were talking business and just topic-jumped to church."

Tyler gently touched Olivia's hand to slow her apparent annoyance. She relaxed in her seat and picked up her spoon. "Thanks for defending me, but I have no problem talking God or church. I go to Crosspoint Community. Where do you two attend?"

"Pines Baptist."

"Neat. What projects are you guys working on at your church right now?"

Dan leaned forward a little. "What? What do you mean what projects are we working on?"

"Like do you volunteer, lead a Sunday school, or help build a building? I don't know, just what's going on?"

Her father didn't respond to that but instead shoved another spoonful of ice cream in his mouth. Tyler could sense her father was upset.

Kora touched Dan's arm gently and peered over at Tyler. "Right now, we're in a season of rest. We haven't been active in serving for a little while now."

"A ten-year season of rest?" Olivia fired at her, increasing the awkwardness.

"*Olivia.*" Tyler's eyes were serious. He didn't want a fight to break out over their dessert. It was already tense, judging by her dad's reaction to the initial question.

"She's right," Kora admitted, eyebrows raised as she turned her head to look at Dan. "We haven't done much in a while outside of going to church."

"We're old and tired." Dan leaped back into the conversation. "Plus, we're helping Olivia with the baby, and the list goes on and on."

"I didn't mean to upset or offend you. Just making small talk."

Dan was quiet for a moment, then his whole posture relaxed as he let out a sigh. "It's okay. Honestly, I think we make excuses when we know we aren't doing the right thing."

Tyler nodded. "You're absolutely right about that, Dan. I'm guilty of it too."

"What about you? You're serving, I take it?" Dan dug into his bowl for ice cream as he looked toward Tyler.

"Yes, I am. I've been out of town for the last week, but in a couple of days, I'll be returning to the church to help out with the youth group. I try to get involved at least a couple of times a month. I used to do nothing at all until last summer when I heard a sermon that knocked the wind out of my sails."

"Your pastor had a good one that got you?" Dan asked.

Tyler shook his head as he recalled his trip to Diamond Lake, the inn, and the good people he met, Charlie and Serenah. "No, actually, it was out at Diamond Lake. I was staying at *The Inn at the Lake*, and the inn's owners run the church out there, so I ventured down that Sunday morning."

Dan's face lit up. "Is Charlie still preaching?"

"Yes. That was him!" Tyler felt excited to hear that Dan knew of the pastor.

"That man is a powerhouse for God. Our pastor has gone out there a few times in the past and said the man is talented and he came back with a notebook of notes. Our church has teamed up with that church on occasion to do some outreach stuff in Spokane in the past. We had a cookout a few summers back down at Riverfront Park with them, if I recall correctly."

"That is so awesome to hear. I need to talk to Crosspoint about doing more connecting stuff with other churches."

"Can't hurt to ask."

The conversation continued to flow easily after that, and Tyler's nervousness fell away, though Olivia didn't say much.

AT TEN O'CLOCK, Olivia yawned widely as she walked with Tyler to go out to his car. As they exited the front door and stepped down the steps in front of her parents' house, she grabbed his hand. At her touch, tingles and warmth traveled up his arm and into his chest, radiating outward and consuming every part of his being. Her parents had been amazing to him and left an imprint on his heart. While he enjoyed the fact that they had faith, a part of him knew it must've been difficult for Olivia to deal with that all her life if she hadn't chosen to believe.

"How were things growing up for you? Like, with your parents being believers?"

She grimaced.

"That bad, huh?" Tyler stopped at the sidewalk and turned to her. He looked her up and down, from head to toe, trying to read her body language, trying to understand her perspective and heart. He was moved with compassion, and he raised both of his hands to hold each of her arms. "Olivia, look at me."

She peered up into his eyes. It was obvious now to him that she was fighting back tears.

"Your parents love you. They've always loved you, and I don't know what your childhood looked like, but I imagine they were critical and strong and firm with you. But that's because they love you so much. Imagine for a second if Molly were about to get hurt. Would you want to stop her from being injured?"

She nodded. "Of course."

"That's what they were doing."

She pulled away. Sniffling, she wiped her eyes as she turned her gaze toward her parents' house. "I know . . . but they could've gone about it differently, though, Tyler."

"You're right, but they did what they could and did the best they knew how. I think you know that."

Olivia turned back to Tyler and nodded, then took a step closer to him. She wrapped her arms around his body. "You're right, and I've been seeing the truth of that more and more since Molly came into my life. You know, there's something about you, Tyler. I feel like you can see right through me."

She laid her head gently against his chest, and he kissed the top of her head, then rested his cheek against her hair. They held each other for a long moment. Tyler didn't want to let go of her, let go of this moment in time. He wanted it to last forever, to never let it slip away. Sadly, though, he knew he had to let go. Gently releasing from her, he kissed her softly on the lips.

"I had a great time today. Let me know when you want to do it again."

"What about tomorrow?"

He smiled. "I'd like that, but I have to work on a few big-ticket items that will take me into the evening. Wednesday, I'm helping with the youth at church."

"Maybe later in the week?"

"Yeah. Let's plan for that."

He grabbed her and pulled her in for one last short kiss, then left to his car.

WHEN HE ARRIVED home at the bowling alley that night, he was pleased to see a large stack of moving boxes lying on his living room floor. Knowing that his brother was the only one with a key at the moment, he smiled. Walking into the kitchen, he saw a handwritten note on the counter from Jonathan. *You're welcome. ~ J*

Later that night, after packing a few items from the bookshelf, as he lay in bed saying his prayers, a thought surfaced to his mind that was unsettling but true. *She doesn't believe.* It was a cold reality that Tyler tried not to dwell too much on. He knew he had no power or strength to save Olivia's soul. It was up to God to do the saving. While it comforted Tyler to know he had no control over that aspect, it also terrified him. *What if she never chooses to believe?* He tossed and turned that night as the fears and the what-ifs tormented his mind. He tried for hours to sleep, then finally, at 2:30 AM, he rose from his bed and went out to the living room.

Opening up his Bible, he began to read in Romans, eventually stopping in chapter three.

This righteousness is given through faith in Jesus Christ to all who believe.
There is no difference between Jew and Gentile,
for all have sinned and fall short of the glory of God,
and all are justified freely by his grace through the redemption that came by Christ Jesus.
Romans 3:22-24

TYLER'S EYES welled with tears as his heart swelled with an overabundance of sorrow and joy. Sorrow because he knew that Olivia could say 'no' and joy because Tyler saw God, over and over again, chasing after that broken girl's heart. He saw it that night on the side of the road out in the country where she almost died. He saw it in God's gift of a precious baby girl that softened Olivia's heart. He saw it in her parents' love for her. Tyler saw God's love written all over the pages of her life, and yet Olivia hadn't come to the saving knowledge of Jesus. *Will she ever have faith?* He wondered grimly. Tyler didn't have answers, but he knew who did. He wiped his eyes and set his Bible on the coffee table. Pushing the coffee table in front of him a few extra feet, he got down on his knees and prayed to God. *I'm drawn to this girl, Lord. I love spending time with her, and I like her parents, and I like the way she makes me feel, but You already know all of this. What I'm getting at, Lord, is this . . . I want You first and foremost in my life. I know a healthy relationship with a woman requires You at the top for both of us. Not just one of us. Lord, I pray that You reveal Yourself to her and bring her to a place of repentance. A place of coming to You. You are not optional, but she is. Let me never forget that. Amen.*

CHAPTER 19

OLIVIA'S THOUGHTS CONSISTED OF ONLY Tyler in the weeks and months that followed his meeting her parents. When they were together, they were inseparable. When they were apart, they'd text and call one another. Tyler made her feel like the queen of his world, and she soaked up every moment and feeling he cultivated inside of her. She felt what the two of them had was the closest to magic she'd ever get. She felt like he was the one like no other man had ever come close to. He cared for her and her emotional wellbeing in a way she hadn't ever experienced in her life. And after three months of dating, Olivia was ready for the next step in the relationship.

Lying on their backs one sunny Saturday afternoon on a blanket sprawled out in the yard behind his house at Diamond Lake, Olivia's thoughts were on him and on Molly. "I think it's time you met her."

He jumped up and turned to her, excitement in his eyes. His joy wasn't a surprise to Olivia. She already knew he loved Molly, just like he loved her. He would listen carefully every time she spoke about her, and he even asked about how she was doing when she wasn't brought up in conversation by Olivia.

"Are you sure?" Tyler held out his hands as he knelt down on his knees. "I know this is a big deal."

She sat up and turned to him, crossing her legs over one another. "Yes. I think it's overdue. I think I've been nervous because once you meet Molly, then you'll have every part of my heart."

Tyler smiled, touching her cheek gently with the palm of his hand. Reaching for a strand of hair, he grabbed it between his index finger and thumb, rolling it between them. "You can trust me, Olivia. You can always trust me."

"I know I can. I'm ready."

He smiled, then stood up. "Let's go."

"Where?"

"To get Molly. I want to meet her now. I've been waiting for this moment for a while. I even know exactly what I want to do. I want to take her to that park near your parents' house. You know the one."

"All right, yeah. Let's go."

He grabbed the blanket and tossed it over his shoulder, then grabbed ahold of Olivia's hand.

AT HER PARENTS' house, Olivia let Tyler go in the front door first. As he walked in, she followed behind him and watched. He smiled deeply as he lowered himself to his knees to see Molly eye-to-eye as she lay in the swing.

"Hi, Molly," he said with a gentle voice. "I'm Tyler, a friend of your mommy. It's nice to meet you."

He offered his index finger to Molly, and she giggled and smiled, then latched her little hand onto it. Olivia's heart was filled with so much joy that it was spilling over in tears coming down her cheeks. She sniffled as she wiped her eyes. Tyler glanced over with a concerned expression on his face.

Shaking her head, Olivia shooed a hand. "Don't mind me."

Kora came into the living room and looked over the event unfolding before her eyes. She smiled, then looked at her daughter Olivia and mouthed, "I love him." Then she proceeded to point at the unaware Tyler.

Standing up from the couch, Olivia smiled and mouthed, "Me too." Then Olivia traveled into the kitchen and her mother followed. Olivia opened a cupboard and pulled a glass out, then retrieved the half-gallon of orange juice from the fridge. Taking the glass and juice over to the island in the kitchen, she poured a glass and then took a long drink.

"You're glowing with joy these days, Daughter." Her mother's head was tilted, her lips curved in a 'satisfied with your decisions' kind of smile. She brought both arms up to the island and rested her elbows on the surface as her eyes stayed on Olivia. "When are you two getting married?"

"Mother!" Olivia jerked her head toward the doorway leading into the living room where Tyler was only a few feet away. "You can't talk about that so loudly! It's *only* been three months."

"Sorry." She shrugged. "For people like your father and me, that is what dating is for, Olivia."

"Maybe, but not for me."

Kora came around the island and touched her arm gently as she spoke softly. "Honey, he's just like your father and me. Marriage is on his mind whether it is for you or not. Obviously, not right this second. You two have only been seeing each other for a few months, but eventually, it'll come."

Olivia wasn't obtuse. She had thought of marriage with Tyler and had even fancied the idea. But all the good that she saw in Tyler was eclipsed by worries that loomed nearby in her mind. She and Bruce were good too while dating—not this good, but pretty good—and look how that turned out. "I don't even want to think about marriage, Mom. It's bad to go there."

"Is your father's and my marriage bad?"

"No. That's not what I meant." Olivia fumbled in her thoughts, and without thinking, she gave her mother what she really thought of her and her dad's marriage. "But you two are a little on the boring side."

Her mom blinked and was quiet for a moment. She smiled. "Oh, honey. Being an adult is boring most of the time, if you're doing things correctly."

"Rachel's life isn't boring. She has plenty of fun and she's an adult."

Her mother lowered an eyebrow as she narrowed her look at Olivia. "Is Rachel's life what you want for yourself?"

"Don't judge her, Mother!" She immediately regretted her outburst in tone as reality filed through her mind. She thought of her schooling for the dental assisting certification. She only had another month and a half or so left and she'd be graduating. If she would've fallen in with Rachel's lifestyle after she and Bruce separated, Olivia would be in a darker place. A shudder ran the length of her spine. "But you're right about not wanting that life. But I also don't think life has to be boring."

"Of course, it doesn't." Tyler's voice startled her as he walked into the kitchen. "Life isn't boring. Well . . . maybe some parts, but that's maintaining all the different things in life while waiting for the next big thing. Life is full of hills and valleys and trials and blessings and good times and bad times. That's life." His eyes fixed on Olivia the next moment, warming her from the inside out. "By the way, Olivia, you make quite the cute children."

Children? Her heart leaped at the thought of a child between the two of them, then it backtracked remembering her mother's words moments earlier about Tyler being the *marriage type*. Olivia already knew Tyler wasn't the kind of guy who would take a dive beneath the sheets before the wedding night, and that meant there would be no children before marriage.

"Thanks, I think so too. How about we head to that park you suggested?" Olivia let out a succession of quick nods as she walked away from her mother and toward Tyler in the doorway. Her eyebrows bounced up and down, trying to signal in some sort of Morse code to Tyler that she wanted to leave.

Tyler let out a gentle laugh, then tipped her a nod. "Yes, let's get going."

Olivia strapped Molly into the stroller out on the front porch while Tyler grabbed the diaper bag from inside. He soon joined the two of them and helped lower the stroller over the curb and onto the sidewalk.

As they headed down the sidewalk toward the park, Tyler put his hand atop Olivia's that was holding one of the handles on the stroller. She peered over at him and smiled, and he leaned in and gave her a peck on the lips.

"I like this. I like us." Olivia beamed as she pushed her baby along with Tyler by her side.

"I do too." He smiled warmly.

At the park, Olivia stayed on a bench with the stroller nearby as Tyler carried Molly on his shoulders over to the playground. She looked so small up there on his shoulders. Olivia smiled as she watched Tyler hold Molly's little hands and guide her around the playground, looking at everything before he finally put her into the baby swing at a slow pace.

Olivia's hand had a sudden pulse of pain rip through it, and she clutched it tightly with her other hand, waiting for it to subside. Fear tangled around her heart as the pain intensified. She hadn't had even a sliver of pain in months, and its sudden return was unnerving. She stared at the cement path beneath her feet and focused as she tried to slow her breathing and wait for the pain to go away. Wave after wave, all within a few minutes. She could hardly think because it bothered her so much. Then, it started to fade, slowly leaving like a tide going out to sea. She sat upright and rested her back against the bench. She started to cry softly.

"Babe?" Tyler said as he approached with Molly. He looked upset, distraught. Quickly, he placed Molly into the stroller and then sat close to Olivia's side and held her hand gently. "Talk to me. What's wrong? What can I do?"

Shaking her head, she wiped her tears and forced a smile. "I'm fine. It was just an old friend coming back for a visit."

Tyler smoothed a hand over his face and stood up. He wasn't happy, starting to pace, and she felt uncomfortable.

"*Tyler.*"

He stopped and looked at her.

"I had some hand pain for a minute. I think I was more startled than anything else. I'm fine, really. Please calm down."

Slipping back to her side on the bench, he grabbed her hand softly, compassion in his eyes. "I have a natural desire to want to protect you, Olivia. To take your pain away. To make you smile. And this pain, it's something I can't do anything about, and the thought that it's returning drives me a little mad. Does that make sense?"

Olivia's lips trembled. She hadn't seen Tyler this worked up since they had started dating, and she didn't like it. She didn't want her pain to hurt anyone else. It had already hurt her enough. She loved Tyler's concern and care for her, but she didn't love how it had hurt him in the process.

"I understand. I'm sure it was just a random bout of pain, Tyler. If it shows up every few months and leaves again, I'm fine with that. Key word being *leaves*."

He nodded in agreement, the wild look in his eyes settling. Then, he lifted her hand to his lips and slowly pressed a kiss on top of her hand.

"My love, wouldst thou gift me a pleasure by walking with me roundeth thee park-eth?"

Olivia tossed her head back as she busted into laughter. "What was that?"

He laughed too, then he kissed her on the lips by surprise. She melted by the sudden brush of her lips against his. He pulled back from the kiss, smiling, and said, "That was Shakespeare. It's romantic."

Shaking her head, she laughed again and smacked his shoulder. "*You* don't need Shakespeare."

Rising from the bench, they journeyed the park's paths, Olivia pushing the stroller. As they traveled, Olivia's thoughts gravitated to the faint pain still present in her hand. She hadn't revealed that the pain was still there to Tyler on purpose. She knew from his reaction just now he'd probably want to fix it, and it would cause him pain when he couldn't. This time, she'd have to do things on her own so no one else would be bothered by it. She resolved by the end of the day that she'd make an appointment for another acupuncture visit on Monday to see if that would resolve it.

CHAPTER 20

*D*R. HALL DID LITTLE TO comfort Olivia over the phone on Monday, two hours after her appointment. She had called him on break at the dealership when waves of pain radiated from her hand while she was typing on the keyboard. The acupuncture hadn't worked, and she hoped there could've been a mistake. With tears in her eyes and all hope draining from her, Olivia ended the call and cried bitterly as she leaned her back against the brick wall out back behind the dealership. She lowered herself down to sit on the pavement. She thought the pain was gone for good, and now that it had returned and stayed, it sent her into despair. She felt as if it would never leave her.

"Olivia?" Jasper's concerned voice carried from a few feet away at the back door of the dealership.

She wiped her eyes and straightened her posture, doing her best to put on a show. "Yes?"

"You okay?"

"I'm okay enough. What's up?"

"There's a customer who needs you to look up some information on their warranty, and tons of people in line

159

behind her. We are super-swamped with this back to school special going on."

Olivia dug deep for strength, scraping against the bottom of the well, and rose to her feet. She wiped the dirt away from the backside of her flowered skirt, wiped her face tear-free one more time, and then went inside. She'd have to work through the pain, at least for today.

After her shift, she was tempted to go to Rachel and see if she could help her get some pills like before, but she didn't want to travel down that path again. Rachel had almost accused her of being an addict last time. She didn't like it and she didn't like putting her daughter in harm's way like she had done previously. On her way to her mother and father's house to pick up Molly, she stopped at the grocery store to pick up Ibuprofen, milk, bread, cereal, and a few other essentials she needed at the apartment. The pain had left her for a moment in the store, and she was relieved when it did. Then, as she was turning down the aisle for water, the pain came on again, this time worse than all the other previous times, and she stopped in the aisle and clenched her eyes closed. *Why can't this be over? Why does it have to hurt so much? What is the point?*

A moment passed and the pain subsided. She opened her eyes and continued pushing the shopping cart down the aisle. Glancing over, she saw wine bottles. She recalled a time earlier in her life when she went with Rachel to a birthday party for a friend and Olivia had fallen off the trampoline and hurt her shoulder. The girls at the party sneaked her a few glasses of their mother's wine and the shoulder pain went away. *A lot safer than street pills,* she thought, grabbing a couple of bottles. She continued through the store and got all the items she needed.

She picked up Molly with little conversation with her mother due to the exhaustion and pain and went home.

Olivia put the groceries away, fed Molly a bottle, and then placed her daughter in the high chair to play with some solids that she was recently approved to start. As she zipped the spoon of rice cereal around in the air, pretending it was an airplane to find its way to Molly's mouth, she smiled and did her best to enjoy the little time she had with Molly before bed and the milestone of her eating solids now. Another shock of pain hit her, and she dropped Molly's spoon, the plane crash landing on the tray. She fought back tears as she waited for the pain to stop, then resumed feeding Molly.

As she cleaned the tray a short while later, her phone buzzed over on the kitchen counter. Wiping Molly's face with some baby wipes in her hand, she unbuckled her and set her down on the blanket in the living room to roll around and let her tummy settle for a bit.

She arrived at her phone in time to answer the call.

It was Tyler.

"What are you up to?"

"Just got home and fed the beebs. I'm going to lay her down soon and then probably binge on Netflix."

He laughed. "You want to hang out? I can bring a movie over and we can just chill."

She peered over into the kitchen and thought about the wine she had bought and about the acupuncturist and the emotional toll the day had inflicted on her. "No, I think I'm going to relax tonight. I'm really tired, Tyler. Though it does sound wonderful. Raincheck?"

Olivia did desire to see him, but she was exhausted from pretending lately. Whether it was at work or with her parents, or even with Tyler. Nobody knew the struggle she was dealing with right now, and she wanted it that way. She didn't want to burden others with her pain. She'd handle it and not put the pressure on those she loved.

"No problem. I need to probably get some more work

done on this new client proposal I'm working on anyway." He let out a sigh, then shifted to a new topic. "You have a good day?"

Such a simple question, yet only a complex answer existed on the other end, locked up in Olivia's heart. She gave him a half-truth. "It was work."

"Ain't that the truth?"

Her phone's call waiting beeped in on their call. It was Rachel.

"Hey, Rachel is calling me."

"Okay, have a good night. Take care."

Switching the call over to Rachel, she greeted her as she went over to Molly and scooped her up from the blanket on the floor.

Rachel was full of energy and using her valley-girl voice. "Hey, giiiiirl."

Olivia laughed lightly and looked at Molly, drawing comfort in her baby's eyes. "I'm not going out or doing anything, before you even ask."

"Um, *why?*"

"Stop doing your valley girl impression. I'm not in the mood. I want to be alone and at home. You can respect that, right?"

A honk came from outside, drawing Olivia to open the apartment door and go out. She walked out with Molly on her hip and peered down the steps and out to the parking lot. She saw Rachel's car parked and she was waving obsessively through the windshield. "I guess I can't respect it. Come on. You're dressed and Molly's ready. Let's go."

She shook her head. "I really don't want to go anywhere, Rach. Plus, Molly is ready for bed."

Rachel got out of the car and walked toward the steps as she hung up the phone. Stopping at the base of the steps, she peered up at Olivia. "Then let me come in. I'm already here."

"Okay. Fine."

Her cousin ran up the steps and into the house. Olivia followed her inside and shook her head.

"Why are you sprinting?"

"I had to get in before you changed your mind." Rachel walked through the living room and into the kitchen. She started to open cupboards. "I'm hungry. Do you have anything to eat?"

"You picked the right day to intrude. Just went to the store. I was going to eat after I put Molly down. Just toss in a pizza from the freezer while I put her to bed."

"Okie dokie."

Going into her daughter's nursery, she placed Molly gently onto the changing table and gave her a new diaper for the night ahead. As she did, she couldn't help but think Rachel was acting more obnoxious than usual, and it annoyed her that it had to be today. She had enough going on without Rachel adding stress. After the change, she placed Molly in the crib, being sure to hit the *On* switch for the Noah's Ark mobile before going out to the kitchen for a pacifier.

Upon entering the kitchen, she found Rachel attempting to set the oven. "How does this blasted thing work?"

"Like most ovens. It has to pre-heat *before* you set the timer, dear." Reaching past her, Olivia set the temperature, then went to the fridge to grab some wine, noticing Molly's binky on the counter.

"Hey, Olivia."

As she picked up the binky to go give it to Molly, she looked up at Rachel. "Yeah?"

"I lost my job today." Rachel's eyes watered, tears flowing down her cheeks a moment later. "That's why I just showed up. I didn't know who else to turn to. You're the only person I really have in my life."

Olivia's heart broke apart and guilt overwhelmed her as she set the binky down on the counter. She rushed to Rachel, throwing her arms around her. "Oh, Rach! I'm sorry for trying to be so brick-wallish with you on the phone. I'm such a bad cousin."

She laughed. "No, you're quite the opposite. You're too good. I'm scared to death I'm going to lose everything. My house, my car . . ."

Releasing from their hold, Olivia shook her head. "No, you won't. With your experience in management? You'll have a job in no time. Hey, let me get this binky to Molly before she has a fit, and I'll be right back out."

Walking down the hall to Molly's bedroom, Olivia felt grieved over her cousin's loss of employment. She didn't really know if things would work out, but she knew that if Rachel wasn't careful, she'd be back to dealing drugs and being on a track going nowhere quick. It was bad enough that she was into the drug scene part-time. If she became desperate for money, it'd only grow into a bigger problem.

As she approached her daughter's crib, Rachel left her mind and the pains of her life melted away in that moment. All she cared about was her precious baby girl. Molly held a smile on her face as she took the binky. She had grown so much in so little time, and Olivia knew she'd only grow more day by day. Giving Molly a motherly gentle brush of her hand along her temple and cheek, Olivia peered into her eyes. "I love you, Molly. Sleep well."

She turned and left, closing the door gently.

POURING her fourth glass of wine later that night, she emptied the last bottle Rachel and she had been sharing. She was a lightweight when it came to drinking, somewhat because of her weight, but also because she never drank the stuff more than a handful of times in her life. Luckily, the wine had done the trick for her pain. She hadn't felt much of anything since her second glass. Olivia walked into the living room, grinning at Rachel as she sat on the couch with her feet up on the coffee table.

"Bottle is out. Oh, well." She plopped onto the couch cushion beside Rachel and leaned her head against her shoulder.

"You never told me what possessed you to get wine in the first place. You don't drink, Olivia, at least not since we were kids."

She shrugged, sitting upright. Her walls were down now, her defenses sent home for the evening. "The pain is back in my hand. I'm so sick of it."

"So, wine helps?"

Olivia closed her eyes, nodding a few times as she turned her way. "I think I'm stuck forever with having the pain. It's so . . . *annoying*. I do the right thing and leave that cheating scumbag, and I get punished with lifelong chronic pain. Yay."

Rachel shook her head. "Things just happen sometimes. I lost my job because of my till being off by $100. I know that jackweed Tommy took it, but I'd let him use my till and that's my responsibility. Things happen. I'll figure out a new job like you were saying, and you'll eventually figure out this pain thing."

"You know what makes me mad, Rach?" She rested a hand on Rachel's shoulder. "You worked at that job for so long, and poof! They toss you out like a sack of garbage at the end of the night. *Zumiez* lost more than an employee today. They lost the best employee they ever had or ever will have."

She laughed. "Sure. Hey, are you still seeing that Tyler guy?"

Realizing that she hadn't seen her cousin in almost two

months, she nodded. "Yes, he met Molly a couple of days ago. Hey, you know what? We need to hang out more."

"I know, right? Maybe if you called me once in a while instead of calling Romeo, we could."

Olivia laughed. "Calling is a two-way street, giiiirl."

As the evening progressed, so did the conversations. Eventually, they stumbled onto their old days, and more specifically, Olivia's old boyfriend, Champ, out in Nine Mile Falls. Olivia called those *the dark years* while Rachel always referred to them as *the golden times of youth*.

"Come on, those were great times!" Rachel shook her head as she paused for a second. "What about that time when we went to Long Lake with Champ and his friend Skully? Remember? We sneaked in the back way after dark."

"Oh, when Skully snapped his collar bone falling down the hill on the way out? Fantastic."

"Forgot about that." Rachel leaned against the couch cushions. "But the rest of that night was fun. We were jumping off the docks in the moonlight and had the music from Champ's boom box blasting. Oh, and when *Forever Young* came on and we all sang at the top of our lungs standing on the edge of the dock."

"We were blitzed." Olivia was sobering up from the wine now, and clarity was coming back to her. "Sure, there were good times sprinkled in, but to say they were nothing but good times is an outright lie. It's just not true."

Rachel shrugged and stood up. "I guess it's a matter of perspective. Did you know Champ moved back from Chicago?"

"What?" Olivia felt her heart stop for a moment. "When did this happen?"

Panic began to fill Olivia's heart. Champ was one person she never wanted to see again. He was a vile and horrific individual, and if there were such a thing as souls, he didn't have one, in her opinion, or if he did, it was as black as night.

"About a week and a half go. He's back out in Nine Mile Falls, actually."

Hearing that Champ was back in the area moved an old and rusted part inside Olivia, a part she didn't like. She and Champ had a short relationship years ago, and he had ended up cheating on her with one of his old ex-girlfriends. When Olivia had heard about it, she went and slashed his Cadillac tires and took a baseball bat to both headlights. "Wow. I never thought I'd hear about him again."

"Right? I went out and saw him a few days back. He seems matured."

"Is he still doing drugs?"

Rachel's lips tightened, forming a thin line.

"Should've figured as much."

"Yeah, that's Champ. So, what about you and this Tyler guy? You two getting close?"

"Yeah, I'd say pretty close." Olivia thought about the wine, the pain she had been hiding from him. "He doesn't know about the pain being back. Nobody does but you."

"Why aren't you telling him?"

She shrugged. "He's a guy. He just wants to fix it."

"Typical guy mode there. Just explain it to him."

Olivia shook her head. "I don't want to burden him, Rach. He's such a good and kind man, and he . . ."

"He what?"

Rachel already knew about the pain. She might as well know about it all. "He deserves someone better than me." Shame had Olivia tilting her head down as she absentmindedly rubbed her wounded hand even though there was no pain at the moment.

"That's not true! You are awesome, and any guy would be lucky to have you!" Rachel seemed outraged that Olivia would think lowly of herself, her voice picking up a couple of octaves.

"Thanks, but he can have someone whole, which it seems like I will never be, at this point." Glancing at her cell phone, Olivia saw it was now past eleven o'clock. She smiled and raised an eyebrow. "I'd better get to bed. You know, Rach, some people have jobs."

They both laughed. Rachel shook her head. "That was a low blow."

"I couldn't resist."

Olivia walked her to the door and shut it behind her. Turning around, she saw the wine bottles sitting on the counter. It had worked, and it didn't put her daughter and herself at risk of anything—that is, as long as Molly didn't need to be rushed to the ER in the middle of the night. This could work out in the long run for a solution to the pain. All she had to do was make sure she didn't overdo it and make a habit of it. Olivia felt a measure of relief in her heart as she headed down the hallway to her bedroom. Finally, she was able to control the pain in her own legal way, without doctors looking at her like she was making stuff up. She didn't have to worry anymore.

CHAPTER 21

WAKING EARLY WEDNESDAY MORNING, TYLER sat up in bed covered in a layer of sweat. Raking a hand through his hair, he glanced over at the clock. It was just shy of four thirty in the morning. He had another dream, the same repeating dream he had been having for a little over two weeks now, ever since the last time he'd heard from Olivia. He blamed it all on stress from the change in his and Olivia's relationship. They had been obsessive in their relationship the last few months. The two of them were seeing each other and talking daily, and now there was a deafening silence between them. She didn't call or text anymore and he'd altogether stopped trying after being ignored repeatedly. He'd even tried going to her work twice, and Jasper had intercepted him, saying she wasn't there and he couldn't give out her work schedule.

He pushed the comforter off with a huff and swung his legs over the edge of the bed. Hunkering over, head almost between his knees, he clasped his hands together and prayed. *God, she's not answering my calls or texts. She doesn't want to see me. I know she's not a believer, but I think she's close to being one. I don't want You to lose her, God, and I don't want to lose her either. Please . . .*

Slipping off his bed, he headed down the hallway toward the kitchen. The dream replayed in his mind as he walked. He was in a forest, the sun was shining down across the tops of the trees, and the birds were singing. He felt joyful, exuberant. It felt as if someone was walking beside him, but when he turned to look, there was nobody there. Then, he came to the end of the path and pushed his way into shrubs and bushes. It was dark, he felt unsure of what was happening, and then he pushed through past the shrubs and was suddenly out on a grassy mountainside. His vision lifted from himself and the whole picture came into view. A lake, and more mountains, and the sun was shining brightly. He was overwhelmed with the scenery, the breathtaking awe he felt in every part of himself, and then poof! He woke up.

After the coffee brewed, he poured himself a mug and took his Bible with him out the sliding glass door that led to the cement patio with a fire pit facing the lake in the east. It wasn't very often that he had a chance to sit in the twilight of the morning and enjoy his coffee and his time with the Lord. He set his mug of steaming-hot liquid on the small table beside the chair and sat down. He looked out to the peaceful lake and thought of God. He thought of how God had spoken into existence such beauty and majesty. Turning his gaze, he followed the tree line around the lake, and in the far distance, he could see houses.

Being overwhelmed by his Creator, Tyler bowed his head. *Forgive me, Lord. I fail time and time again to trust You. It's You who holds the breath in my lungs and it's You who knows the future. My insecurities and shortcomings are all flesh, and I pray You help me to take my eyes off myself and place them on You alone. Now I ask You to please clear away the gunk from my heart and let me be open to Your Word and Your truths. Amen.*

Opening the Scriptures, Tyler began to read the story about Jesus and how He had calmed the storm. As he read, the truth of God's Word tore open his eyes and heart, putting Tyler in his place.

That day when evening came, he said to his disciples, "Let us go over to the other side." Leaving the crowd behind, they took him along, just as he was, in the boat. There were also other boats with him. A furious squall came up, and the waves broke over the boat, so that it was nearly swamped. Jesus was in the stern, sleeping on a cushion. The disciples woke him and said to him, "Teacher, don't you care if we drown?" He got up, rebuked the wind and said to the waves, "Quiet! Be still!" Then the wind died down and it was completely calm. He said to his disciples, "Why are you so afraid? Do you still have no faith?"
Mark 4:35-40

TYLER'S EYES welled and his heart twisted in agony at the light being shed on his sin. Tyler knew where he would be on that boat that day, and he wouldn't have cozied up next to Jesus on that cushion, taking a nap. No, he would've been with the rest of the disciples and in an all-out panic. He had not spoken with the girl he liked for just two weeks and was losing sleep over that fact alone. Wiping his moistened eyes, Tyler saw the words that twisted the dagger of conviction tighter in his soul. It was the words Jesus had spoken. *'Why are you so afraid? Do you still have no faith?'*

His heart heavy, Tyler had to pause his reading and let the words trickle through his entire being. He had to let them soak into every bone and find every corner of his life. Then, after a few minutes, he prayed. *Oh, how I long to be one who would be napping on the pillow in the boat beside You, Lord. Yes, at peace while the storms whip around me, resting in Your security. I need Your help, Lord. Not with Olivia per se, but with me. I'm broken and I am flawed and I need to rely on You only and stop fretting. Loose me from this bond that I have inflicted on myself by getting too close to Olivia. Let me only have eyes for You, Lord. Only eyes for You . . .*

ARRIVING at the office at eight o'clock, Tyler put another pot of coffee on, then went and got settled in his office. Still having an hour before Jonathan would be in to go over the proposal for the new youth building for the YMCA, Tyler decided to do some side-work on filing the physical copies of invoices. It wasn't a very important task since everything was digitalized, but good recordkeeping of hard copies was still considered a good business practice. As he filed each invoice going back over the last year, he noticed an unsettling recurring theme—a lot of freebies. Anger began to fill Tyler.

Giving Jonathan the benefit of the doubt, he took the stack of invoices that had been zeroed out and went to his computer to double-check the digital records. He didn't want to accuse his brother of something until he first had all the facts. First, he checked the digital copies—they all were zeroed out also. His anger grew. Then he went and checked the receivables to make sure there hadn't been payments that were being diverted somewhere else. Tyler then breathed a heavy sigh of relief to find that wasn't the case. That would've meant his brother was stealing. At the end of it all, it appeared to be exactly what he had seen in the beginning. His brother was working for free and doing it often, without Tyler knowing. *How could he do this to me?* Tyler wondered as he felt betrayal and hurt pressing on his heart.

Hearing the *Willow Design* office door open, Tyler jumped

from his seat and headed for the door to go confront him. He was in such a hurry he almost forgot the stack of papers and had to double back to his desk to get them. He was full of anger toward his brother for working for free. He knew he had done it a few times here and there, but not this many.

Tyler walked out into the lobby area as Jonathan was pouring himself a cup of coffee.

"We need to talk."

"Whoa." Jonathan chuckled. "Let me get a cup of coffee in before we *talk*."

"No, this is serious."

Jonathan obliged and they went into Jonathan's office. He took his coffee with him and took a seat behind his desk. Tyler tossed the stack of invoices on the desk and they slid to Jonathan.

He picked up the invoices and flipped through the first couple silently. Then, he set them on the desk and peered at Tyler. "Okay?"

"*Okay?*" Tyler clenched his jaw and walked away from the desk, going over to the window. He was so angry he couldn't speak. His brother stood up from behind his desk and came around the front of it and up behind Tyler.

Tyler turned his head slightly over his shoulder without fully turning around. "Why do you not care about this company?"

"I do, Tyler."

He whipped around and looked Jonathan squarely in the eyes. "Then why do you work so much for free? I don't get it. *Please*, explain it to me."

Jonathan held open his hands and lowered his head. "I can explain."

"Good! Do it."

"Come sit down." Jonathan walked over to his desk and sat down. Tyler did also, sitting across from him. Jonathan brought his hands up on the desk and opened his arms, palms up. "It was wrong of me not to disclose each invoice we zeroed out. I will admit that."

"You bet it was wrong!" Tyler snapped, then he leaned forward over the desk and tapped the table. "I've worked just as hard as you, and for you to tell people we don't want money without talking to me at all? My goodness, Jonathan. It's not fair of you. If you want to give your portion of your earnings back to clients, whatever, but don't volunteer my money!"

"You're right." Jonathan nodded in agreement, no anger in his words or expression. Tyler was calmed by his brother's calmness over the matter.

"Okay. So why? Why do you do it, Jonathan?"

He glanced toward the window for a moment as he was silent. Then he looked back at Tyler. "I can go through every invoice and tell you a story with each one, but what good would that really do? The fact is I do feel I have enough money in life, and a few free invoices don't bother me. I don't care about the money once my bills are paid and my family is taken care of. After that . . . I just care about helping people."

"Helping them with designing their buildings?"

"Yes. It's what I do. It's my gift to give to the world when I can. Again, I'm sorry I brought your money into the equation. That was wrong, and a lack of thinking on my part. In fact, figure out what you lost and I'll write you a check."

Tyler shook his head and a smile broke across his face for the first time that morning since he arrived at the office. "You make it so hard to not like you, brother."

Jonathan laughed. "Good."

"No, really, man." Tyler raked a hand through his hair. His anger had all melted away. "You're my role model in life. I think God gave me a brother like you because He knew I'd need someone like you."

"Right back at you, Brother."

As Tyler was leaving work that day, he received a text. He didn't expect it to be Olivia when he pulled his phone out, but it was, and she was asking if he'd come over and see her. He felt unsure of what to do. He had just been praying to God earlier that morning to let her go from his mind. Now, here she was, back in his life again. It didn't matter if he wanted to see her or not because of his plans tonight with the youth group. It wasn't just a normal Wednesday night service at Crosspoint, but instead, they were all meeting at the church to load up in vans and go out to his house to play games, roast hot dogs, and make s'mores. He thought maybe this was God's way of saying he needed to invite her. Instead of trying to reply to the text, he called her.

"Hey. I know it's a long shot, but I figured I might try and it's too much to text."

"Oh?" Olivia sounded curious more than she did nervous.

"It's Wednesday, and—"

"I'm not going to church, Tyler." Anger appeared in her voice but it didn't deter him.

"No, no. Hear me out. It's different. The youth and I are all going out to my house to play games and roast hot dogs and stuff. It'll be fun. It's laidback."

There was a long pause on her end of the phone, then finally, she said, "I can do that."

"Really?" Tyler's heart swelled with an overwhelming joy. "I have to warn you, there will be a message from the Bible."

"You'll be doing it?"

"Yes."

"That's okay too. I really want to see you. I've missed you."

"I've missed you too. Meet us out at my place at seven. I am meeting the kids at the church and then we'll be out."

As he hung up with Olivia, he could feel the waves lap against his heart with confusion. She had re-emerged from nowhere and gave no explanation to where she had been for the last couple of weeks. Tyler had to fight the urge to text her about it and ask why she had blown him off, but he didn't give in. Instead, he laid down next to Jesus on the boat. He refused to give in to the panic running amok in his thoughts. He didn't understand why Olivia had vanished for two weeks, but he was going to be grateful that she reached out and trust God through it.

CHAPTER 22

*A*S THE KIDS LOADED INTO the Crosspoint church vans, one of the youths, a thirteen-year-old boy named Parker, came over to Tyler in the parking lot.

"What's up, Parker?" Tyler asked, acknowledging him standing nearby.

"I need to talk to you for a second, Mr. D."

Turning to one of the other adults, he caught Daisy's gaze. "I'll be right back. I'm going to chat with Parker." She nodded with a curious look on her face before directing herself to the other teens.

They fell into step together and traveled away from the other kids and vans in the parking lot. Parker leaned his back against a car and crossed his arms and immediately teared up. "My dad left."

"What?" Tyler's heart broke at hearing the child's words, and he placed a hand on the boy's shoulder. "You okay?" Compassion flowed through him, and anger that a man could leave his family like that. Not wanting to portray his anger to a child, Tyler kept a poker face as he listened on.

"Mamma said he had to go away for work, but she was

locked up in her room all day crying." Parker sniffled as he wiped his nose with his sleeve.

Closing his eyes to prevent himself from tearing up, Tyler cleared his thoughts and prayed for strength. Then, he got down on one knee and looked Parker squarely in the eyes. "You remember that talk we had a few weeks ago at youth group?"

He shook his head, wiping his nose again as he looked at Tyler in confusion. "No."

"You remember. The one about trusting God no matter what. You remember that at all?"

"Yeah, a little." His small nod backed up that he really did remember, urging Tyler to continue on.

"Listen, I know things are tough right now and things don't make a lot of sense, but you keep your eyes on Jesus, Parker. God is in control, and He is never going to leave your side or let you down. God is the answer to every heartache and every broken spirit. You need to trust in Him. Come on, let's pray."

He rested a hand on the child's shoulder and they bowed their heads. "Lord, I come to You right now with Parker. He's upset, scared, and worried. Lord, I know You know our hearts better than anyone else, and I pray that You wrap Your arms around this child right now and comfort him. Please help him to find peace, please help him to find a calmness that only You can provide. In Your precious and Heavenly, name, Lord, I pray these things. Amen."

Tyler looked at Parker. "If you need someone to talk to, you can call me anytime, day or night. You got it?"

He nodded quickly and then leaped forward unexpectedly and hugged Tyler. Fighting tears off, Tyler slowly brought his arms up and put them around the boy. "It's going to be okay, Parker."

As they walked back toward the vans, Tyler felt his own

preaching to Parker hit his own heart. *I know things are tough right now and things don't make a lot of sense, but you keep your eyes on Jesus.* Parker climbed into a van with the other kids. Daisy and Pastor Carson, the other adult leaders, found their way over to Tyler.

"Is he okay?" Daisy asked.

"No, he's not." Tyler's eyes were narrowed on the van, thinking about the heartbreak that little boy was going through at the moment, all because of the selfishness of mankind. Tyler needed to be selfless, and this was a good reminder. Then, he turned to Daisy. "He's not okay, but he will be."

The leaders each got into a van and started the caravan out to Diamond Lake and to Tyler's house.

Arriving a short time later, they all piled out and ran through the yard to the volleyball net he had set up the night before in preparation of the day's activities. The adult leaders walked in step together to the back side of the house. Daisy and Carson both gave compliments about the property, the lake, and the house. Carson asked, "Why's the dirt road keep going further on the property? What's behind that bend of trees?"

"A cabin. It was given to me by an old friend last year after he passed away. Before he passed, he gave me part of his property to build this house. I couldn't have lived out on Diamond Lake without him."

"Now that's the kind of friend to have." Daisy nodded, peering toward the patch of trees.

Peering over at Jessica, one of the freshmen in high school, he saw her serve the volleyball. Then, Tyler turned to Daisy as they all closed the last few feet to the kids. "She looks pro. Does your niece play at school?"

"She sure does. Varsity, in fact."

"Nice."

Hearing a car pull up the driveway, Tyler saw Olivia's car coming to a stop behind the vans. His heart began to beat faster, and he turned to Carson and patted his shoulder. "Olivia's here. I'll be right back."

Tyler tried to walk, but it inevitably turned into a run as she got out of the car and adrenaline surged through him. He had to reach her as quickly as he humanly could, maybe even faster, if possible.

Arriving to Olivia, he launched her up into his arms and spun her around. His heart warmed and he loved how it felt to have her in his arms again. He lifted his eyes to her and some of her hair brushed against his face. She peered down into his eyes with a warming smile. They kissed as he set her down, then Tyler gently pushed her hair out of the way and delicately placed it behind her ear. She was back in his life, and he couldn't help but be happy about it even if things felt shaky in their relationship.

"Oh, how I have longed to kiss you again." He tilted his head, sensing something off about her. "You okay? It's been awhile since I saw you last. I was starting to worry."

"I'm okay." She smiled, but he could see it was labored. He let it go and decided that she'd talk about it if she wanted to talk about it. "Have you all been here long? I was hoping to meet you out here about the same time."

"Just got here." Tyler grabbed her hand, linking his fingers between hers, and led her over to the group. His heart was overwhelmed with happiness, but he didn't let go of what he had learned that morning in the twilight when he was with the Lord. He wouldn't be caught in a panic again.

AFTER VOLLEYBALL, all the kids were hot from the sun and wanted to take a dip in the lake. Everyone changed inside and then headed for the water. Parker, though, was sitting in a chair up on the patio. On his way with Olivia to the water, Tyler noticed Parker and stopped short of the shore.

"What is it?" Olivia turned to see what Tyler was looking at. He was staring at Parker. "Why's that kid not getting in?"

"He's going through a hard time right now. His dad left him and his mom yesterday."

Her eyes stayed fixed on the child. "That's so sad."

"Yeah. He told me back at the church before we loaded up in the vans. I think I'm going to go talk to him again."

Olivia touched Tyler's chest and shook her head. "Let me? I know I'm not a dude or a youth leader, but I know about a hurting heart. When you're in a place like that, you just need someone to be there with you. There doesn't have to be a lot of words going on."

"If you're sure you want to do it."

She nodded. "I do. You go hang out with the other kids. I'm not really dressed to swim anyway."

"Okay." He leaned in and kissed her cheek and then booked it down to the water to join the others. He kicked off his flip-flops and threw off his white V-neck on the shore and then entered the water quickly, following up with a dive in to cool off from the heat. The cold lake water plummeted his body temperature in an instant and he exploded to the surface.

"Whoa. That is refreshing!" He laughed and wiped the water from his face. A few of the kids laughed and then Carson worked his way through the water and over to him.

"She looks like she's pretty good with kids." Carson nodded toward the house where Olivia was sitting with Parker. Tyler turned and saw her. It was nice to see Olivia in this kind of light, and it made Tyler desire her all the more.

Tyler agreed with a nod.

"Hey, Mr. D. Can we play Marco Polo?" Tyson, one of the

youth, asked. All the other kids agreed they wanted to play also.

"Yep. I'll be Marco. Ready? I'm going down."

He went down beneath the surface of the water and counted off ten with his hands above the water. Then he came up, eyes clenched.

"*Marco . . .*" He moved around the water carefully, paying attention to the water moving around and the light sound of giggles. He laughed. Tyler loved the youth group and he couldn't imagine his life without the kids being a part of it now. When he first started serving at Crosspoint at the end of last summer, he had never expected he'd fall in love with not only the kids, but the church family as a whole.

HOT DOGS WERE A HIT, then after that, it was right on to the s'mores as night began to fill the sky. As the teens munched on their treats and sat on a log that Carson and a youth had dragged out of the woods, Tyler went inside the house to grab his Bible. As he was walking through the kitchen, heading for the sliding glass door to go back outside, Olivia entered.

"Hey." Her voice was soft, gentle, and a pleasant interruption to his plan at the moment.

"What's up?" He couldn't help but smile at her. This was turning into a perfect occasion.

"Where are we all sleeping?"

"There are sleeping bags in the vans. Just haven't pulled them out yet. It will be girls at Chet's cabin and boys here at my house. That cool?"

"I'm cool with that. My mom was fine with watching Molly overnight. I just got off the phone with her." She shrugged and smiled. "I don't know how much I am okay with being away from my little girl, though, it being the first time."

Acknowledging the big deal it was to her, Tyler set his Bible down on the counter and came closer to her. Bringing his hands up to her arms, he gently touched her and peered into her captivating eyes. "It's going to be okay. You trust your mother with Molly, right?"

"I do."

He caressed her arm. "Then let it be. I know it's a big deal, but you have to trust God."

She blinked.

Tyler retracted inwardly, bringing to fact within himself that she didn't acknowledge or believe in God. "Oh, right. Sorry, I'm in God-mode hardcore right now."

Her gaze landed on the Bible, and when it did, she smiled. Tyler thought for a moment that maybe, just maybe, she was starting to believe. He clung to that hope in the moment. All she had to say, though, were three simple words in response. "I see that."

"You're going to hang out and listen, right? You don't have to, but you never know. You might like it."

"I planned on it. I just wanted to steal one more kiss from you." She leaned in and kissed him. His heart warmed, knowing that she'd be willingly listening about God for the first time since he knew her.

He smiled. "You can steal those anytime. I won't mind. Let's go back out."

"Okay." She grabbed his Bible and handed it to him.

They walked outside and the kids were all about done with their s'mores and were now drinking their sodas and waiting for the talk.

"Let's pray and then we'll dive into the Word of God."

He stood in front of the fire, facing the youth who were opposite him. The adults were nearby, sitting in lawn chairs.

The fire was crackling from the new log someone had added to the fire, and hot embers and ash floated up into the starry night sky above the fire pit.

Bowing his head, Tyler prayed aloud. "Lord, thank You. Thank You for this group of wonderful, talented, and smart teenagers. Thank You for all the fun we had today. Help us now to open our hearts to Your Word and to learn from You. Help me to get out of the way and for You to minister to Your young people. Amen."

Tyler opened up the Scriptures and read aloud.

"Psalm 119:105 states, 'Your word is a lamp for my feet, a light on my path.' This is the verse we're going to stay in tonight for our talk. Let me ask you something. Do you have the lamp of God lighting your path in this world? Take a moment and think about it."

Tyler closed the Bible and paced in front of the fire, then he stopped and pointed to the fire. "God's light is bright like this fire. It illuminates the space, and with it, we are able to see where we're going. In this life, you will face many tribulations. It happens to everybody. People will let you down. That new girlfriend or boyfriend you have? A let-down. Guaranteed. You see, the thing is, there's a part of ourselves that only God can satisfy." He was quiet for a moment as he surveyed the young people's faces. His gaze stopped on Parker. "I'm preaching to myself too, right now. We all go through difficulties and darkness . . . and the only way we can get through those tough times and not be stuck in the dark is when we let the light that only God can provide guide us in everything we do."

Leaving the fire pit and patio, Tyler went off into the darkness of the yard and turned toward the kids still at the fire. He peered up at the moon, then back at the teens. "Ignore the moon for a second. Listen, when I'm trying to walk without God in my life, it's like I'm falling all over the place because I can't see where I'm going. It's dark. When I'm walking with the Lord, though . . ." He came back onto the patio near the fire. "When I'm walking with the Lord, I can see *clearly*. And you know what?" His gaze landed on Parker again. "Sometimes, even with the light, we can't understand what's going on in our lives, but we can trust God when everything else seems a mess. He is our guide through this life. He is our everlasting light. He knows everything and loves us and will carry us if we let Him."

CHAPTER 23

OLIVIA EXCUSED HERSELF FROM THE group after Tyler closed the message with a word of prayer. She didn't need to use the restroom, but she did need the space for a moment. Inside Tyler's bathroom in his house, she flipped on the light, shut the door, and locked it. Then, peering into the mirror, she looked at herself. Was she lost and in darkness like Tyler had spoken about in his message to the kids? Was she walking without the lamp of God? She felt okay, well, kind of. She was a good mom and was close to getting her certificate for dental assisting.

A knock came on the bathroom door moments later, startling her. She walked over to the door.

"Yeah?"

"You okay in there?" Tyler's voice was gentle, muffled through the wood that separated the two of them.

Olivia opened the door. "Yes, I'm okay. Was that message about me, Tyler?"

He shook his head. "No. Not necessarily. I had been planning the message for a week and a half now. I didn't know you were coming till earlier today."

"Oh." Her voice softened as she criticized herself for self-ishly thinking it was about her. But Tyler brought a hand up and touched her arm, giving her some reassuring comfort as he gazed into her eyes.

"Don't feel bad. It happens to a lot of people. God knew you would be here tonight, though, so maybe *He* planned on your hearing it. I just know I didn't."

"Tyler, we need to talk."

His eyes went wide. "Okay. Let's talk."

"I've been avoiding you."

A light laugh escaped his lips. "Oh? I hadn't noticed."

"I want to be honest with you. The pain came back in my hand, and this time, it's been worse. It's really hard to deal with and I was trying to hide it from you, and the only way I could do that was avoiding you altogether." Her eyes welled as her heart ached. "I didn't want to worry you or bother you."

He tilted his head and frowned. "It's not a bother, Olivia." He raised his eyebrows. "Just go back to Dr. Hall. I'm sure he can get you in again."

She raised a hand, palm down as she shook her head. "I already did that. You can't fix it this time."

He was quiet for a long moment. "I'm sorry. What can I do?"

"I don't know. But I don't want to hide it from you anymore. Being away from you is too painful."

"So, instead of telling me so we could work on it together, you just ghosted me and stopped returning my calls and texts?"

Her heart twisted as she nodded, still hiding the fact that she had been drinking her pain away with wine for two weeks now. She was drinking more and more to attempt to stay on top of the pain. Olivia had come to see Tyler tonight in the hope that if she spent enough time around him and told Tyler she was in pain, that in some way it would help her be more careful with the drinking, maybe even help her slow the train down. But honestly, she had been thinking about having a drink the whole time she had been at the lake that evening. The only time the thought left her was when she was with Parker, talking to him about his mother and father.

Olivia came close to Tyler and hugged him, soaking up his comfort like she'd longed for so desperately as of late. "I'm sorry I hid it from you, and I'm sorry for avoiding you. I honestly just didn't want to burden you."

His jaw clenched, he shook his head. "You're *never* a burden to me, Olivia."

"Why do you seem mad?"

"Because I am mad! You keep saying you're a bother and a burden. You know? And instead of confiding in me, you avoided me, and it hurt."

"I'm sorry, Tyler."

"Yeah, well, maybe this can't work if this is how you deal with issues."

Olivia's heart splintered. She had hurt Tyler by her choice that she thought would keep him from being hurt. Tears started down her cheeks, and when he saw them, his entire demeanor shifted to a softer one. He came closer and smoothed his hand over her cheeks, wiping the tears away. Then he leaned in and gently pressed his lips against hers, reminding her that he still, in fact, cared deeply for her.

"Olivia, I know this can still work. I'm sorry for saying that. Let's get back to the others and we'll talk more later. The girls are about to head to the cabin."

She pulled away from their embrace and nodded, wiping a stray tear. "Okay. I'll join up with them. Maybe we can chat in the morning?"

"Meet me on my patio at eight o'clock tomorrow after I

cook breakfast, and we'll chat more about this. You're important to me, and I'm sorry you felt like you had to keep it from
me. I want to be there for you, but you have to let me."

Warmth swirled in Olivia's chest knowing that Tyler
wasn't holding against her the fact that she had ignored him
for two weeks. He had forgiven her. Though she was craving
a drink tonight, it was pleasant to be around Tyler again. Her
affections for him hadn't dulled in the slightest. If anything,
they were increasing. He came in close and planted a gentle
kiss on her lips, melting her insides.

DAISY CHOSE the spare room and its bed, while insisting that
Olivia take the master bedroom for herself. She tried to resist
the kind youth group volunteer, but her attempts at changing
her mind were futile. It was quickly becoming apparent that
this group of people weren't like the people she had encoun-
tered growing up at her parents' church. These people had a
faith that they not only believed in but lived out through
their actions. After the lights were out and all the teen girls
tucked away into their sleeping bags, Daisy and Olivia went
outside the cabin.

They both let out a sigh of relief as they sat down in a
pair of lawn chairs facing the lake. The moon was high and
large, almost full, and reflected down across the smooth
surface of the lake. It was quiet and peaceful, nothing like
the patio off Olivia's apartment in Spokane. It reminded her
of how much she'd missed not only Tyler, but visiting him
out here in the quiet. She was a fool to try and push
him away.

"A person could get used to this kind of living," Daisy said
with a slow nod as her eyes stayed fixed on the lake in front
of them.

"Right? I love it out here in the country."

Daisy turned toward Olivia. "I like you and I want to clear the air about something."

Olivia tilted her head, smiling. "Okay? Go ahead."

"Tyler and I went on one date a while back and it led *nowhere*. We stayed friends, obviously, but I just wanted you to know."

Olivia didn't like that they had gone on a date, but she was thankful Daisy liked her enough to tell her. "Thanks for telling me."

"You're welcome. You two are sure cute together."

Olivia was glad to hear someone pay a compliment to her about the two of them. "He's the sunshine in my world right now."

Daisy nodded and then looked out to the water in front of them. "I see the way he looks at you. I hope you know he loves you deeply."

Olivia was surprised to hear her say the word *love* and her heart melted. "You think?"

"Yep. I've known Tyler for a while now, long before he joined the youth group at the church, and I've never seen him look at a woman the way he looks at you. That's saying something."

Hearing it from someone other than herself and Tyler helped confirm the feelings Olivia was experiencing about Tyler's affections, and she was thankful. "Thank you. That means a lot to me."

Olivia began to think about the preaching Tyler had done earlier, then about her pained hand, and nervousness flooded her whole body, but she braced herself to talk. "Daisy, can I ask you something?"

"Yes, of course. What is it?"

"How do you know God is real?"

She smiled and looked over at Olivia. "There's a long answer and a short answer with that question, but I'll give you both. *God's chosen people* is the short version. The long version goes like this. When I was young, I didn't go to church with my family, but I did go when I visited my grandma and grandpa in the summer. I went to VBS and Sunday school when I stayed with them. I remember one teacher in Sunday school in particular. Mrs. Neko. She taught about the love of God and how God was our Heavenly Father, not our earthly one. I had lost my biological father at a young age, and it was the anniversary of his death a couple of days prior to that particular day, so I was thinking a lot of him. The way I see it, Olivia, is this. God doesn't make the bad things happen in our lives, but He does use them. He uses the bad to lead us to Him, which always results in good. He's perfect in all of His ways, and He wants our hearts, wants all of us. We just have to accept Him, and unlike my earthly father, He will never go away. God's unconditional and undeserved love was *always* highlighted at VBS, and it was during one of those summers that I accepted God into my heart as my Lord and Savior. It was because of His chosen people sprinkled in my life here and there that I felt His love then and even to this day. I now can look back and see that every one of those leaders and volunteers was placed there by God to gently lead me into His presence. He knew that I wouldn't fall instantly into it and that I needed time and guidance, and He used everyone around me to bring me to that."

Olivia nodded and let Daisy's words wash over and through her. She'd spent her whole childhood resisting her parents and resisting going to church. She had spent a great deal of time being adamantly opposed to God, Jesus, and all things religious. Since she had been in the wreck, she had begun to soften little by little. It started with her mother and how she was after the wreck. Then it grew a little more when she started dating Tyler.

"Can I be really honest for a moment?" Olivia asked.

"Yes."

Olivia turned more toward her. "When I think seriously about the idea of God out there, I struggle. I can't wrap my head around an all-knowing, all-powerful being."

"Neither can I."

Olivia's eyebrows rose. "You can't?"

"Not fully. Our little three-pound brains cannot possibly comprehend Him fully. If we could, He wouldn't be God."

Something in Olivia shifted a fraction, though she wasn't exactly sure what it was. "That makes sense. I also see the Bible as a list of rules that you have to follow, and if you don't, you will be struck down and punished."

Daisy shook her head. "That's what the world and Satan want you to think. That it's just a bunch of rules and restrictions placed on you by some big, mean God. The truth is the total opposite. There are no rules. They are instructions and guidelines that God gives to us to help us live our lives in a way that is pleasing to Him, and ultimately, to a life worth living in freedom. You see, you find true freedom in a relationship with your Savior. In obedience to Him, we find His abiding joy in our hearts. Could I go watch that filthy South Park cartoon like I used to years ago? Sure. But I no longer have a desire to do so. Yes, back in the day, I took pleasure in that crude humor, but not anymore. It's not because I'm trying to follow a set of rules given to me by the Bible. It's because God has given me a new nature and He is refining me day by day. He is molding me and shaping me to be like Jesus a little more every day."

Olivia relaxed into her chair and looked out at the water again, silent. Her pulse began to speed up and she was feeling uncomfortable. Had she misunderstood the Scriptures she was raised with? Had she misunderstood God as He truly was this whole time? Or was all this just one woman's experience and one woman's opinion? She wasn't sure, but her mind felt overwhelmed and her eyes grew heavy with a desire to sleep.

"Thanks for the chat. I think I'm heading to bed." Olivia stood up as she yawned, and a second later, Daisy rose out of her seat too.

"It's been a good talk. Anytime you want to talk, let me know."

"Thank you."

OLIVIA FELL ASLEEP QUICKLY ENOUGH, but only a couple of hours later, she woke with pain. She clutched her hand as she sat up in bed. *If You exist, please make this pain stop! Please!* A moment later, she regretted her prayer. She realized if there were a God out there, a forced demand was probably not the way to go about asking for anything. Rising from the bed, she walked over to the window and peered out to the yard toward the tree line and road that led up to Tyler's house. Her heart longed for him to be holding her right now. Maybe if he was able to be there for her in these intense moments of pain, she'd be able to manage her emotions a little better.

Walking away from the window, she turned on the lamp atop the dresser in the room and a picture frame came into view. It was of Chet and Margret. She remembered what they looked like from the pictures Tyler had showed her. The pain soon subsided, and she let out a heavy sigh of relief. *Finally.* She turned the lamp off and crawled back into the bed.

An hour passed and the pain once again woke her from sleep. Her eyes watered as she sat in the moonlight streaming into the bedroom and onto the bed. She felt utterly hopeless and alone in her suffering.

CHAPTER 24

*T*YLER WOKE BEFORE THE REST of the house the next morning. After his morning coffee and devotions, he got busy in the kitchen preparing a large breakfast for the entire youth group. He went all out, cooking pancakes, eggs, toast, hash browns, bacon, and sausage. He also had bagels, gluten-free bagels, cream cheese, sliced fruit, and two pitchers of milk and orange juice. It was a feast fit for kings and queens, and in his heart, each one of those kids was just that. He held the truth in his heart that these kids would soon be the leaders of the church, the ones who would be marching into the darkness ahead for the world, and the more he could encourage them and support them now, the better the future could be.

Parker was the first boy up that morning, and he came strolling into the kitchen at a quarter after seven o'clock. He rubbed his eyes of sleep as he staggered his steps over to a stool at the large butcher's block counter.

"What's that yummy smell?" he inquired, peering around the kitchen.

Tyler tapped the oven door. "Breakfast. All that is left to

make is a few more pieces of toast. You want to take over and I'll go to the cabin and get the girls?"

Parker perked up and nodded. "Yeah! That'd be awesome, Mr. D!"

He laughed and pulled the hand towel off his shoulder, handing it to Parker. "Now remember, this hand towel puts you in charge. Don't burn the toast."

Parker looked at the hand towel as if it was a gold fleece and placed it over his shoulder. With all seriousness in his face, he nodded to Tyler. "Got it."

Tyler walked outside to the van still parked there. He did a double-take when he noticed that Olivia's car was missing. His heart felt as if it dipped into his stomach. *She left?* He remembered their date at eight o'clock that morning and he became discontented. *I trust You, God. It's her I have a hard time with.* Unsettled by the fact that she had left, he drove a van down the path to the cabin.

Upon entering the cabin, he approached Daisy.

"When did she leave?"

Daisy shrugged. "I guess during the night. I don't know. When we woke up, she wasn't here."

"Okay. Load the girls up in the vans. I made breakfast up at the house." Slipping his cell phone out of his pocket, he dialed Olivia. His heart pounded with each ring on the phone. He had just gotten her back in his life and he didn't want to lose her again. It went to voicemail. Frustrated but submissive to God, he let go.

He returned his phone to his pocket and pushed it all aside in his mind. Joining Daisy and the girls outside as they got into the vans, Tyler focused his heart and mind on serving the youth and not being distracted by Olivia. For the rest of the morning, he was able to focus on the youth and enjoy the time with them, but as soon as the vans pulled away from his driveway at a quarter to noon, he pulled his cell phone out one last time.

There were no messages or missed calls.

His jaw clenched and he peered up at the sky. *What is the point of all this, Lord? What is going on? What is Your will regarding Olivia and me?* Looking forward, he noticed a bird perched on a tree branch. It was the same colored bird he had seen that day at the inn. Blue on top, white on its belly. He was able to recall his mindset during that time at the inn. He was learning to appreciate the small things. He prayed again. *Forgive me. Help me to appreciate the small things again and to be content, Lord. Amen.*

Turning, he went inside and got ready for work.

ARRIVING at *Willow Design* a short while later at one o'clock in the afternoon, he was greeted by his brother.

"You seem distracted. At first, I thought you were just tired from having the youth at your house all night, but it's different than that, I suspect." Jonathan's comment came as they were in the middle of discussing the proposal for the Astro account in Phoenix.

"How?"

"All short answers and your eyebrows are furrowed. You still upset about Olivia not talking to you?"

Tyler explained what had happened and how she had joined the youth and him last night. Jonathan processed and was quiet for a long moment.

"You know, the message out of the Word you delivered last night could've spooked her."

"Yeah, it could've." Tyler sat at his desk pensively, debating and mulling the situation over in his mind. "I'm going to go to her apartment."

"Isn't she at work?"

"That's true. I'll go to her work." Determined, Tyler rose from his desk chair and went for the door, but Jonathan caught his arm, concern evident on his face.

"You sure you want to do this? If she wants to be left alone, Brother, she might . . . I don't know . . . want to be left alone?"

"I know she's in pain right now, Jonathan. Whether that's physical, emotional, or both, I want to be there for her. She came out to the lake with the youth group willingly and sat and listened to me talk about God. She is struggling right now, and I'm . . . I'm going to go to her."

"Okay. Just mentally prepare yourself in case she's not receptive." Tyler nodded. "Hey. Don't forget to buy those airplane tickets for us. If we buy them now, a few months out in advance, we'll save big."

"I know. I already added it to my to-do list on my phone. I'll see you."

Leaving the office, Tyler felt nervous but confident. He didn't know if this was God's will, but he did know he loved her enough to want to be there for her. He got in his car and drove down to the dealership. As he walked into the dealership and didn't see her at the receptionist desk, he felt something in his gut tell him that something was wrong. Jasper walked up to him.

"Can I help you?"

"Where's Olivia?"

"She's not here today. Is there something I can help you with?"

"No."

Turning around, he tried calling her again on his way out to the car. There was no answer. His heart pounded and he got into his car, then drove to her apartment.

Climbing the stairs to her apartment, he noticed broken glass on the cement just outside her door. Confused thoughts swirled in his mind as he stepped over the glass and knocked on the door. As he did, the door swung open. Three empty bottles of wine sat on the coffee table, another few on the counter in the kitchen. His heart dipped as he entered and surveyed the scene before him. *She drinks?* He walked in and called out for her.

"Olivia?"

There was no answer, but he could hear Molly let out a whimper in a room down the hall. Moving quickly through the hallway, he opened the nursery door and saw Molly in the crib. He went over and scooped her up into his arms. Holding her close to his chest, he rubbed her back and spoke gently to her, trying to calm her.

"What are you doing here?" Olivia's voice was sharp, her eyes bloodshot, and an annoyed look was on her face as she stood in the doorway of the nursery. He turned toward her, the smell of something vile making him pause. It appeared she had become ill and it was on the front of her shirt. He held her gaze and doing so caused his heart to splinter. She looked at him as if she hated him.

"You left last night. I was worried and you weren't answering your phone. You didn't go to work."

Her eyebrows furrowed and a look of fire lit in her eyes. She rushed over to him and took Molly from his hands. "How dare you walk into my house, Tyler!"

"The door was open. What's with all the wine bottles? Why'd you leave last night? What is going on? You don't look too good right now, Olivia. What can I do to help?"

"You need to leave. That is what you can do to help." She turned and walked toward the door, lightly bouncing Molly up and down as she rubbed her back.

Tyler stepped toward her, determined, his heart pounding. "No. I want answers."

Olivia stopped and turned around, a fire lit again in those

bloodshot eyes. "You want answers, Tyler? How about the fact that my mother called me in the middle of the night because Molly was throwing up and she couldn't bring her fever down? How about the fact that I just got home from the ER, after being there since 3:00 AM? I honestly thought about texting you, but then my daughter would throw up again." She scoffed. "You want answers . . ." She shook her head. "Those wine bottles are from the last couple of weeks of my trying to keep my pain down. But that doesn't matter, does it? You walked right into my home and judged me, thinking they were from a couple of days rather than weeks. Admit it."

Guilt weighed heavy on Tyler's thoughts as he stood in silence. "You're right. When I saw the broken glass, the wine bottles, and the open door, and when you randomly left last night . . . I thought the worst."

He came closer to her and tried to embrace her, but she pushed him back forcefully and caused him to stagger his steps.

"Finally!" She sounded relieved, and a crazed laugh escaped her.

"Finally, *what?*" Tyler took a step toward her, eyebrows furrowed. "What's that mean?"

"Finally, you act like a typical *Christian*! Accusing me of something I am not. Finally, you can start to not like me, and finally, we can be done with this charade. You have to face it, Tyler. I'm not a good person. Those wine bottles? That's how I deal with difficulties. I don't pray to a God that doesn't exist and rely on a false crutch of faith to get by. I rely on what I see, what is real, and I rely on myself! Now, kindly, please get out of my house!"

He was quiet for a long moment, regretting ever coming over to her apartment, and then he took a few more steps closer to her. Peering into her eyes, he looked longingly into them. He loved her and wanted to be with her, but he knew this wouldn't work. He knew from the beginning, when he had read about the unequally yoked Scripture, that they would ultimately arrive at a place like they were now. A place where they separate and go their own ways. It hurt him more than anything had ever hurt him before. Then, he leaned in and kissed her gently on the lips.

"You couldn't see with your eyes what we had, but I know you felt it. Not everything is based on seeing as you seem to think it is, Olivia. Hopefully, one day, you'll understand that. I hope Molly is okay. Goodbye."

A BROKEN HEART and a memory of a dream of what could've been were all that Tyler had as he left her apartment that day. He didn't go back to work, but instead, he went to his old bowling alley and sat in his favorite stool at a high table and sipped on a cola while he watched the bowlers.

He took a swig of his ice-cold cola and let out a heavy sigh. He remembered the day he had met Olivia like it was yesterday. Upstairs in his flat, explaining to his brother how he wanted a life like the one he had, he'd desired a woman, a wife, a family. Then he met Olivia that same night. Over the last few months, he had seen a glimpse of the possibility of a future with Olivia. One where they were married and had a family together. Now, those dreams had melted away just like the ice cubes were now doing in his glass.

"Hey, man. Long time, no see!"

Tyler turned to see who was speaking. It was Vinny, the manager of the bowling alley and longtime friend. He smiled and stood up, embracing his old friend in a hug.

"How's your mom?"

"Good, good. I never thought I'd see you again after you

left. I have to say I was a little disappointed I hadn't heard from you since you moved."

Vinny sat down at the table with Tyler.

"I'm sorry, Vinny. I got busy with the house and work, and you know . . ." Guilt plagued Tyler as he thought about letting yet another person down.

"I get you, man. Hey, my wife finally had that baby girl."

"What'd you name her?"

"Hope."

"Cute name." Tyler picked up his glass and took another drink from it. It was hard for him to be genuinely happy for Vinny since he was in such a dark place of despair, focused on himself. A wave of conviction washed over him in the moment as he thought about his reading from the other morning, in the twilight. He thought of the boat and Jesus's words. He prayed, asking God to help him be more loving and trusting in Him.

"You doing good?" A concerned look rested on Vinny's face. It was obvious that he could sense something was wrong with Tyler. "I mean, you're sitting in this old bowling alley alone, drinking a Coke. I know you used to sit down here when things weren't going the best for you in life."

"You know me too well." Tyler shrugged a shoulder and let out a sigh. "I'm just a little confused in life. I'll be okay."

"Of course, you'll be okay. You're Tyler Dunken." He let out a laugh. "You want to bowl? I'll give you a free hour or two."

He shook his head. "That's okay, man. I'm about to leave."

"All right." Vinny reached a hand out and they shook hands. "You take care of yourself, and if you ever need anything, let me know."

He slid off the stool and headed back to work behind the counter. As his old friend walked away, Tyler thought more of the situation and more about the boat where Jesus had been napping. He wasn't going to let this situation drag him down and bankrupt him of joy. He had to push forward and get his mind off Olivia and onto God. His first and foremost love wasn't Olivia. It was Jesus. Tyler depended on God, and that's who would never leave him nor forsake him in this life.

CHAPTER 25

OLDING MOLLY CLOSE TO HER heart as she sat on the couch in tears that afternoon, Olivia wondered what the future held for her. Last night had been a disaster, a slow-moving train wreck in progress. When she got the call from her mother, she had already had less than a few minutes of sleep. It hurt to get out of bed and drive the distance over to her mother and father's house to pick up Molly. Then at the hospital, things only worsened. Fighting against sleep as she waited in the hospital room in the low lighting, she had to clean up vomit from Molly every twenty minutes as they waited for help. This all happened as her hand throbbed in pain.

On her way home, with little sleep and fighting pain at six in the morning, she pulled into a gas station and almost went in for a bottle of wine. She didn't go in though. Instead, she left the gas station and went home. Once at home and with Molly in her crib, she tried to sleep. Then, she awoke to the sound of someone in her apartment. Though she was relieved to find it was Tyler, at the same time, her anger was set ablaze. He had seen her dark secret scattered across the apartment. He had seen what she had worked so hard to keep from everyone.

Her phone suddenly rang. It was her mother returning her call.

"Is Molly okay?" Her mother's voice carried a motherly concern with it.

"Yes, she's going to be fine. They got the vomiting under control and then pumped her full of fluids because she was bordering on dehydration. It's just a stomach virus, and they got the fever down in the ER, and as long as we stay on top of it, she should be fine. I was wondering if you could take her for a while, so I can sleep? I hardly got any shuteye last night and only a few hours this morning. I'm dragging here."

"I can, but you'll have to pick her up by six o'clock this evening. Your father and I have a potluck at the church."

"She can't go?"

There was a long moment of silence, then Olivia jumped to correct herself.

"Never mind. Duh, she's sick. Six o'clock, no later. Got it. I'll drop her off in fifteen minutes or so."

Hanging up with her mother, she put together Molly's diaper bag and left for her parents' house. She did her best to fix her makeup and hide the fact she had been crying. Kora was a good mom and could sense whenever Olivia had been crying and would ask questions she didn't want to answer. If her mother began to ask questions, Olivia might break down and spill all, and she couldn't risk that happening. Olivia couldn't bear the thought of her parents being disappointed in her. She arrived at her parents' house at three o'clock and handed Molly off.

"Olivia?" Her mother's voice was laced with concern and stopped Olivia's heart as she was almost out the door.

She turned. "Yeah?"

"Did she have a prescription for her sickness?"

"Just the Tylenol." Olivia's heart settled. "It's in the diaper bag. Her next dose is at 4:30 PM. Don't be late or her fever could spike again."

"Okay, great. Get some sleep, dear."

Shutting the front door, Olivia's guilt and shame intensified. She was using her mother when her child was sick. It should be Molly's *own* mother caring for her, not her grandmother. Olivia knew she couldn't take care of her right now. She felt if she didn't get at least a couple of hours of sleep in today, she'd fall apart and not be able to function at all, and that wouldn't be good for Molly. As she pulled into the parking lot at her apartment complex, her hand began to throb intensely, the pain returning. *No!* Her thoughts screamed out as she grabbed her hand. *No, please, no!* She was about to turn the key and go get another bottle of wine, but she knew she couldn't. She had to drive in a few hours to get Molly and there would be no driving while drunk.

Climbing her apartment stairs, she made it inside, down the hallway, and into the bedroom. She collapsed onto the bed atop the comforter and pillows.

Sleep was almost to her when her hand began to hurt again. Was it never going to end? Exhausted, she rolled over onto her back and pulled out her cell phone. She called Rachel.

"I need something for this pain, Rach."

"Wine works, right?"

"Yes, but I can't drink right now. I have to go pick up Molly in a few hours."

"And you think you can drive on Hydros?"

"Well, yeah. I did when I was pregnant. I know how they affect me. I can manage that."

Rachel was quiet for a moment. "I just texted you Alex's address. I don't have any right now."

"Thanks."

Hanging up, she dragged herself out of bed and headed out to her car, disappointment in herself bringing her lower than ever before, but the pain was louder than her self-loathing.

A MAN WITH LONG, ratted brown hair and an unshaven face answered the door at the address in Newport. The appearance of the man was unsettling to Olivia, but she pushed her discomfort aside and focused on the pain relief she was seeking.

"Alex?"

He shook his head. "No, I'm Carlos. Alex is in back. Come on in."

He stepped aside and let her in, holding the door open. She walked in with cautiousness in her steps and worry in her heart. She hadn't been in this kind of place since she was in her youth, and it filled her with a measure of uneasiness as she proceeded deeper into the house. Going down the hallway that Carlos had pointed out, she came to the end of it and saw the open bedroom door. Stealing a glance inside, she saw a man with a shaved head, unbuttoned shirt and jeans on. She went in.

"You must be Alex."

"That's me. What can I do for you?"

"I need Hydros. I'm in a lot of pain and the doctors won't prescribe me anything, and—"

"Baby, I'm not a priest and this ain't confession. You're Rachel's cousin, yeah?"

Her face reddened. "Yes, I am."

He slid off the bed and began to button up his shirt. Then, he reached over and grabbed his wallet. "I don't have anything here, but I have a connection outside of town, due south. It's just shy of an hour from here."

"What? Why'd I come here then?"

"Whoa. Calm down. You couldn't just go there without me. This guy isn't as chill as me. I do have another option." He turned and opened his nightstand and pulled out a small baggie. Seeing the contents, she knew it was heroin. "It'll take all that pain away, guaranteed. A heck of a lot better than some hydrocodone."

"No, thanks." Olivia was disturbed and turned to the doorway. "Let's go. I'm in a hurry."

He laughed and shut the nightstand drawer. "We're all in a hurry, baby. But the reality is we don't know where we're going. Just chill. You're lucky I ain't got nothin' else going on right now and can escort you myself."

She shook her head and walked straight through the house and out the door. As she got in her car, she did the math on time and realized she'd be cutting it close. As Alex emerged from the house, she approached him.

"I need to follow behind your car. I can't take you in mine. I have to pick my daughter up at six from my parents' house and it'd take too much time to bring you back here."

"You talk a lot."

Her cheeks reddened again. "Sorry."

"Just follow me then." He got into his car and led the way.

They cut through Spokane and headed south toward Nine Mile Falls. As they entered the Nine Mile Falls area and then Suncrest, she became uncomfortable, remembering that Champ had returned to the area. *Please don't let it be Champ,* she thought to herself. Suncrest was the little town outside Spokane that she had spent a lot of time in when she was young and in her drug days. As they came to the top of the hill, where the town of Suncrest began, she immediately noticed new buildings. A fast-food joint, among other places. A lot had changed and that brought a measure of comfort to her because she knew she had changed too.

Turning down Meadowview Lane, Alex pulled into a house's driveway. The property was about an acre in size and had a small roundabout to the left of the long driveway. It looked rather civil and not the rowdy kind of place like Alex's house did in Newport. This brought her another measure of comfort.

Alex got out of his car and walked over to her as she stood near the front bumper of her own car.

"Stay here and I'll go talk to my friend."

She peered around at the yard and noticed a towering pine tree nearby. She peered up at the branches and needles. Pine cones dotted the branches and she was reminded of Tyler's friend Chet. Then she started thinking more of Tyler. *Maybe I was too harsh on him.* As she waited, she resolved in her heart to go find Tyler and confess all. She wanted to be with him, and she knew in her heart she had to let him in on all parts of her life and self if it could ever work out. *I love him.*

The front door opened, and Alex came out, smiling big as he did, a bag full of white powder in hand. Shutting the door, he came down the cement steps and out to Olivia.

"He's looking forward to seeing you."

"That's kind of odd. Don't you think?" Her nerves inflamed and she leaned to the right, glancing at the house. "His name isn't Champ, by chance, is it?"

"No, it's Tony. It'll be fine. Go ahead inside. I'm heading back to Newport."

"Thanks for the help."

"Baby, you don't have to thank me. It's been my pleasure helping an angel like you out. You come see me if you ever need anything other than Hydros."

He got in his car and started backing out of the driveway. She rolled her eyes and headed for the door. She knocked lightly and then let herself in as Alex had told her to do. She entered. Again, she was cautious, unsure of what to expect.

"Hello?" she called out. The kitchen ahead was empty, and the living room to the left of the entrance had two burly big men in it.

One of the men looked away from the television set and looked at her. "He's downstairs."

She walked down the steps, holding the railing as she did. Seeing an open door to the right, she walked in.

There on the bed was Champ, her ex-boyfriend. Alex had lied. Her stomach twisted and she turned to leave.

"Olivia!" He stopped her with his words. "Where you going? There's no hard feelings about the past here. My Cadillac is fixed. I've changed."

"Why do I find that hard to believe?"

He laughed and shooed a hand. "It's all good. It's history. Here's the Hydros you need."

Champ tossed a full pill bottle with no label through the air toward her. She caught them and relief spread to the core of her being.

"Thanks." Joy filled her, knowing she'd be pain-free in moments. She turned to leave when he spoke again.

"What happened to you, O?"

"I got clean and married." She left it at that. She didn't want him knowing that she was single at the moment.

"You're not wearing a wedding ring."

"It's being repaired." Olivia's lying capabilities were on-point. They had to be though. She wasn't talking to someone like Tyler who wouldn't push boundaries. Champ was the complete opposite of Tyler. He was ruthless and unkind and would take whatever he wanted whenever he wanted it. She grew uncomfortable. "Well, it was nice seeing you again. I'd better get going. Thanks again!"

"Olivia." His words were ice-cold, sending a chill up her spine. She turned to him.

"Yeah?"

"What about payment?"

"Oh. I'm sorry, of course. It's just been a weird day or I would've remembered." She dug through her purse with trembling fingers and pulled out a fifty-dollar bill, then came over closer to him. "Is this enough?"

When he reached out to grab the money, he skipped the cash and grabbed her wrist. He jerked her toward him and onto his lap on the bed. Her heart beat faster and her insides froze. Her eyes went wide, knowing this was not good. The pain in her hand didn't matter anymore, not right now. All that mattered was getting out of that house. She struggled to free herself and almost made it out of his grip, but then he slapped her in the side of the head and held her arms down.

"That fifty dollars doesn't even begin to cover what you owe *me*, O."

His hand came up to her arm, and he jammed a needle from out of nowhere into the side of her arm. Terror overtook her, and her eyes widened as she watched the liquid inject into her arm.

"What was that?"

"Just consider it an *old friend*." He laughed maniacally, and her body suddenly relaxed to a state she hadn't been in for a long, long time. She willingly slid off his lap and lay on the bed as the drugs ran their course. All her muscles loosened and her thoughts slowed. She suddenly didn't care about anything or anyone as she was brought to the edge of reality where death was only inches away.

CHAPTER 26

THREE MONTHS LATER, TYLER awoke in a cold sweat the day he and Jonathan were set to fly out to meet a new client in Phoenix. Glancing at the alarm clock, it read six o'clock. He had the dream again, the same one from the last time he wasn't on talking terms with Olivia. Hanging his legs off the edge of the bed, he pondered the dream. He wondered if it meant something or if it was just chance. He still thought of Olivia every day since that fateful end in her apartment three months ago. He wondered how she was faring in life. Was she working at some dental office now that she had gained her certificate? He also pondered little Molly, and his heart ached as it brushed against memories. He had resisted each time he felt the urge to pick up his phone to reach out. Olivia's angry expression as she kicked him out that last time he saw her still pained him.

Rising from his bed, he went out into his kitchen and made a pot of coffee. The dream replayed through his mind as he placed the coffee canister in the cupboard. The walk on the forest path, the feeling that someone was next to him, and then the struggle in the bushes before finding himself on a grassy mountainside near a lake. By the time he finished his coffee and devotions that morning, it was seven thirty, still five and a half hours before he had to be at the airport.

He walked to the sliding glass door and peered out to his patio and fire pit. A light dusting of snow had fallen last night and had covered it in a blanket of white. He thought of Olivia again. An urge too powerful to ignore came over him to go to her. He hadn't felt like this since that day in the apartment. He was trusting God, but this urge now felt divine. He had the perfect excuse to swing by her apartment. He had been holding onto this particular excuse for months. He had another dress for Molly from Chet's old things in the barn. He found it sitting in a woven pine-needle basket with a woven lid. He knew it must've been special. If nothing else came of it, he'd at least get a chance to see if she was doing well or had moved on, unlike himself.

Parking in a guest parking spot at the apartment, he noticed her car wasn't in her reserved apartment spot beneath the covering. A different car was there. He almost stopped and left, thinking it could be another man's car, and the pain gutted him with the thought. But he decided to go knock anyway. He needed to know for sure.

"Hello?" An elderly lady answered the door. He didn't recognize her. Confusion was on both of their faces.

Rubbing his coat arms to keep warm, he held the woman's gaze. "Is Olivia here?"

"Nobody by that name lives here. Sorry." The door closed a moment later. Tyler's heart took flight with worry as to where Olivia was now. He walked through the parking lot and back toward his car. *Maybe she moved?* He thought for a moment but then dismissed it, knowing she was in a lease. Nothing was making sense. Suddenly, an uneasiness settled across him. He started to regret giving her space the last three months like he had done. But then he doubled back on his thoughts as he recalled her coldness in the apartment that last day. *This is what Olivia wanted.* He just wished he knew what *this* was. Clutching the dress he had for Molly in his hand, he felt like he was lost in a sea of confusion. He got into his car and turned the key over and prayed. *God, I don't know where she is or what she's doing, but I pray she's okay. Please, Lord. Please help bring me clarity on this matter. Amen.*

Lifting his gaze as he turned the key over, he recalled her parents' house. He could go there. Surely, she had to be there if not at her apartment. Tyler drove to her parents' house, and upon pulling into the driveway, he noticed Kora walking out to her car with Molly on her hip. Tyler's heart lightened with joy upon seeing Molly. Olivia was here. *Thank You, Jesus,* he thought, getting out of the car. He approached Kora in the driveway.

"Hey, Kora."

"Oh, hey, Tyler!" She smiled big and opened her free arm to embrace him with a hug. He was surprised by the affection but welcomed it and hugged her back.

"How is everything going?" Kora inquired as she opened her rear car door and set Molly in the car seat.

"Great. Is Olivia inside? Can I go see her?" Tyler was excited he was so close to her.

Kora finished buckling Molly and stood upright, turning around to Tyler. Her face grimaced and she didn't say a word.

"What? Is she sad? Still in pain?"

Olivia's mother's eyes watered and she lifted a hand to cover her mouth slightly. *"You don't know."*

"Know what?" Tyler's heart downshifted from feeling good, to okay, and now to panic. He took a step closer, frazzled and contrite over his lack of involvement in Olivia's life for months now.

Olivia's father came walking out the front door and down the steps, joining Tyler and Kora at the car.

"Hi, Tyler! You come by to see Molly?" His grin was huge as he patted Tyler on the back like the two of them were old friends.

Kora, with tears in her eyes, turned toward him. With a soft voice, she spoke to her husband. "He doesn't know, Dan."

"What's going on?" Tyler shook his head and glanced at Molly through the open car door, then back at the two of them. "Please tell me." Without answers, Tyler was going to worst-case scenario in his mind . . . of Olivia being dead.

Dan nodded, his eyes moist. "Molly lives with us now."

Tyler's pulse jumped. "What? Why? What happened to Olivia?" *She's dead,* Tyler thought to himself. *I've lost Olivia forever now.* The thought of Olivia being in Hell sent a cold shudder through his body. His eyes welled with tears. *Oh, God! No. How can this be? Please, Lord, let this not be true.* Tyler prayed to God he was wrong in those moments while Olivia's parents looked at each other and whispered to one another.

A teary-eyed Kora couldn't handle the conversation anymore and shut Molly's car door, then got into the passenger side of the car. Dan stepped closer and placed an arm around Tyler. "A few months ago, Olivia dropped Molly off with us for a few hours. She was feeling tired and needed the sleep since they were in the ER earlier that day. We thought nothing of it and agreed but told her we had a thing a little later that evening and needed her picked up by six. Six o'clock came and she didn't show. Then we called, and she didn't answer. Then we canceled our evening plans and stayed by the phone, waiting for word from our daughter. It never happened. We waited two days and then had the police get involved." At this point, Olivia's father got choked up on his words and paused to regain control of himself.

Tyler waited eagerly for him to continue, wanting all the details, all the information. *Please be alive,* he thought to himself.

Dan dabbed his eyes with a handkerchief from his back pocket, then continued. "Anyway, they found her out in Suncrest, with some known druggie loser. She was high, they suspected, but with no evidence of drugs on the scene and her being able to communicate that she was safe and okay, the police had to leave."

Tyler was moved with happiness at hearing Olivia was alive, but a deep sadness set in quickly afterward at hearing of her state. He took a step back. This didn't seem like her to him. It didn't seem like the Olivia he had fallen for over the summer. "What's the address?"

"I don't have it."

"Where's Rachel? Can I get *her* address?"

"Sure. She hasn't talked to her much, but she did a little after we figured out where she was. Rachel was where we went first too. Here, just a second." Dan put his reading glasses on, then retrieved his cell phone from his pocket. "Here's the address." Dan was pure business at this point. Tyler wondered if he had to separate his emotions from it all to survive these days.

After Tyler entered the address into his phone's navigation, he thanked Dan and headed to his car.

"Hey, Tyler."

Stopping at Dan's words, Tyler turned at his driver's-side door, facing the serious man before him.

"She can't come around Molly right now. We have to put Molly's safety and wellbeing first."

"Of course. I understand." Tyler was well aware of situations like this after watching Jonathan go through a similar one with his old sister-in-law.

Leaving Olivia's parents' driveway, he headed to Rachel's

house. As he drove, he replayed the conversation with Dan in his head, still unable to fully wrap his mind around it. He was beyond thankful she was still alive, but being doped up wasn't Olivia. Sure, he knew about her past, but he refused to believe that she had returned to it like a dog returning to vomit. Memories bubbled to the surface of his mind. He remembered at the park when he caught Olivia looking at Molly with so much love and joy, and his heart broke. There was no way she'd throw her relationship with Molly away for drugs, no matter how bad that pain in her hand had gotten. As he got closer to Rachel's home, he thought of Olivia losing that job and the fact that she had been so close to finishing school, and his heart ached bitterly. Then he thought again of her past with drugs. He couldn't deny her past existed, nor the Scriptures that specifically say people return to their old ways. The reality was that the evidence was stacked on both sides. He didn't know what really happened, but he knew God did and prayed the rest of the drive.

RACHEL LET Tyler into her house upon his arrival and made him a cup of coffee as they sat together at her kitchen table.

"I'll ask you once more, Rachel. Where is she staying out in Suncrest?" Tyler was losing patience fast, his heart yearning to find Olivia sooner rather than later.

She squirmed at the question. Guilt hadn't left her face ever since she answered the door. "Do you need more sugar for your coffee?"

Tyler slammed his fist against the top of the table, rattling their cups of coffee. His jaw was clenched. "Just tell me!"

"I'm not only her cousin, Tyler. I'm her best friend. What kind of friend would I be if I ratted her out?"

"When I couldn't find her at her apartment and her

parents were tight-lipped and sad at first, I thought Olivia was *dead.* For that brief moment in time, a part of me died too. Listen, Rachel, I know you want to do the right thing here. It doesn't matter how mad she'll be at you for it. Please help me get to her." Tears surfaced in Tyler's eyes, waiting for a response from Rachel.

"And your plan is to do what when you get to her?" Rachel was moved by his speech but seemed to be holding back for some reason unbeknownst to Tyler.

He shook his head. "Don't worry about it. I'll take care of her."

"Like . . ." Rachel slid a thumb across her throat and then laughed. Tyler didn't join her in the laugh. "Sorry. I shouldn't laugh, especially since you actually thought she was dead."

"Stop delaying and tell me where the woman I love is, *right now.*"

Her shoulders loosened and she tilted her head as she peered into Tyler's eyes. "You really do love her. Don't you?"

"I do."

"We'll see about that. You want to know where she is? Fine. She's with Champ, her ex-boyfriend from back in the day. They did heroin together for years, and that's what she's on right now, and she's with him right now. She doesn't want to see anyone, not even me, and I'm sure, especially not you. I wouldn't go after her, Tyler. Just let her be."

He stood up. "Thanks for the coffee. You have the address of Champ's house, I take it?"

She hesitated, giving away the fact that she knew exactly where it was.

"Give it to me. I'm not playing games anymore, Rachel."

She jotted the address down on a slip of paper and handed it to him. "He's a drug dealer, *Tyler.* He has guns and bodyguards. He'll kill you if you show up there."

"He won't kill me, and I'll get her out of there."

Her eyes widened, and she appeared surprised by his confidence. "Doesn't this all create even an ounce of fear within you?"

Folding the note, he shoved it in his coat pocket. He shook his head as absolute confidence emboldened him. "No, I have God on my side."

He turned and left her house. On his way out to his car in the driveway, he recalled his brother Jonathan and their flight to Phoenix. Knowing his brother was probably doing final touches on the design sketches in the office, he stopped in at *Willow Design* downtown to speak with him. As he walked into Jonathan's office, his brother set down his pencil.

"You're not going."

Tyler was surprised to hear him guess correctly. He nodded but held a perplexed look on his face. "Yeah. How'd you know?"

"You have that fire back in your eyes. The same one you had when you were dating Olivia. I'll cover for the two of us in Phoenix. What's going on?" Jonathan crossed his arms as his eyebrows went up. He appeared curious yet fascinated too.

Tyler felt nervous but confident about what he had to do. "She's in trouble, Brother. I have to go rescue her out of a dark place."

"Go get your girl."

As Tyler came closer, Jonathan stood up and they embraced in a brotherly hug. Jonathan patted his back and then released him.

"Be careful, Tyler."

"I will be."

Tyler left the office and headed to the address on the slip of paper. It was about an hour away from downtown, out in the Nine Mile Falls area. He prayed every moment of the way out to the location in Suncrest. Tyler thought more about Molly being at her grandparents' house, and he was thankful that they'd stepped up and taken care of her. Molly needed solid people, people who were stable and able to care fully for her, and that wasn't Olivia, not right now. He knew that Olivia would have to act quickly if she ever wanted a chance to get Molly back before it was too late. He knew from Jonathan's conversations with counselors and mental health experts that children don't do well with shifting homes frequently in their lives. More than one time, Jonathan was told by professionals that even seven or eight months away from a mother and in a new home was long enough to where the child couldn't go back without suffering in the process.

Arriving at the address on the slip of paper that Rachel had given him, Tyler reached over to the glove box and popped it open. His pistol fell into view and he prayed. "God, I don't know what I'm doing here outside of rescuing this woman. Please don't make me use this weapon. I don't want to hurt anybody. I just want her for you, God."

Grabbing it, he checked to make sure it was loaded and then switched the safety off. He got out of his car and walked the driveway toward the front door. His pulse raced.

Arriving at the front door, he opened it and proceeded inside, praying no one could hear how loudly his heart was beating. A person came in from the living room and he punched him in the nose as he swept the leg, sending the man dropping to his backside and to the floor. He snatched the man's handgun and quietly placed it in the freezer in the kitchen, feeling a sense of calmness now that the main body-guard was gone. Then he headed upstairs. Room after room, he found nothing but drugged-out people lying in beds. Some appeared to be younger than eighteen. The horrific sights were unsettling to him, but he knew now that the police would have a good reason for searching the home. He went downstairs to the lower level. Opening the first door on the right, he found Olivia and a man in bed.

His heart flinched, pain crushing him at the sight of what was going on. It was a sight he hoped to forget but knew he never would. It broke a piece of him.

"Get off her!" Tyler held his gun firmly in both of his hands, pointing it at the man who was in nothing but boxers.

The guy jumped off the bed and off Olivia. His steps fell back to the closet. He fell backward and onto his butt in the closet. He held his hands up with a fear-ridden expression in his eyes.

"Don't shoot me, man!"

Tyler moved quickly to the bed and wrapped Olivia in a black blanket. Then, he hoisted her into his arms, keeping his gun pointed at the man.

"You need Jesus, Sir," Tyler said coolly and calmly, and then he fired two bullets into a container of white powder on the nightstand and left the room.

Out at the car, he delicately placed her in the back seat and shut the door. Taking a look at the house once more, he shook his head and pulled out his phone. He called the police and told them about what was going on inside the house. With the dusting of white powder covering most of his room, plus the underage children, Champ would be a chump in a prison somewhere soon. Then, he got into the car and put it in reverse to leave.

CHAPTER 27

*H*ER EYES HURT, HER HEAD hurt, and every muscle in her body cried out in a deep and agonizing pain. Peering around the room, she didn't recognize her surroundings right away. It didn't look like Champ's bedroom. She sat up and promptly threw up in a metal pot by the bed. She continued to throw up until she was dry-heaving. Afterward, she then realized she was in Chet's cabin, in his bedroom and in his bed. Confusion swirled about in her mind endlessly. Her headache worsened and she turned and saw a glass of water on the night stand. There beside the glass were a few ibuprofen. She grabbed both and took them, then collapsed back into the pillows.

Waking again sometime later, she felt a little clearer-headed and she was able to slide her legs over the edge of the bed. Nearby, a foot away from the bed, was a metal chair, and on top of it, the metal pot she had thrown up in earlier, but it was cleaned out. Still confused, she set her feet on the floor and stood up. Her legs ached and she tried to stretch them. It helped with the muscle aches, but only a fraction. She staggered toward the door. Her legs weakened, and she grabbed hold of the dresser, clutching on for dear life. After a moment, she was stable enough to walk again. She proceeded out of the room and down the hallway, nausea keeping her movements slow.

As she entered the living room, she saw Tyler sitting on the couch. He set his Bible down and rose to his feet. More confusion poured into her thoughts. *Why am I here? How did I get here? Why do I hurt all over?*

"Hey, how are you feeling?" Tyler looked relieved to see her up and about.

"I feel like death. Why am I here?" Olivia's head pounded and the bed called her name, but she needed answers.

He moved around the coffee table and closer to her, but she took a step back.

"You're here because you're alive. And you're going to get sobered up and get your daughter back."

"She's gone *forever*, Tyler. My parents took her." Thinking of Champ, but more specifically about the drugs, she shook her head. "I need to leave."

As she tried to go for the door, she stumbled, but Tyler was able to move quickly and caught her in his arms. She peered up at him, barely able to concentrate.

"No, you're staying here with me. You need to get better." His voice was even more comforting than she remembered, but it didn't touch the agony she was in.

"I hurt all over and I want to die. You don't understand. All I need to do is get a little in my system and this sickness and pain will go away. Just a little bit, I promise." *Just make it all stop*, Olivia begged herself in her mind.

Tyler didn't respond right away and instead helped her over to the couch to sit down. "You don't really want to do that, Olivia."

A sardonic laugh escaped her lips and she shook her head. "You don't know what I want."

"Can I get you a glass of water?"

"No, you can get me out of here and back to Champ's house where I was before you thought it'd be a good idea to take me away against my will."

"Okay." Tyler stood up and grabbed the keys off the coffee table. "You can go back to the drugs and just be a zombie until you inevitably die. Molly has two capable people in her life to care for her. You're right. She doesn't *need* you." He was walking to the door to open it, disappointment evident on his face.

A light flickered beneath the pain in her muscles. She did want her daughter. She wanted to see her and be with her. Tyler knew what she wanted even more than she did.

"I want to see Molly. Take me to her first."

He sat back down and set the keys on the coffee table. He turned to Olivia and took both of her hands into his hands. "You can't do that right now. But if you get yourself cleaned up and back on track, I know for a fact that they'll let you see her and eventually have her back." Compassion lit up his face, love shone through his eyes, and his voice held the truth.

Her heart started to ache. The pain was far worse than all the pain in her body at the moment. She let herself fall against the back of the couch cushions as she wept. "*No.* They'll never let me see her or take her back. I'm done for as a mother!"

"It's only been three months, not three years, Olivia. You can do this. They want you to do this."

A wave of aches washed over her body. Her hand pain became apparent too. She sat upright and let her head fall to the side and looked into Tyler's eyes. "You don't understand a thing, Tyler. You don't get what happened to me."

"Tell me what happened."

Olivia's heart felt heavy as memories flipped through her

mind. The needle in her arm, the pain in her hand going away. "Champ didn't just give me drugs. He took my pain away. He did it when you and all the doctors couldn't."

Tyler grimaced. "It wasn't real."

"Yes, it was real! My pain was gone, and now . . . now, I hurt more than ever, thanks to you." Olivia shook her head, more tears coming down her cheeks. "Why didn't you leave me there to die? Why'd you come, Tyler? Huh? Why'd you come? Why do you hate me so much?"

He stood up without a word and walked into the kitchen. He opened a cupboard, then she heard the faucet turn on. Returning a short while later, he handed Olivia a cup of water. "Take sips when you can. If you get hungry, there are leftovers in the fridge. If you need anything, come outside and call for me. I'll be cutting firewood."

He went over to the door and put his coat on, then left. Olivia felt restless, but at the same time, exhausted and in pain. She wanted so desperately to just get a little bit of heroin in her system so she could feel okay again, but she knew there was no chance of getting any unless she left this cabin and property. After Tyler left, she forced herself off the couch and began to search for her cell phone or a phone of any kind to call Champ, but she found none.

As a cold flash came on a short while later, Olivia crawled back into the bed in Chet's room and covered up with all the blankets on the bed. The chill in her body could not be touched no matter how many blankets she layered on. So, after a few minutes, she pushed herself out from the covers and went down the hall to the bathroom. Turning on the shower as hot as she could stand it, she climbed in and let the water wash over her. Finally, relief. As she stood in the shower and let the steaming hot water rain down over her, she stared down at the drain, thinking about how all her dreams and hopes in life had been washed away. She wept. All the withdrawals she was experiencing at the moment were nothing new to Olivia. She had gone through the same thing the last time she came off heroin in her youth. She hated Champ for what he had done to her by jamming that needle into her arm like that, but then again, she didn't. A part of her still wanted to go back, just so she could feel okay again.

"Olivia?"

Her annoyance inflamed at hearing Tyler's voice, and she cursed, then yelled at him. "What do you want? You obviously know I'm in the shower. Do you have a habit of just walking into bathrooms when people are showering?"

He was silent for a moment.

"I made you some eggs and toast. Just wanted to let you know." His voice carried zero attitude with it, and it only drove her anger toward him deeper. Tyler was holding her hostage in that cabin against her will, and he'd made sure she had no way to contact the outside world. Not only was her phone nowhere to be found, but the land line in the cabin was shut off, and the Internet didn't work on the computer in the living room.

She got done in the shower and wrapped herself in a towel. Exiting the bathroom, she went down the hallway and out to the kitchen where Tyler was sitting at the table eating.

"Hey. Are there clothes here I can wear?"

His eyes were wide, obviously distracted by her lack of clothing and only a towel wrapped around her delicate frame. He paused for a second. "Yes, there is a closet full of your clothes in Chet's room. I hung them all up for you. Other items that don't hang are in the dresser."

"*My* clothes?"

He nodded, finishing another bite of his egg. He wiped his mouth with a napkin. "Your mother gave them to me."

"My mother knows I'm here with you?"

"Yes. She's rooting for you to get better, Olivia. We all are so you can get Molly back and get your life on track again."

She didn't speak a word but left the kitchen feeling annoyed and headed down the hall toward Chet's room. As she entered the room, the pains all over her body that had vanished in the hot shower came back to existence. Wanting to be done with it, she took the picture of Chet and his wife off the dresser and chucked it against the wall so hard the glass shattered and the frame fell to the floor.

Silence followed and Olivia sat on the bed. She needed to leave and get back to Champ's house if she was ever going to feel better again. Resolving to make her escape that night, she went over to the closet and picked out an outfit to wear.

SHE WAITED for night to fall that evening and for Tyler to be asleep on the couch before she left Chet's bedroom. Carefully, even though she was in pain, she sneaked out of the window in the bedroom. As she made it out, she tumbled to the ground with a painful thump. Landing on her shoulder, she cried out in agony as it sent shockwaves through her already aching muscles. Teary-eyed and still exhausted and in pain, she pushed herself up off the cold snow-dusted ground and started to walk over to Tyler's car in the driveway.

She cupped her hands around her eyes and peered in. It was locked and the security light was blinking. Olivia let out a defeated sigh and peered at the snow-covered dirt road leading up to the main road that would lead toward the highway back to Spokane. If she could make it there, maybe someone would be driving by and be willing to give her a ride to the nearest gas station so she could call Champ. Each step up the snowy, muddied road was more painful than the one before it, but she pushed through the aching muscles. A quick hit with Champ would be all she needed, and then she could go get real help in Spokane. She just needed a little to maintain, a little to feel normal.

As she came up to the main road, she collapsed to her knees and puked from the pain. Wiping her mouth, she stood up and glanced both directions. She could see her breath and darkness in both directions. The only faint light was provided by the moon. The November air was chilly and the coat she had found in Chet's closet wasn't doing a very good job at keeping the cold out. She tugged on it as she crossed her arms and tried to keep her warmth as she waited for a car to come by. An hour passed without a car in sight in either direction. Each passing moment felt like eternity to Olivia.

Her eyes turned back to the road, and then finally, she decided to walk. She headed in the direction she knew she needed to go. Traveling down the side of the country road on the shoulder, she rubbed her cold arms to attempt to give herself more warmth. She felt miserable, alone, and in a great deal of pain.

As she rounded a corner a mile down the road, a car's headlights shone behind her and she leaped with joy as she flipped around to face the car. She waved and jumped up and down with joy as best as she could, considering the pain was still present. Finally, someone had come to rescue her from this godforsaken cold winter night. As the car pulled off the road and she approached it, she came closer and realized it wasn't just anybody—it was Tyler.

When she didn't touch the door handle, he rolled down the window.

"This car is heated up really good, and there's a fire in the fireplace back at the cabin. Get in and we'll go warm up. We can chat, and I'll make us some tea to settle your stomach." Memories of their time together filtered through her mind briefly. She remembered their long talks together. They were special to her at one time. A moment passed, then a gust of cold air pressed against her cheeks, causing a burning sensation that led her to suspect that her coldness was shifting into the first stage of frostbite.

"Fine! I'll come back, but I'm not sitting by the fire and having some tea and conversation with you. I'm sick and I want to die, Tyler." She got into the car and slammed the door, tears trickling down her chilled cheeks. He turned the car around and took her back to the cabin. As they slowed in front of the cabin and then came to a stop, she turned to Tyler.

"Why are you doing this?" She couldn't understand this man at all. Who gives up their life for a time to help someone else?

"*I love you*, Olivia." Tyler looked like he meant those words, but she didn't know how.

"Yeah." She laughed, turning her head as she directed her gaze to the cabin and crossed her arms. "Some love you have. Coming over to my apartment and accusing me of being a bad mom and a drunk."

He was quiet for a moment. "I never said those things. You know, it doesn't matter. I'm not trying to say I'm perfect here, and I'm sorry for any pain I have brought to you." He shook his head and then bowed his head. Olivia assumed he was praying when he did that. Then, he turned to talk to her again. "Listen, I thought you were dead. Then I found out you were alive, so here I am. I am here to help you, and I'm going to do all that I can for you. If you run a hundred times, I'll go after you a hundred times."

"You have to go to work sometime. I'll leave the second you do."

"I'm not doing a thing in my life until I see you better. If you don't want to be with me at the end of all this, I'm fine with that, but that little girl isn't going to grow up without her mom."

"Oh, whatever. You already told me she had capable people."

"Yes, she does, but that doesn't mean that's the best fit. You are the best fit, Olivia."

"Don't you worry about *my* daughter, Tyler. I'm sure Bruce will take her when he gets wind of what has happened."

"Bruce already said he is only interested in sending a check to your parents. He's not interested in caring for a kid. He was annoyed at your mom for even asking when he'd already made that clear to you. As for her not being my daughter, I'm well aware. She isn't my daughter in any sense of the word, but she is a child and she doesn't have a say in any of this. Someone has to speak up for her. And, Olivia, if she did have a say, I know for a fact that she'd want you. You are a good mom, and you will get clean because you do love your daughter more than drugs."

His directness settled Olivia's nerves a fraction. Just like when he had met her, he was still seeing right through her.

"You're right about me loving my daughter. I do with all my heart." Olivia felt some strength return when she said those words.

"Then prove it by getting clean and getting her back before it's too late and she's damaged."

With that, Tyler got out and shut the door behind him, heading inside the cabin. A shift occurred in Olivia in that very moment. She knew by Tyler's words that this wasn't about Tyler fixing her up so she could be the model girlfriend he wanted. This was truly about her getting better for herself and her life, but most of all, her daughter. She couldn't understand why he was helping her, but a portion of her heart had now become grateful that he was. But as she got out of the car, anger returned as the pain in her body flared once again. She couldn't let go of her desire to be pain-free and get drugs, and Tyler stood in her way of relief.

CHAPTER 28

TYLER WATCHED AS OLIVIA WALKED past him in the living room and went down the hallway to her bedroom. She slammed the door behind her. He flinched at not only the sound of the door, but at the state she was currently in. Tyler had done research when she was busy vomiting and in and out of consciousness the first couple of days. He read over all the withdrawal symptoms that were possible as she was coming off heroin. He knew it'd be difficult for a while before it ever became easy, and at the end of it, he most likely wouldn't be with her due to his connection to the past with her. He was fine with whatever the outcome was between them relationship-wise. This all was far beyond that now. This was a matter of life and death, and he wasn't going to give up on her when everybody else had already done so.

Tyler had already slept a collective five hours that night. He didn't need a wink more. Taking a split log from the pile beside the fireplace, he tossed it in and sat down in Chet's rocking chair that sat near the fireplace, Margret's only a few feet away. He had brought them in when the cold settled in, fearful that the weather would damage them.

After feeding the fire, he bowed his head and prayed. He had been doing a whole lot more praying lately, and he had a feeling it wasn't going to change anytime soon. Olivia was worse off than he'd anticipated going into it. Originally, he had no idea she'd desire to leave, though he had read they tend to be obsessed with the idea of getting high during detox because they want to outrun their sickness.

After his prayer, he read the Bible. An hour passed and he returned the Bible to the coffee table and went to check in on her. Opening the door carefully, he peered in. She was asleep, but she was sweating and shivering at the same time as she held herself. He moved into the room and came up to her, pressing the back of his hand gently against her head. She felt warm. Tyler went down the hall to the bathroom and dampened a wash cloth with cold water and rang it out. Then, he returned to the room and laid it across her forehead.

He peered up at the ceiling and in a whisper said, "Have mercy on her, God. *Please*."

THE FOLLOWING MORNING, Olivia emerged from the bedroom while Tyler was sitting on the couch reading his Bible. When his eyes caught a glimpse into her sea-blue eyes, he smiled. Though she hadn't been the most pleasant to be around lately, he knew the girl beneath the levels of addiction and was still happy to see her. He closed his Bible and set it down on the coffee table.

"Eggs?"

"Yes, please. I'm a little hungry." She looked away from his glance and pushed a strand of hair behind her ear as she walked into the kitchen and took a seat at the table. Olivia appeared tired and worn out. He hoped that today, she'd be a little more relaxed and she'd be able to settle in more comfortably as she recovered. Standing up from the couch, he went into the kitchen and prepared the two of them breakfast. As he served the eggs onto plates on the table, she peered up at him.

"What are you thinking about, Olivia?" He wanted to get inside her mind, to spend time with her heart. He felt if he could climb over those walls she had put up, he'd be able to reach her, help her, and comfort her in this time of need.

She glanced around the cabin, then back at Tyler. "I'm thinking you deserve to love a woman who can treat you a lot better than I do, Tyler. That's the honest truth."

"How do you know what I deserve?" He inquired, hoping to keep the conversation moving forward with her.

She laughed as she shook her head and lifted her fork. "Where do I start?"

Tyler sat down and reached a hand over, gently touching the top of hers. "Love is a choice, Olivia, and I choose you."

"Bad choice." She shook her head, a blush reddening her cheeks. "I've done nothing but disappoint you."

"That's not true, and I don't care what you've done. You can't *earn* my affection, Olivia. You have it already."

She was quiet for a long moment. Then, she started to eat. He stood up and retrieved two glasses from the cupboard. He poured two glasses of milk over at the counter. He turned toward her. "What do you want to do today?"

Shrugging, she set her fork down after taking a bite. "I'd like to see my daughter."

Remembering the photo that Kora had given Tyler of Molly, he left the glasses of milk on the counter and went into the living room for a moment. He grabbed his Bible from the coffee table and snatched the photo from inside.

He returned to the kitchen and handed the picture to Olivia.

"In time, Olivia. In time. I promise you." Tyler watched her for a moment as she took the photo and stared at it. He could sense a wellspring of hope bloom inside her in that very moment. He smiled and then grabbed the glasses from the counter and brought them over to the table. He set one glass down in front of Olivia and one in front of his plate, then took his seat.

"What made you come find me?" she asked, setting the photograph down.

"I had been thinking about you a lot. I also had something for Molly, another dress."

"I see." Her eyes gravitated to the picture of Molly near her plate, and Tyler could see her becoming upset the more she focused on Molly. He tried to help by changing her focus.

"I brought down a bunch of books from the house, some magazines too. The books are beside the couch in the living room, magazines under the coffee table. There is also a large variety of DVDs in the tote next to the TV."

Olivia nodded and took a sip of her milk. "Thanks. I'll keep that in mind. What will you be doing?"

"I need to work more on the firewood. I have none up at the house and barely anything left here."

"Okay. Why are we out here and not at your house?"

"You'll spend most of your recovery in this cabin, and I'll be at my own house. I'm just here right now to help make sure you get through the first little part. It's better this way."

Lifting his plate off the table as he stood, Tyler walked it over to the sink.

"Hey, Tyler?"

He turned toward her.

"When can I see her?"

"You'll want to take this slow. After you are feeling better and you're not withdrawing, start talking with your parents and learning what has been going on for the last three months with your daughter."

She nodded, and he came over to her at the table. He was thankful to see her more understanding and less argumentative today. He leaned his arms over the chair he had been sitting in and clasped his hands together. Noticing her thinking face, he asked, "What's on your mind?"

"It's *my* daughter. I don't see why I have to start anywhere other than seeing her."

He paused for a moment. "You love your daughter, Olivia, and just seeing how she is doing is where you have to begin to build trust with your parents. Your parents have sole responsibility and custody of Molly right now. It's not up to you what happens. This is what they've laid out."

"But that's not fair, Tyler!"

Opening his hands, he shook his head. "Your actions have consequences. It's not a matter of what's fair or not in your mind. This is the reality you live in now."

Olivia went quiet, the fight in her trampled down by some withdrawal symptom, Tyler suspected. She pressed a hand against her forehead. He came closer to her and bent over, kissing the side of her head.

"I'll be outside if you need me for anything." He wished he could spend all day with her, but since he was home from work, he really needed to work on firewood and now was as good a time as any.

Tyler went and slipped on a pair of sturdy work boots and laced them tight. Then, he put on his flannel jacket and headed outside. Once at the wood pile, he pulled the axe out of the chopping stump and set a log up to split. He chopped wood for the next hour and a half, stacking the wood neatly beneath the tin roof with the rest. When he was done, he returned the axe to the stump and peered around the property as he wiped sweat from his forehead. He hadn't spent so much time on the land since he took ownership of it, and he felt remorseful for not doing so. He'd had hopes of notching down his workload last year after his vacation to Diamond Lake, but he hadn't gotten around to really doing so. Tyler sat on the stump next to the axe and surveyed the white coat of snow across the land. It was magnificent. He bowed his head in prayer. He prayed for himself and for Olivia.

He felt a deep struggle in his soul as the woman he loved was fighting her way back from the hell on earth known as addiction. He didn't know what the lasting impacts of what had happened the last three months would be, but he prayed to God they wouldn't be so severe that the two of them could never be together again. *Your will, not mine, Lord.* His desire to be with Olivia was tossed back and forth across the waves of unsure feelings. Initially, it had vanished when he saw her and Champ in bed together. He wasn't able to dislodge the horror of what he had seen happening when he busted down the door to the bedroom. His love was still in his heart, but he didn't like witnessing that. He prayed again for help.

Rising from the stump, he went into the cabin to get the keys to Chet's work truck that was parked alongside the barn. He needed to repair a broken part of the fence he had spotted the night before when he had gone out searching for Olivia. When he walked into the cabin, he saw Olivia sprawled out on the couch asleep, a movie playing on the television.

He smiled. Tyler hadn't seen her look so peaceful since he brought her to the cabin four days ago. He walked quietly up to the couch. Pulling up the blanket, he covered her and then went into the kitchen for the keys. He grabbed the keys from the small pottery bowl near the sink and then proceeded out the back door toward the barn.

Arriving at the fence a short time later in the truck, a few yards from the dirt road between the cabin and his house, he shut off the truck and got out. The snow crunched beneath his boots as he went around to the back of the truck and retrieved his toolbox. The sound of scurrying in the tall grass sticking out from the snow caught his attention nearby. Curious, he set the toolbox down near the post and went to investigate. He was surprised to find a medium-sized dog in the snow, and it barked as he approached.

"Hey, boy." He bent a knee down and slowly reached out to pet the Border collie.

The dog lowered its head in almost a cowering manner as it inched closer to Tyler's hand. He went the rest of the way and patted the dog's head, then rubbed behind its ear. Tyler's heart filled with warmth as he saw the dog's tail wag excitedly. It was refreshing to his soul to see something alive that was so happy to see him. It had been a long four days without interaction with anybody besides Olivia outside of a few brief calls with his brother.

"Come on, boy. You can help me with the fence." Tyler stood up and walked toward his toolbox, but the dog didn't follow. Tyler whistled and patted his jeans, and the dog skipped forward through the snow to follow. The dog stayed by Tyler's side as he worked to repair the broken barbed-wire fence. After he was done, he bent down to the dog and gave him another rub behind the ear.

"Who do you belong to? A good dog like you must have an owner."

He checked for a tag but found none. "Well, I'll post some signs up in town and call the neighbors. For now, you'll be named . . . Ace. I like that name."

Tyler opened his driver's-side door of the truck and then placed the toolbox into the bed. Ace jumped right into the cab and situated himself in a prone position on the bench. *He for sure belongs to someone. He's too well-behaved.* Tyler turned the truck around and returned to the snowy road and to the cabin. At the cabin, he left Ace outside and went in and grabbed a bowl of water and the leftover lasagna from two nights ago. Returning outside, he surveyed the area in wonderment as the dog was gone.

"Ace," he called out loudly. Tyler felt immediately dumb as he realized he had barely given the dog the name. Surely, he couldn't come by hearing the name. To Tyler's surprise, just the sound of his voice beckoned the dog back to the cabin. He came darting through the snow toward the cabin and stopped just short of Tyler.

He lowered the food and water to the icy ground and the dog dove right into the lasagna.

"Where'd the dog come from?"

Tyler turned around to see Olivia rubbing sleep out of her eyes as she stood in the doorway of the cabin in one of Chet's oversized jackets. She stepped out onto the porch and down the steps to the yard.

"I don't know. I found him up the path toward the house. No tags."

She smiled as she looked at the dog and approached. She bent her knees and patted the dog's head and then rubbed his side. The dog stopped eating and rolled onto its back, and she rubbed his belly, her smile widening. Tyler was glad to see Olivia smile. She hadn't done that since her arrival.

"I named him Ace, by the way." Tyler laughed. "Obedient dog, whoever he belongs to. I'm going to head inside and call the neighbors. Here in a little bit, I'm going to go into town and put up flyers if no neighbors claim him."

Glancing at Tyler, she nodded. "I'm sure whoever the dog belongs to misses him. He's cute."

Tyler agreed and headed up the steps of the porch to the cabin.

CHAPTER 29

*C*URLED UP ON THE COUCH in pain after Tyler had left for Newport to hang flyers about Ace, Olivia cried in the silence as the fire burned hot in the fireplace. Another wave of aches had filled her muscles and brought her to the edge of her sanity. She just wanted the pain to end. Earlier, she had been feeling a little better and thought the end of the withdrawals was near, but they had simply taken a short reprieve. How long would her punishment last? When she wasn't in agony, her mind and thoughts were there to condemn her and to demonize her for all the wrong she had done to the people she loved. She had hurt Tyler, Molly, and her parents with her decision to stay with Champ like she had done. The guilt was crushing her. *I could've left so many times, and I didn't.*

Stretching herself out on the couch to bring a fraction of comfort to the muscles in her legs, she let a hand hang over her head and off the couch. She jerked in surprise when she felt a lick on her hand. Relaxing, she put her hand down to the side of the couch and patted the dog on the head. Ace had been a welcomed addition to the cabin. She sat up on the couch and beckoned the dog to climb up. She snuggled the furry warm animal, and the warmth of him brought a measure of happiness to her spirit. The waves ended, and she spotted a pile of magazines tucked beneath the coffee table. Olivia grabbed a few and started to thumb through them.

Deciding on a gardening magazine, she tossed the rest onto the coffee table and opened it up. She flipped through page after page and stopped on an ad that showcased a woman's hands holding a bountiful basket of brightly-colored vegetables. It made her think of the garden in Colville when she had still been married to Bruce. She had loved and tended that garden daily with her hands, and she could still taste the juices of that first tomato she'd ever harvested. She longed to have a garden again, to be able to work the soil with her hands and let the sun warm her cheeks. Most people loathed the task of pulling weeds, but not Olivia. She loved removing the bad, leaving only the good. The work made sense to her, and in a way, she felt it made her confusing world with Bruce tolerable. She always had the garden to go to when she needed it.

It only took ten minutes before more withdrawal symptoms pulled her away from the magazine. A cold sweat covered her in an instant as dull aches flashed once more in her muscles. Pulling the magazine from her lap, she placed it on the coffee table and lay down on the couch. Ace was still on the couch with her. He was right there in her arms. Covering herself and the dog with the blanket, she held the dog close and tried to think of her garden, pushing away the pain and the cold flashes.

When she woke sometime later, she noticed the magazines were put away. *Tyler must've returned,* she thought. She stood up and went over to the window that faced the front yard of the cabin, Ace by her side. He wasn't at the wood pile. Then, Olivia and the dog went to the back of the house and she peered out the kitchen window. He wasn't back there either. *Where is he?* She wondered.

Grabbing an oversized coat of Chet's from the coat hook near the front door, she slipped it on along with her boots and then she and the dog went outside. She came around the corner of the house and found Tyler on his hands and knees in the midst of a few large pine trees.

"What are you doing down in the snow?"

He sat back on his knees and took off his pair of work gloves, smiling at her as he did. "I'm trying to see if this soil down here is good for planting."

Tyler pulled a plastic bag from his pocket and then filled it with dirt.

"What are you going to plant? There are trees all around here."

"I'll clear it. I won't be doing the planting. You will be. You like gardens, right? I envision this whole left side of the cabin can be your garden, with a white picket fence and all."

She liked gardens, yes, but she didn't like hearing his plans for her future. It was winter, and she wouldn't be able to plant anything until the spring.

"How long do you plan to keep me hostage here, exactly?" Panic came through in her voice.

He laughed as he pocketed the baggie with the soil sample. Then he shook a hand in the air. "Let me back up for a moment. I figured you could live at the cabin once you get Molly back. It can be yours."

Olivia shook her head, overwhelmed by the offer. "No, I can't take this cabin, Tyler."

"Why not?"

Why not? She thought inwardly. "Because I have done nothing to deserve it or any of the unwarranted favor you've been showing me. Plus, I don't need handouts. I can carry my own." She turned and started to walk away, but she felt she

243

had been harsh with her words and she turned back to Tyler. "I'm sorry. It was a nice offer, don't get me wrong."

He nodded and stood up, patting off the snow from his pants. He fell into step with her and Ace on the way to the front of the cabin.

"I shouldn't have assumed you'd take it. That was wrong on my part."

"It's okay. You were just being nice." As they went up the steps and onto the porch, she stopped and turned to him. She peered into his eyes for the first time since he had brought her to the cabin, and just as she expected, it only added to the hurt she was feeling in her heart. She had wronged this perfect man in so many ways. Quickly, she turned away, but he caught her chin with a finger and pulled her view back to his eyes.

"Don't look away, Olivia."

"But it hurts, Tyler." Olivia's words broke apart and her eyes welled. She clenched her eyes shut.

Tyler's voice was smooth and soothing to her as he continued. "Open your eyes."

She did. The pain intensified in her chest, and the emotional turmoil was too much to bear. Pulling away from his hold, she went inside. He left her alone after that.

THAT EVENING, Olivia's symptoms were less severe, and she had a desire to cook for the two of them. She wanted to give back to this generous man who gave so much and asked for nothing in return. Rising from the couch, she went into the kitchen and started to look around in the pantry and fridge. Tyler got up from Chet's rocking chair and put another log on the fire, then walked into the kitchen just as she started a pot of water on the stove.

"What are you doing?"

She turned to him and raised an eyebrow. "What do you think I'm doing? I'm cooking us a meal."

"You sure you feel okay to do that?"

"Yes, and don't worry, it won't be pudding cups this time." She smiled. The memory caught in her mind of how their time together that day had been so pleasant.

He laughed and then raised his hands. "All right."

As she strained the noodles through the colander in the sink, he returned to the living room. Her right hand felt a sharp pain surge through it out of nowhere, and she dropped the pot, clanking it loudly against the sink. Tyler rushed into the kitchen.

"You okay?"

Olivia was anything but okay. She didn't respond but instead clutched her hand as the pain radiated. He slowly moved closer.

He gently placed a hand on her back, adding to the emotional turmoil inside of her, yet at the same time providing her the comfort that she needed.

Eyes watering and heartbroken, she turned and looked Tyler in the eyes. "Do you get it now, Tyler? Reality is painful and insufferable."

He was quiet for a long moment. "There's doctors who can help."

She snapped. "Doctors don't help! They just judge me, like you did!"

Tyler was silent.

The pain faded a moment later and she returned to the sink. She pulled the pot out and set it down on the counter and returned the noodles to the pot. She stopped and glanced at him over her shoulder. "You should've just left me. Sure, I didn't have Molly, but you know what I had, Tyler? Relief."

"No."

"What?" She turned around and faced him, placing a hand on her hip.

"No," he snapped, his voice loud. Tyler took a step closer to her as his anger flared. "You're lying to yourself, Olivia, and you're trying to lie to me. Remember? I can see through it all. You didn't have relief at Champ's doing what you were doing there. You were miserable! Sure, your hand didn't hurt, but you were dead inside. Your soul hurt. Admit it!"

Tyler hadn't ever been this loud with her before, and it caused her to recoil slightly within herself, then she got mad. She shook her head and yelled back at him. "No, I won't admit that!"

He took a step closer, his voice lowering, softer now. "Admit it not to me, but to yourself. You were dead inside, Olivia."

She quieted. "No."

One step more, and he was only inches away from her. He brought a hand up and let the back of his hand glide softly against her cheek, and then he slid his fingers into her hair. His delicate touch conjured all the good she had felt with him while they were together. It ignited her soul and stirred within her a warmth that radiated comfort, security, and joy. He stared into her eyes, causing a rip in her soul that was both painful and pleasurable at the same time.

"*Olivia.* This is real, this life. If you don't think that, then look at me and tell me you want to go back to Champ's house, and I'll take you there right now, and you'll never see me again."

She folded and jerked her head away, looking anywhere but into his eyes. "I can't tell you it's not real."

Tyler adjusted and got in front of her eyes. "Why can't you say it? If that's really what you want, then say it."

"Because it's not true! I know I don't belong there. I don't want to belong there either." She pulled away from Tyler, her heart pounding as she did. She grabbed the pot of noodles and returned it to the stove. Slamming it down on the stove, she turned to Tyler. "You're right, Tyler. Is that what you want to hear? You were right. I don't belong there. It's just so hard to be in pain every day, and this isn't something you can just *fix*. I'm not your little project!"

Tyler's expression softened to a somber one, and he came over to the stove as she went to grab a pot from the cupboard to make the sauce. When his hands gently found her shoulders, it made her melt inside. His touch was so soft, so loving, so perfect. She turned to him, and with hot tears running down her cheeks, she frowned.

"*Tyler,* I don't deserve a good man like you. I don't."

He shook his head. "It doesn't matter what you think you deserve. It's what you have. The sooner you embrace that, Olivia, the better."

She didn't know what to say, so she said nothing in response. "I need to make the sauce before the noodles get cold."

Tyler waited a few moments more, then directed his words at her once more. "I'm going up to the house for a moment. I'll be back in five minutes."

She nodded. As he left the kitchen, she poured the jar of Alfredo sauce into the small pot on the stove and turned on the burner. As the front door closed, she walked over to the kitchen table and sat down. She peered into the living room at Ace as he lay on the carpet near the crackling fireplace. Olivia's eyes watered more as she thought about all she had done to Tyler. She had ruined a perfectly good man. All those hopes she held in her heart for a better man in her life had come true, and what had she done? She'd mistreated him and put his heart through the wringer. Covering her mouth, she shook her head as her own guilt weighed heavier and heavier on her heart.

CHAPTER 30

TYLER WENT INTO HIS HOUSE and flipped on the lights as he went into the kitchen. He grabbed the watering can from beneath the sink and filled it. Going to the living room, he went over to the coffee table and watered his ficus plant. Setting the can down, he rubbed a leaf between his fingers. The plant had done well without water for the last few days, and he was relieved it hadn't started the dying process. He let out a relieved sigh and sat down on the couch for a moment. Olivia's words pressed against his mind. *Doctor's don't help. You should've left me there. Champ gave me relief when you never could.*

Scooting to the edge of the couch, his shoulders sagged and he bowed his head in prayer. *Help me, Lord. I don't know how to get through to this woman. Only You can soften the soil of her heart. Amen.*

He rose from the couch and looked again at the ficus. Slipping his phone out from his pocket, he saw a text from Olivia's mother, Kora.

Kora: How is she doing? Hope all is well.

Tyler felt it was now time to move on to the next step in

the process. It was a little soon, but he felt it was the right time to get Kora and Olivia speaking with one another. A short step, but a big leap toward Olivia's moving in the right direction. She was still in pain, but Tyler knew that the pain she was experiencing wasn't one that would go away anytime soon. On his way out the door, he called Kora and pitched her the idea of the two of them chatting.

"I'm ready for it. I have a lot to tell her, too." There was an edge in her tone that Tyler knew wouldn't help the situation.

"Listen, I mean this with all respect, but she can't handle any negativity right now."

"She needs to understand what she has done, Tyler!"

He was quiet for a moment, letting his initial anger cool before he spoke. "I agree, and I think she understands it, and with time, she'll understand it more. We have to let God be involved in this process too, Kora. Not just ourselves."

"Hearing you mention God in this brings my heart such a joy. You're right, Tyler. We have to let God do the heavy lifting here, not us. It's He who can save her soul. All we can do is sprinkle the seeds of His Word. I will stick with information on how Molly is doing and encourage her the best I can when we talk. Thank you for your words, and I can't thank you enough for all that you've been willing to do."

"Everybody deserves a chance to redeem themselves."

Ending the call with Kora as he pulled his car to the cabin, he paused before going inside. *Lord, I need You right now. I need You all the time, but right now, I really need Your help. I know she's going to want to jump into seeing Molly right now, and she can't. Please help her understand that. Please help me sow seeds of truth into her life in word and deed. Amen.*

As THEIR DINNER came to an end, Tyler offered to do the dishes and Olivia accepted with a smile. She seemed exhausted and went straight for the couch after leaving the kitchen table. As Tyler washed the dishes by hand in the kitchen, he called for Olivia. She came in.

"How do you feel about calling your mom? You can see how Molly is and—"

"Yes!" She retracted, lowering her excitement as she shrugged a shoulder. "I mean, yeah, that'd be cool."

"In my left pocket." He nodded toward his back jeans pocket, and she came up behind him. As she slipped her hand into his pocket, Tyler felt a twinge of tingles crawl up his spine at her touch. With the phone in hand, she went down the hallway and into Chet's room, shutting the door behind her. Tyler almost stopped doing the dishes to go follow her to make sure she was calling only her mother, but instead, he lifted his eyes to the ceiling. *God, You know I'm worried she's going to call Champ to come get her out of here. You can see my fears. Please settle them. Please let her just call her mom.* He added, *Scratch that. Help me to trust You more fully and not worry.*

He finished stacking the clean dishes into the dish drainer and wiped his hands on the hand towel hanging from the stove. He started down the hallway but stopped short of the door and turned around, refusing to go in. *Trust God.* He went and sat in the rocking chair beside the fire across from Margret's rocking chair. Tyler stared into the embers burning hot orange. An hour passed, and he thought about what she and Kora could be speaking about for so long. *Trust.* Then, in the hopes of distracting his thoughts away from the situation, he noticed it was about time for another log. Glancing at the empty metal rack where the wood sat next to the fireplace, he knew he had to go get more firewood. He got up and put his jacket on and went out to the wood pile. He grabbed a bundle of split wood and headed to the cabin, and as he did, a car came down the dirt road.

251

Tyler glanced at the night sky and said, "Really?" Anger and frustration filled him as he stepped to the edge of the yard and waited for the car to arrive.

He breathed a sigh of relief when he saw Jonathan's gaze through the passenger-side window.

Jonathan shut off the car and got out.

"Figured you might like a visitor." He held up a case of Coke. "And some energy."

Tyler laughed. "Man am I happy to see you! For a second, I was worried. Come on in. I was just grabbing some wood."

Walking inside together, Jonathan shut the door as Tyler placed the wood beside the fire. Tyler's brother looked around the living room and stole a glance into the kitchen. "Where is she?"

"In Chet's bedroom, talking to her mom."

"I see." Jonathan raised his eyebrows and lowered his voice as he sat down on the couch. Tyler tossed a log on the fire and joined him. "How is she?"

"Really good. Well, her hand pain came back to her, but outside of that, she seems to be on the good side of recovery so far."

"Did she ever do the acupuncturist? Dr. Hall?"

Tyler nodded, smoothing a hand over his face as his heart went out for Olivia. "Yes. At first, it helped, she thinks, but not the second time. She doesn't know what else to do. The doctors aren't much help."

"That's got to be hard for anybody." Jonathan rubbed his hands together, appearing to be in thought. "I wonder if some diet changes could help? Marie had a friend who went gluten-free and it helped with her nerve pain."

He shrugged. "I don't know. Anything is better than black-tar heroin. That's all I know."

Jonathan nodded. "Yeah, that's for sure!"

The bedroom door opened down the hall and their conversation shifted right away.

"Rose is reading now. She's brilliant." Jonathan beamed, directing conversation to his daughter.

"I always had a feeling she'd be a quick learner once she started school." Tyler peered at Olivia as she emerged from the hallway with tear-filled eyes. She looked away immediately and went into the kitchen. Jonathan shooed Tyler off the couch to go after her, and he did.

Entering the kitchen, Tyler came closer to her as she was standing at the sink, a hand resting on the counter. He didn't know what was ailing her, but he was moved with compassion.

His tone soft and gentle, he came up to her side and put a hand on her back. "Everything okay, Olivia?"

She sniffled. "It's fine."

"What happened?"

She turned around and looked into Tyler's eyes. He was overwhelmed as he could see her pain and hurt from the phone call. "My mom said that I can't have my girl back until I'm stable and surviving on my own without help."

"So what? You can do that. You would want the same for Molly if it were reversed."

"*So what?*" She shook her head. "I have nothing! I don't have a job, a place of my own, not even a car anymore!"

"What *did* happen to your car?"

She sighed. "Some addict wrecked it when I was at Champ's house." She shooed a hand through the air and went over to the table. She sat down in a chair and her face fell into her hands. "I'm so lost, Tyler."

When she said she was lost, Tyler's soul stirred within him. He knew God was prompting him to take the opportunity. He tried to think what he was going to say, but he felt the moment slipping. "It's going to be okay, Olivia. You just have to give all of this time. And my offer still stands. You can have the cabin. It's just sitting here."

"You love me more than anyone else in this world ever has or ever will, and I can't comprehend it for a second."

Tyler's soul again stirred. It was a second chance for him to witness to her, and he sat down at the kitchen table. His thoughts tried to worry him, to pull him away from witnessing. His mind even called to fact that his brother was sitting alone in the other room. The enemy threw one more excuse, reminding him how much Olivia had voiced her hatred for God. Despite all the fiery darts, Tyler's courage strengthened in the moment.

"Actually, there is someone who loves you more than me."

She lifted her gaze, an inquisitive look about her. "What? *Who?*"

"Jesus." He paused, waiting for her to stop him or storm out of the kitchen, but she didn't. She waited for him to go on. "His love for us is unconditional, Olivia. No matter how many times we mess up and do everything wrong, He is there and ready to take us into His loving arms. All we have to do is accept Him, believe in Him."

"No, there are rules you have to live by." She laughed, but it appeared to be out of nerves more than anything else. She wiped tears and continued. "Believe me, I know. I lived by those rules growing up in a *Christian* home."

"What rules?"

"Go to church. Read your Bible. Never curse. Never touch alcohol. Never do drugs. Always listen to your parents. Put others before yourself. The list goes on and on."

"Your parents were trying to help you by making those rules. Think about it. If you read your Bible and go to church, what is that going to do to you?"

"I don't know, brainwash me?"

Tyler shook his head and the insult away, not letting it

affect his tone or demeanor. He was still strong in spirit. "No, you're going to be putting God into your heart. And not drinking? How many news stories do you hear that involve violence, broken families, and death that are alcohol-related? Sin leads to death, Olivia. True Christianity is not a list of rules you need to follow. Those *rules* you are talking about are just simply some of the evidences of a transformed heart and guidelines that protect you because God loves you so much."

"Whatever they are, they aren't me." She laughed, shaking her head. "Plus, Tyler, I've done more sins in just a few months than most good church kids like yourself do in a lifetime."

"Jesus said that if you even hate a man in your heart, you have committed murder. I've killed, I've lusted, and I've done all the bad things a person can do when you peel it down to the heart. You see, humanity has a heart condition, not a behavior one. The behavior is just the result of a heart gone wrong."

"So we're all hopeless. Great news!"

"No, we're not hopeless. Jesus is the good news. God loves you so much, Olivia, way more than I could ever love you. He loved you so much that He came down in human form and died on a cross. God, who breathed into existence all the beauty and wonder we see in the world, came down to His creation and took on an earthly body, then He died so we can have freedom, so we could have a relationship with Him. Think about that for a moment. He died for us when we were already convicted and guilty and deserving of Hell. Sin leads to death no matter what the choice of poison is. It's evident in our world all around us. Drugs, for example. They've ruined your life in the last three months and made you dead inside, and you temporarily lost your daughter. Adultery rips marriages and families apart and crushes dreams and hopes. Hate leads to wars and broken relation-ships. You don't have to go very far to see how painful life is with sin in it, how it leads to death. This fallen world needs a Savior to save us from Hell, and that Savior is Jesus."

Olivia was quiet as Tyler spoke, then for a moment after-ward. Then, she looked at him. "How do you know you have the right God? There are tons of gods all over the world."

"I know because I believe in Jesus as my Savior. After I made that choice in my heart to accept Him and believe in Him, the Holy Spirit came inside me and continues to bear witness to that truth, that there is one God. Ephesians 4:6 says, 'there is one God,' plus many other countless verses in the Bible say it too, and I believe the Bible is true." Reaching a hand out, Tyler touched hers gently, seeing she was still listening. "Salvation is simple, Olivia. Believing in Jesus as your Lord and Savior and believing that God raised Him from the dead. You confess that, and you are saved. Chris-tianity is not like the religions of the world. They desire to complicate it, though I do understand why they would do that. They complicate it because we, as humans, feel like we need to earn everything we get, but we can't earn Salvation. The reality is it's a free gift from God received by faith alone. He saves us from ourselves and from Hell. Ephesians 2:8-9 says, 'For by grace you have been saved through faith, and that not of yourselves; it is the gift of God, not of works, lest anyone should boast.' God loves us, Olivia, and He has sent us a way out of our heartache and pain, not only in this life, but in eternity. John 3:16 says, 'For God so loved the world that He gave His only begotten Son, that whoever believes in Him should not perish, but have everlasting life.' "

CHAPTER 31

OLIVIA'S HEART POUNDED AS SWEAT formed on her forehead. She didn't feel well, but at the same time, she wanted to keep listening to Tyler. The way he spoke about God, about salvation, about love resonated with her heart at the moment. The only sad part for Olivia was the fact that as he communicated God's love to her, she couldn't shake the feeling of being unworthy. Not after the talk with her mom she just had on the phone, and not after hearing from her father all about how much pain she had inflicted on the family through her three-month hiatus with Champ.

Tyler was silent, seeming to be waiting for her to say something. Olivia didn't know what to say or how to respond. "I think I need to lie down. I don't feel well."

As she stood up from the kitchen table, she was light-headed and her legs gave out, but Tyler somehow got to her in time and caught her in his arms.

"You have a habit of catching me, don't you?" She smiled softly as her eyes were half-shut. He lifted her into his arms and carried her down the hallway.

He smiled. "I guess I do."

Pushing open the bedroom door, Tyler walked over to the bed and laid her down gently. He turned on the standing fan and pointed it toward her.

"Good?"

She nodded. As he left the room, Olivia felt the pounding in her chest still there. She thought of what Tyler had told her about Jesus, that God's love was far beyond any love that Tyler had shown her. She thought that was impossible, but then again, she'd thought a man like Tyler was impossible too, at one time. If there was a God out there, she knew she didn't deserve His love. She felt worthless and undeserving of merely Tyler's love. How could she ever feel like she could have God's love that surpassed it? As her mind spun around the idea of God and His love for her, her thoughts came to a standstill. Like a beckoning light, her thoughts drifted back in time.

She was at the night around the fire pit with the youth group at Tyler's house. He was speaking about God being a lamp that lit the way we should go in life. She could see the embers lifting into the star-filled night sky and smell the logs on the fire still burning. Her mind leapt again, all the way back to the car wreck two summers ago, Tyler pulling her out of the wreckage. Tyler, who gave all the credit to God. God had saved her from death that night. She realized it was the truth. And not just a physical death. She had been given a second chance to find Him. Again, her thoughts traveled. She was now driving out on the streets of Newport, looking for Alex. Farther up ahead, she saw Tyler walking down the sidewalk. It was right after he had lost Chet. Then finally, when she was lying in that bed with Champ, seeking death as her eyes rolled from the drugs hitting her system. Tyler broke through the bedroom door, saving her yet again, giving credit to God, yet again.

Olivia's thoughts came back to reality. She recalled the

talk she had with Daisy and how she'd said that God had placed people in her life. She realized God had been guiding her, calling her, and using Tyler and others to do it. Her whole body tingled as she was suddenly overwhelmed by the revelation and everything coming together perfectly.

As a new reality, a new belief set into her mind and heart, all pointing to the fact that God does exist and God does love her, waves of guilt lapped against her. The weight of her own sins she had committed toward the God she now knew existed weighed heavily on her soul. The turmoil in her heart was far more grievous than anything she had ever experienced, and she could barely breathe from the weight of the crushing guilt inside her. As the darkness clamped down on her heart, she cried out to God, hot tears running down her cheeks.

"Save me, Jesus! Forgive me! I want to know who You are, and I need You to be my Savior!"

In that very moment, as she confessed with her tongue, the weight and darkness vanished. A strange sensation of tingles washed over her whole body, and she sat up in her bed. She looked around Chet's room. Everything was the same, but she knew it was different inside her soul. There was no more weight, no more burden. She still held remorse for her actions, but the guilt and condemnation had left her. Bowing her head, she prayed to God, tears still flowing, but these tears were from the joy of being saved.

"Lord." She paused, crying and heaving as she replayed the horrible things she'd thought and said about God. "Thank You for saving a horrible person like me, Jesus." She found the name to be pleasant on her tongue. She had never liked the name before. She said it again. "*Jesus*. Oh, how sweet that name sounds *now* on my lips." She wiped her eyes and continued. "I don't know what I'm doing and I don't know where I'm going from here, but thank You so much. Please be the light that guides me in my life. I'm so sorry it took so long to see the truth of who You are. And thank You for saving me. Amen."

There was silence in the room.

Remembering her talks with her father earlier in life, she knew that the Bible was how God spoke to His people, not through voices in their heads. Promptly, she got out of bed and went down the hallway toward the living room. As she entered, both Tyler and the other man she had seen earlier were sitting on the couch. They both looked at her.

"I don't believe I got a chance to introduce myself earlier. Sorry about that. I'm Olivia." She stuck out a hand, and both of them just stared at her for a whole moment.

The man jumped off the couch a moment later and shook her hand. "I'm Jonathan, Tyler's brother. I've heard a lot about you."

"You feeling better?" Tyler inquired as he stood up, seeming to recognize something was different about her.

Olivia nodded. "A whole lot better! I just gave my heart to God!"

"That's fantastic, Olivia!" Jonathan smiled and came over and hugged her. "Welcome to the family! You're a sister in Christ now."

Tyler came over after her and Jonathan's embrace and hugged her too. As he released her, he looked into her eyes. She could feel herself melting at the love she could see in him.

"I'm glad you found Jesus."

"I feel so much better already. Thank you for not giving up on me. You still spoke to me about Jesus even though you knew I didn't want to hear it. You allowed Him to use you to get to me, and I am so grateful for that." Olivia smiled. Even though she had physical pains still present in her body, they had seemed to take a break for the moment. She lifted the

Bible off the coffee table. "I'd better go and hear what God has to say."

"You want me to join you?" She could see Tyler's eyes twinkle with hope to join her, but she declined, shaking her head.

"I think right now, no. I hope that doesn't offend you. God and I have a lot of catching up to do."

"Okay." Tyler's lips tipped a smile.

Olivia turned and headed back to Chet's room. Once in the room, she climbed onto the bed and flipped open the Bible with a deep hunger in her soul. She prayed and asked for help to understand the Book that in the past was more like hieroglyphics than the living, breathing Word of God. As she opened her eyes from prayer, she saw highlights and underlines all through the pages in the Bible. *These must be important passages to Tyler,* she thought as she thumbed through Psalms. She continued for a while and then came to Psalm 119. She wept as she read. The verses resonated with her heart in a deep and painful but pleasant way. She saw connections not only to herself, but with Tyler and her parents. The lives of those she loved were woven right there into the Scriptures. The life-giving Words of God were moving mountains in her heart and mind and giving new life to her soul.

Before I was afflicted I went astray, but now I obey your word.
Psalm 119:67

THE VERSE STOPPED her cold in her tracks as she read it. A chill ran the length of her spine and she wept at realizing that she would've never found God if it weren't for her pain, if it weren't for the car wreck which ultimately led her to tonight. And now, though the pain was still present, she had God, she had a Savior who loved her more than anyone, and she knew it. Her hand pulsed in pain right then, and she grabbed it, but this time, she prayed. *I don't want drugs to fix this, Lord. I want You to fix it, and if You won't, I'll be okay with that too.*

There was no miracle for Olivia that night, but the pain did subside a few moments later. She kept reading, letting her soul soak up the Words of truth and of life that she had missed out on for years.

A WHILE LATER, after his brother had left, Tyler came and knocked lightly on the bedroom door.

"Come in."

He walked in and his gaze fell to his Bible on her lap. "You've been reading a while, huh?"

"I have." She slipped the Bible off her lap and set it to the side and got out of the bed. Olivia was glad to see Tyler and had a newfound appreciation for the man who had been so instrumental in her finding Jesus. She hugged him. "Thank you, Tyler, for everything."

"You're welcome." They released from a long embrace and his eyes found the Bible on the bed again. "What have you been reading?"

"A lot." Olivia turned toward the bed. "I've been in here for hours just poring over the Scriptures. A lot of verses I knew from growing up with my parents, but they took on a whole new life to me now that I have Jesus." Olivia felt guilt for the wasted time and went and sat on the edge of the bed, her shoulders sagging. "I can't believe I resisted for so long. I feel kind of bad."

Tyler joined her side and put his arm around her shoulders. "Don't focus on that. Focus on the fact that you belong to Jesus now. You have a new life. You are born again. Focus on what a future with God at the center looks like for you and for Molly."

She smiled and nodded, her shoulders straightening. "I think life is going to be different now that I know I have God with me."

"Yep. He doesn't promise life will go smoothly, but knowing Your Savior intimately helps a great deal when there are bumps along the way." He stood up and headed for the door. Ace strolled in through the doorway, tail wagging. "By the way, no calls yet for Ace. I think between that and the fact that none of the neighbors knew about him, we have a good chance of his staying around."

"Awesome. He's kind of growing on me."

"Me too. Hey, Jonathan wants us to join him and his family for dinner this Friday. Do you think you might be up for it?"

"Yeah, that should be fine. I'd like to meet his family. Hey, would you mind teaching me more about being born-again and the life of Jesus? I don't know where to look, really."

Tyler smiled. "I would love to. Come out into the living room and we'll study together."

"Why can't we stay in here?"

He laughed, his gaze turning to the bed. "Less temptation in the living room."

Olivia grabbed the Bible and got up off the bed. She didn't say what went through her heart and mind in that moment, but she sure felt it inside her heart. She didn't have a desire to be with Tyler anymore, at least not right now. He was loving and kind and pure and all sorts of right, but she knew who had the first spot in her heart, and that was her Lord and Savior, Jesus Christ.

CHAPTER 32

TYLER WOKE EARLY AND BREWED a pot of coffee. After his coffee was ready, he slipped a jacket on and went outside onto the patio with his Bible and mug. He dusted the light snow off a chair and table and took a seat facing the lake. His heart's desire for Olivia to find God, to find salvation in Jesus Christ, had come into existence merely two weeks ago, and he was overwhelmed with a never-ending joy in his heart. He couldn't say thank you enough to God. Every time the Lord crossed his mind since that fateful evening in the cabin, Tyler lifted praise and admiration to God for His transforming grace. Olivia's new nature in Christ was growing each day, and Tyler saw change after change. Even at dinner with Jonathan's family, she was easily staying in the conversation around the dinner table when it pertained to God. She had come so far from who she was when he talked to her that day at the inn. All this talk of God was good, but they hadn't once touched the subject of their future together.

His phone rang in his coat pocket. He set his coffee down

on the table beside him next to his Bible. He pulled it out of his coat pocket and smiled, seeing it was Olivia.

"Did you get snow?" she asked.

A laugh escaped his lips. "Of course, I did. I'm merely a half-acre away from you."

"It's only a dusting, but it's refreshing after all that rain washed away the little snow we had. It looks like a beautiful white blanket, and with the backdrop of the lake, wow. Isn't God good?"

A smile curved on his lips. Tyler's love for Olivia had grown even deeper and wider the last couple of weeks as he watched her take baby steps in faith and leaps in trusting God. One leap in particular was when she agreed to the terms set forth by her mother and father about only having conversations with them for an unspecified amount of time. She spoke with her mother daily in the evenings, right at eight o'clock, shortly after Molly was put to sleep, and was filled in on all the happenings. Though she didn't like being subjected to her parents' control over her daughter, she told Tyler that she fully trusted God with the situation.

"You're right. God is good, Olivia. It's a gorgeous view from this vantage point. Are you looking forward to getting back into school today?"

"Yes, I'm thankful that they let me come back to finish, but I'm a little nervous to leave the cabin, if I'm totally honest about it. I don't trust myself."

"You don't have to trust yourself. Just trust God."

"You're right. Thanks again for letting me use Chet's truck and his cabin and everything. I don't think I'll ever be able to say thank you enough."

Tyler was quiet for a moment, then his gaze caught the Bible out of the corner of his eye. "I'll be praying for you today, Olivia. I'd better get my reading done before I head to work."

"Okay. And thank you. See you tonight for dinner?"

"I'll be at the cabin by six."

Hanging up with Olivia, Tyler returned the phone to his pocket. He thought about the dinner tonight and his plan to bring up the topic of their future together. He recalled the moment a few days ago where they almost kissed in the barn when they were doing some cleaning and organizing. It was when Olivia was reaching over Tyler's arms to grab hold of a box that was about to fall off a shelf. After she had pushed it back into place and she was only an inch or two away from his face, he started to lean, but she pulled back and away. Ever since that moment, he had become concerned about where the two of them were heading in their relationship, if they were heading anywhere at all. If she didn't want to pursue a relationship together, that was okay with him—or rather, it would be with time and prayer, but he needed to find out and stop feeling as if he was in a never-ending limbo.

Picking up his Bible, he opened it. Before he started to read, he prayed. *God, let me understand what I'm about to read. Help me to let You guide me in all my thoughts, actions, and words today, and especially tonight. Amen.* He read for the next hour, taking sips of his coffee every so often and letting the Word of God sink down into his bones. After he was colder than he could handle any longer, he went inside and got ready for work.

JONATHAN WAS ALREADY hard at work sketching on his new architect desk in his office that morning. After dropping off his jacket in his own office, Tyler walked across the way to Jonathan's and knocked on the door frame.

"Hey, Brother."

He set his pencil down and peered up at Tyler. "Hey. I

267

didn't even hear you come in. By the way, Rose was asking about Olivia last night and when the next time she was coming over. No mention of you, though."

Tyler laughed. "Rose knows who to gravitate to, doesn't she?"

"She sure does." Jonathan smiled and stood up from his seat and walked over to his office desk. Scooping up a folder, he brought it over to Tyler. "In the efforts of staying completely honest and transparent, I wanted to show you what I'm working on for free in the spring. If you don't want to do it for free, that's fine. I'll pay you for what I would've charged, like we discussed before."

Opening the folder, Tyler saw it was a design mock-up for a new children's museum downtown. Notes toward the bottom were jotted down. ***Noah's Ark, Nativity Scene, Interactive Exploration of the Bible.*** His heart was moved upon seeing it was going to be dedicated to teaching children the Scriptures in a fun way. Peering up at his brother, Tyler closed the folder and handed it back to him.

"I'm in."

"You sure? You seemed pretty upset back in August about my freebies before."

"I know. But if something furthers the kingdom of God and spreads the good news, I want to be a part of it at no cost."

"The other projects were related to kingdom building too. Some were just brothers and sisters in Christ in need. I have stories."

Tyler took a step closer and rested a hand on his brother's shoulder. "That may be true, but you didn't tell me those stories up front before you did it. I just felt robbed of the choice."

Jonathan nodded, and it appeared as if a light had turned on in his brain. "That makes sense. I'm sorry about that."

"It's okay. I'm sorry too. I should've listened and not been so hasty. We're good now. Chances are, if you're down for it to be free, I probably will be too. Just talk to me."

"Sounds good."

Tyler headed into his office and started making calls to current clients and potential new ones. As he worked, he thought of Olivia and wondered how she was doing back in the real world for the first time in a while. She hadn't left the cabin alone since she'd arrived two and a half weeks ago, and he knew the temptation of old sins were very present. She had confessed the night before over dinner that she had thought about Champ and the feelings of being high on more than one occasion, but she had prayed through the inner struggle. He had worries about her, but he knew God was ultimately in control, and it'd take her relying on Him alone to make it through. He had showed her in the Bible that same evening where Jesus was tempted and how He'd rested in God alone to get through those trying times.

AT LUNCH, Tyler headed down the block to Hayden's Bistro and ordered a ham and cheese sandwich. Jonathan didn't join him but instead ordered in for lunch. As Tyler sat near one of the windows in the bistro, he watched the passersby as they went up and down Main Avenue in downtown Spokane. His phone rang as he was three-quarters of the way through his sandwich, and he set it down to answer the call. It was Olivia.

"Everything is great! No offense, but it's nice to see some faces besides those of you and your family."

A chuckle escaped Tyler's lips and he shook his head. "No offense taken. You getting back into the swing of things okay?"

"Yep. I sure am! Hey, if it's okay with you, I want to raincheck on our dinner tonight. My father invited me out for a dinner to talk. I haven't spoken more than a few words with him since his blowup a couple of weeks ago on the phone. My mom made it sound like he wants to reconcile."

Worry flared in Tyler's soul as he considered the fact that she could be lying to sneak off to Champ's house. The truths of God's Word written upon his heart rose up, though, and put the fire out. *Trust God.*

"Okay. What time do you think you'll be back at the cabin?"

She was quiet for a moment, only fanning the fire of worry. When she finally did speak, she sounded edgy and annoyed. "However long it takes. I don't want to put a time on it. It's my dad, you know?"

"I understand." Tyler picked up the remainder of his sandwich and tossed it into his mouth, chewing as he did.

"Please don't be mad, Tyler."

"I'm not mad. I just wanted to talk about something tonight."

"Well, I'll stop at your house on the way to the cabin and we'll talk then. Okay?"

Her tone was confident, and his worries settled, feeling it was a signal that she was being truthful. "That will work."

AFTER TYLER GOT off work later that day, he bought dog food on the way home for Ace and went down to the cabin to feed him. Walking inside the cabin without Olivia there brought a measure of uneasiness to him. He felt like he was invading her private space. He made his way straight through the living room and to the kitchen, where the food dish and water bowl sat for Ace. He poured the food into the dish and then put the bag away in the coat closet where they kept the dog food. As he turned to leave the kitchen, he saw a scribble of something on a sticky note on the counter. He almost went to it but stopped short of it. *I can't,* he told himself and walked away. Then he leashed Ace and left.

That evening, as he waited at his house for Olivia to show, Ace stayed nestled up to his side on the couch. Tyler patted Ace's head as he stared at the clock above the fireplace mantle in the living room as it struck nine o'clock. *This is maddening,* he thought, and rising from the couch, he went into the kitchen and pulled down his box of assorted teas from the cupboard.

Snatching the bag of chamomile tea, he hoped it'd help settle him down for the night. He warmed a mug of water in the microwave and then steeped the tea in it. As he stirred the tea and sugar, his mind raced. *What if she's with Champ right now? What if she's hurt? What if she's high? What if I should've waited longer before letting her go back out into the real world?* His mind halted suddenly, and he pulled the spoon out of the cup. *Trust God.* He took his cup of tea and went and sat down at the dining room table. The light above his head illuminated the table and parts of the room, but the shadows from the darkness outside pressed in through the windows. He opened up to God in a real and raw way with his emotions. *I don't want to trust. Trusting and patience aren't easy, Lord. What's easy is to worry, to be mad, and to panic. Which I'm doing a swell job of right now!* Tyler swallowed a big gulp of his tea. The warmth traveled down his throat. He knew it didn't matter how his flesh felt in this moment of weakness. The only thing that mattered was what God had to say about it, and he knew he needed to trust Him more than anything right now.

The doorbell rang.

Praise the Lord! Tyler thought as he rose from his seat, leaving his tea at the table.

CHAPTER 33

OLIVIA WAITED FOR TYLER TO answer the door as she stood on the snow-covered steps of his porch. She was elated by the conversation that had taken place with her father and she couldn't wait to tell Tyler all about it. When he opened the door, she was confused by the worry she saw in his eyes.

"What's wrong?"

Tyler shook his head. "Nothing now. Come in."

Now? What did that mean? she wondered as she crossed the threshold into his house. As they walked through the foyer and into the living room, she noticed Ace curled up on the couch. Olivia turned to him. "Why's Ace here? You went into the cabin? And what did 'nothing now' mean?"

He held his hands up in defense. "I bought him food. He was out, and I was worried. It was your first time out of the cabin since . . ."

"Go ahead and finish it, Tyler. Since you took me away from the drugs and Champ. Since I became a Christian. You were worried I wouldn't survive out in the real world." Olivia's heart took a strong dive downward at the realization of how Tyler had been feeling. She knew the two of them couldn't work out. She just wasn't sure why, and now it was becoming clearer to her. He wouldn't be able to let go of her past. Sure, she still had some strings holding onto the past, but it was her past, not his, and he'd be stuck in it until he let go. She tossed her purse on the couch and sat down. "Wow, Tyler. So you spent all day worried about me? I guess I'm not the miserable one now."

"No, listen, I—"

"No, you listen, Tyler." She paused as he sat down on the couch beside her, and she made sure to look him in the eyes as she continued. "I love what you did for me, for Molly, for my whole family, essentially, but I think God used you for a purpose. To bring me to Him, to the Cross. I don't think it was for us to get a happily ever after. I just can't see that happening. These last two weeks of living at the cabin have been wonderful, but it hasn't been about me and you. It's been about me and God. It's God who holds the rank of first in my life, and when that happened two weeks ago, it honestly knocked you out of position."

Listening quietly, Tyler's eyes glossed over and he stood up. Walking away, he started to leave the room and Olivia got up and took a step toward him.

"Where are you going?"

"I need to grab my tea. Do you want some?"

"What? Tea? No. I want to finish our conversation. You can go get your tea." He left the room, and Olivia was left to her own thoughts and feelings for a moment. She was upset he didn't trust her, but she wasn't surprised by it in the slightest. She'd had a sneaking suspicion that something like this might happen once she was out from under his watchful eye, but she'd also prayed it wouldn't. The few moments he was out of the room gave Olivia enough time to realize that

Tyler couldn't simply forget what had happened even though she knew he had forgiven it.

He returned with his tea and sat down on the couch. "Listen, Olivia. I love you, and I want to pursue our relationship now."

"Tyler, you're a sweet guy, and I love you too."

He lit up at her words and she instantly wished to take them back as he had received them incorrectly.

"No, don't misunderstand me. I know you can't forget what has happened in the past, and it pains me that any of it ever happened."

Tyler shook his head, moving closer to her on the couch. "It's forgotten. You know I forgave you or I wouldn't ever have been able to take you in and care for you if it were untrue."

"I know. I don't doubt your forgiveness. I doubt your ability to trust me."

"Trust takes time, right?" Tyler shrugged, opening his palms. "We have to give it time, Olivia."

Olivia reached a hand out and touched the inside of his palm, lowering it. "Listen to me. I need time to love God and to seek after Him. Me and you right now?" Olivia's lips pressed together to form a thin line and she shook her head lightly. "It can't be."

He was quiet for a moment, and then he agreed with a nod. "I'll wait for you."

She tipped a sad smile from the corner of her lips. It was a sweet gesture, but she didn't want that. "No, Tyler. You don't need to do that. I don't want you to do that."

"I know, but I've waited for you my whole life, and I can wait a little longer."

Olivia hated the hope she could see in his eyes and sense in his words. She didn't want this to be painful, yet that's exactly what it had become. "I can't promise you anything at all."

"You don't need to. I'll be here when you're ready. How'd it go with your dad?" He asked, shifting the topic.

"He was forgiving and happy to discuss my newfound faith in the Lord. He also gave me this cool bookmark." Reaching over to her purse, she pulled it close and retrieved it, handing it to Tyler to inspect. "Emergency Bible Verses. Kind of a neat little thing, isn't it?"

"Wow, that is cool." He handed it back. "So it went well?"

"Yes, it went better than I could've imagined. Honestly, I was terrified about meeting with him. I wasn't sure if it was another lecture or a sentencing hearing to send me to Hell for my misdeeds of the past. But I guess he went to a men's conference a few days back, and they talked about the importance of true forgiveness and how our decisions affect our families. He didn't realize how bad he was until he heard about himself on stage from another man. Some guy talked about how he had mistreated his own daughter so badly that she'd ended up committing suicide. It really had a profound impact on him. Anyway, it was a good dinner and our relationship is on the mend now."

"Praise the Lord! That's great news, Olivia."

"It gets better! Next week, starting on Sunday at their church, they want me to start going with them and I'll be able to see Molly for a few minutes after service while we're having coffee and donuts."

"Wow!" Tyler's eyes went wide.

Olivia thought of how she and Tyler had been spending every Sunday together at Crosspoint and Wednesday nights with the youth. "I hope Daisy and Carson and even you will be okay without my being there."

"We'll get along just fine, Olivia. Truly, everybody will be thrilled to know you're back to seeing your daughter and taking the correct steps to move forward. I wouldn't worry about it for a second."

As exhaustion crept in, the pain in her hand started in again with it. Olivia took it as a cue to go home.

"I need to get to bed. I'm exhausted."

"All right." Tyler stood up with her and walked her to the door. They embraced in a long hug.

"Thank you for being understanding about the whole friendship thing between us."

"You're welcome, Olivia. I never did any of this just to make you mine. That wasn't my intention then, and it's not my intention now."

She smiled and beckoned Ace to join her. He sauntered from beside Tyler to her, then she headed out to the car. Tyler shut the door as she walked away. Her heart radiated with a mixture of feelings. On one hand, she loved the man for all that he had done and she wanted to be with him forever, but on the other hand, she knew this was what was best for her.

OVER THE DAYS THAT FOLLOWED, Olivia saw very little of Tyler. He stopped coming over for dinner and his lights were out every evening when she arrived home from school. She almost sent a text or called him on several occasions but resisted the urge, knowing that he most likely needed time to process and accept the new reality that existed for the two of them. It hurt Olivia that they weren't even on speaking terms now, but she used all her extra time and energy to pour herself into the Scriptures and her final weeks of school.

On Saturday morning, she woke to the noise of what sounded like a chainsaw outside her window. Spooked by the sound, she stood up and went to her bedroom window. She spotted Tyler sawing up a tree not more than a few feet away.

Hurrying through the cabin, she put a coat and a pair of winter boots on and headed outside.

"What are you doing? It's Saturday morning, Tyler!"

He shut off the chainsaw and stared blankly at her for a moment. "What?"

"What's going on? What are you doing?"

"I'm cutting up a tree. Isn't that kind of obvious?" Tyler smirked, clearly amused at how frazzled she looked.

She furrowed her eyebrows, putting her hands on her hips. "Don't be rude to me."

"I need more firewood for my place so I figured I'd take this tree."

"Right by my window when I get to sleep in this one day of the week?"

He laughed. "Just a coincidence. I had no idea it's your only day, and I'm sorry about it."

"Just stop it, please?"

"I'm already done, so okay."

Olivia trekked through the snow back to the front of the cabin and went in. Taking off her coat, she hung it up and returned to the warm covers on her bed. Glancing at the clock, she knew she could steal at least a couple more hours of sleep before she met up with Rachel in the city for lunch. As she drifted in and out of sleep, she could hear Tyler bring the truck around to the side of the house. Then she heard the sound of a chain jingling. She pulled a pillow over her head to block out the sound.

A couple of hours later, she woke up confused at first and then jumped out of bed and went to the window. He was gone, and she felt a twinge of dissatisfaction over that fact. It had been the first time she had seen him in days, and all she had done was yell at him for something he didn't even know about. If she wanted a civil relationship with Tyler, she hadn't done a very good job at making that apparent during the little interaction she had with him. Feeling awful as she got dressed, she decided to stop by his house on her way to town.

She gave the door a few solid knocks, but there was no answer. She peered in through the living room window and could see the television was on, then the channel changed. She knocked again, this time harder. Still no answer. Having had enough of his ignoring her, she grabbed the doorknob and walked inside.

"How dare you ignore me!" She headed through the foyer toward the living room as she continued, her heart beating wildly in her chest. "Here I am, coming over to apologize, and you can't even answer the door?"

She stopped cold in her steps and speech as she came around the corner to see Tyler on the couch, sprawled out with a bloodied gash on his forehead. Her heart trembled.

"What happened?" Her voice softened as she approached him.

"Just go, Olivia. I didn't answer because I didn't want this to happen. I don't want you worried about me. I'm fine." He looked worn out, the earlier smirk gone and, in its place, sadness.

Bending her knee, she inspected it closer and saw dirt in it. "You need it cleaned out. Where do you keep the antiseptic?"

"What?" He looked at Olivia, appearing to gauge what she was getting at.

"Hydrogen peroxide, Tyler?"

"Cupboard next to the sink. You don't have to do this."

"Hush." Leaving him, she went into the kitchen and pulled the bottle down from the cupboard. Then, she grabbed one over-sized bandage and took a paper towel from the roll on the counter. She went back to the living room. As she bent down and started to clean the wound, she asked again, "What happened?"

"I don't want to talk about it."

"What are you hiding from me?" Olivia patted his wound with the paper towel a little firmer.

"Ouch!" He clenched his jaw, then relaxed. "*Fine.* I slipped on a piece of ice and overcorrected so I wouldn't hit more ice and ended up slamming my head into a section of the tree hanging off the bed of the truck."

She smiled. "Serves you right, coming down so early in the morning and waking me up."

Laughing, he peered into her eyes, catching her gaze, and her heart flinched. He held her gaze with his, affection radiating in his look. "How'd I know you would say something like that?"

Olivia smiled again and finished cleaning his forehead, then she put the bandage on over it. As she rose up from the couch, she had a feeling come over her that made her want to stay. She knew that'd send him the wrong message, though, and she turned to leave, but he caught her arm, stopping her.

His eyes peered up at her, touching the very fabric of her soul. "What if you stayed?"

Her heart pounded, and warmth radiated from the center of her chest, covering her from head to toe. She bent a knee down and peered into his eyes. "What if I did? Then what, Tyler? You'd take care me? You and I would get married and live out here on the lake? I can't do that, and I'm sorry."

She leaned over, kissed him gently on the lips and then rose to her feet and left.

CHAPTER 34

*A*S OLIVIA WALKED INTO THE fellowship hall the next day on Sunday to join her parents for coffee and donuts, her gaze fell on her daughter, Molly. Her heart finally felt whole again, and tears flowed down her cheeks as she stared at her little girl sitting perched on her mother's hip. She had been waiting for this moment for months, but then again, it had been years in the making. She knew she could love her child in a new and full way, like never before, not because of her own strength, but because of the strength of God she now relied on. Molly was young enough that she'd never have to remember her mom before God saved her, and that brought Olivia a measure of comfort.

Coming closer, Olivia recognized the heartbreaking truth of how much Molly had grown since she'd seen her last, and it tore at Olivia's heart. It wasn't only the drugs that kept her from her daughter, but also her own decisions. She chose drugs before Champ ever jammed that needle into her arm, and worst of all, she chose to stay with him after he did. One of the biggest moments Olivia had missed was when Molly learned to crawl. Her mother had informed her almost immediately when they began speaking on the phone that Molly had crawled across the carpet to Papa. It broke her then, and it broke her now.

She fought the tears back and wiped her cheeks, then Kora turned and handed Molly to Olivia. She held Molly close to her chest, kissing her all over her face, wanting to never let go of her or that moment. As she held her baby, Molly began to cry.

Holding her out from her chest, she shook her head. "What's wrong?"

Kora touched Olivia's shoulder softly, then went to grab Molly, bringing her right into her arms.

"It's okay, Molly. It's okay."

Her mother didn't have the heart to say it, but it didn't take Olivia long to realize what had happened. Molly had forgotten her. Covering her mouth with two hands, she wept, knowing that her daughter didn't know who she was anymore. It was her worst nightmare come true. Her heart ached, and she went and sat down in a nearby metal chair for a moment.

After settling her emotions, Olivia rose and came back to Molly and her mother. This time, she didn't take Molly but instead only smoothed a hand over the back of her head and down to her back. *Little steps, like Tyler said,* she reminded herself as she tried not to make it too apparent to Molly that she was overly emotional right now. She knew her daughter didn't need overacting and dramatics, just love. Once Olivia's emotions calmed a measure more, she turned and caught the gaze of her mother.

"That was a good sermon, wasn't it?"

"It was very good." Her mother nodded. "I liked how the pastor used Genesis 1:1, 'In the beginning, God created the heavens and the earth,' to demonstrate the foundation of his sermon on God's greatness. I think sometimes we—well, I mean me, specifically, right now—get too caught up in the happenings in our life that we forget just how powerful our God truly is. You for instance. I never thought in a million years that you'd be able to find your way to Jesus. Even when you were thirteen, you were against God in every way imaginable. But here you are, decades later, and a follower of Jesus Christ. Such a powerful demonstration of God's greatness."

"I agree. It really is a demonstration of Him. I find it strange there was a time I didn't believe in God even though that was only a couple of weeks ago." Olivia's gaze fell on Molly. "I wouldn't have Molly here with me, though, if I had God back when I was younger. Bruce and I wouldn't have ever gotten together."

"But God works all things together for good for those who love Him and are called according to His purpose. He was able to bring the blessing of Molly into all of our lives, and now, we couldn't imagine life without her."

Olivia's father turned around after chatting with another man and leaned in, hugging Olivia. "Heya, kid."

"Hey, Dad."

"Oh! There's Hank. He has my weed eater. I'll be back!"

Olivia and her mother laughed as Dan made his way across the room in a flurry of steps toward an elderly gentleman.

"Your dad has come around a lot, Olivia." Kora's eyes were filled with a spark in them as she watched her husband across the room.

Olivia turned to peer over at him. "I've noticed. Must've been *some* men's conference."

"Yep. I feel like God has been teaching me a lot lately about *His* timing overruling my own timing for things."

"Yeah? How's that been going?"

Her mother laughed, then said, "Each lesson is painful!"

Olivia hung out with her parents and Molly until the

fellowship hall emptied and her parents were ready to leave and Molly was ready for her afternoon nap. Saying goodbye to Molly was the worst kind of pain her heart had felt that day. Her eyes welled up, and she shook her head, embarrassed.

"I'm sorry."

"Don't be sorry, Olive." Her dad came in close and patted her shoulder. "It's painful. We understand that. It's painful for us too. We just want what's best for Molly."

They left the fellowship hall and Olivia went and sat down at a table. She needed to calm down before she made the drive back out to Diamond Lake and to her home at the cabin. Dabbing the tears from her eyes with a napkin, she prayed. *God, it hurts my heart to not have her, and I long for Your comfort. It'd be so easy to go home and over to Tyler's house and just let him hold me, but I don't want to rely on him. I want to rely on You to hold me in this moment. Please teach my heart to rely on You alone, Lord. You alone. Amen.*

LEAVING THE CHURCH, she headed home. As she drove, she remembered she needed to pick up a few items from the grocery store so she passed her turn and went into the town of Newport. She pulled Chet's truck into the parking lot of the grocery store and noticed Alex walking out from the store to his car. She parked quickly and lay down on the bench, hoping he hadn't already spotted her. Her heart raced even though she was driving a truck and not the car that she had been in when she first met him. Praying, she asked God for help and protection. *Please, Lord, let this pass. I don't want to see him or talk to him!*

Ten minutes passed and she felt confident enough to get out and go inside. As she walked through the store and retrieved needed items from the shelves, she checked over her shoulder every few moments. Her heart ached with worry of running into him, and it almost made her decide to leave, but instead, she hurried as best she could.

Turning down the coffee aisle, she glanced over her shoulder toward the poultry. He wasn't there. Directing her gaze forward down the aisle a moment later, she was suddenly face-to-face with Alex. Her heart jumped and panic filled her to the brim. She tried to keep a straight face even though she was terrified to run into the man.

"I thought that was you." He smirked and approached her cart. She tried to push past him, but he grabbed hold of the cart's metal frame, stopping it. "Where you going? I haven't seen you in a while. You know, Champ asks about you."

Hearing Champ's name made her blood boil as the memory of his sticking her with a needle resurfaced amid other things.

"I've moved on, *Alex*. Let my cart go."

Alex moved closer, a menacing look on his face, standing only a foot away from her now. Her pulse soared and she could feel her throat close.

"What do you want, Alex?"

"Where's your boyfriend at? I need to talk to him."

"Leave him out of this. He has nothing to do with it. What do you want?"

He shook his head. "Actually, he has a lot to do with what I want. You see, Champ doesn't take too kindly to people breaking into his house and stealing away his girls and destroying his drugs and getting the cops to come over."

"I'm not his girl."

"Oh, yeah? That's not how I hear those months together went." He took another step closer as he leered, but just then, a cop appeared in the aisle and started toward the two of them.

"Officer, this man is harassing me and threatening me."

The officer shifted into cop mode and set the loaf of bread down from his hand onto the shelf, then approached quickly.

"What did you do to this poor gal, Alex?"

Alex shooed a hand at the cop who knew him by name. "Save it, Brody. Go back to picking off speeders out by the freeway. I'm just talking."

"Don't miss a good chance to shut your mouth. Beat it, *Alex.*" Officer Brody pointed down the aisle to motion for Alex to leave. Once he vanished, he stepped closer to Olivia. "You okay, ma'am?"

"No, I'm not. I'm scared. Alex is a drug addict, and his drug dealer friend is upset with me."

"I know *all* about Alex. You need an escort out of the store?"

Comfort at the thought set Olivia's nerves at ease, but she knew he could be waiting for her outside. "And home, if you don't mind?"

"Not a problem."

As she walked with Officer Brody out through the light snow coming down outside in the parking lot, Olivia thought of Tyler and his head wound. If he had to fight in the condition he was in right now, he'd most likely lose, possibly even lose his life, especially if Alex showed up with a gun. The thought sent tremors of worry through her heart. She couldn't let that happen after all the good he had done for her. Stopping, she turned to the officer.

"Sir?"

"Yes?"

"I'm not going home. I'm going to drive into Spokane to my parents' house. I can't lead Alex to where my boyfriend is located. I fear he might harm him."

"All right. I'll follow you for as long as I can and make sure you don't have a tail on you. Then, you go on to

Spokane. I'm sure if you return tomorrow, things will be okay."

"Thank you."

She climbed into her truck and started for Spokane, Brody's police car behind her. On her way, she called Tyler and filled him in on what was happening.

"Let him come. I'll kill him and chump Champ."

Olivia knew he was only speaking that way from a place of fear. She knew him enough to know he wasn't the type to kill or harm or he would've the day he rescued her from Champ's house.

"Tyler, this is serious, and I know you know you can't kill a person. That's why you didn't shoot Champ when you had the chance."

He let out a heavy sigh. "You're right. Well, keep me updated and stay safe. I want to know when you're safe and locked in for the night, please."

"Okay. Your head feeling okay?"

"Yes, it's doing fine."

Hanging up with Tyler, she called her parents' house. Her mom answered with a lace of confusion around her tone. Olivia told her what was happening.

"But you can't stay here. *Molly.*"

Olivia started to cry, and Kora began to also. Her father got on the phone.

"You'll stay at the DoubleTree Hotel. It's even close to a police station if you have trouble. I just called and booked you a room a moment ago. Let me try to figure out what we're going to do."

Hanging up the phone with her parents, she wiped her eyes. She knew what her heart wanted. It wanted to be with her daughter, not locked up in some hotel room away from everyone she loved and cared about. That wasn't a solution.

· · ·

HER FATHER CALLED LATER that evening after she had checked into the hotel. It was about six o'clock.

"Your mother and I came up with a plan we think is suitable."

Her heart leaped at the idea of leaving the hotel and going to their house to stay with them and Molly. Everything would be perfect and she'd be back to seeing her daughter day in and day out, just like how it had been previously.

"We are willing to pay first and last months' rent, plus deposit and a month of rent until you get a dental office job. That way, you have your own apartment and you're ready for when the time comes to take Molly back into your care."

She shook her head as she thought of Tyler and the cabin. "What? Why? I can keep using the cabin."

"Olive, it's not fair to live in Tyler's cabin and not have any romantic interest in him the way he does in you. We love him for what he's done for us and you, so it's especially not right to use him in that way. Plus, now you have this *Alex* guy looking around for you, and the cabin is pretty secluded. It's only a matter of time before he spots you going to the cabin and things become worse, especially for Tyler. He is such a good man and doesn't deserve a drug dealer after him. At an apartment in Spokane, Alex and Champ wouldn't be able to find you as easily as if you stayed out there."

"I guess you have some good points." Olivia was conflicted with the idea of not being out at Diamond Lake any longer. Her heart had grown accustomed to the beauty of each morning and the silence every night. If she was being honest, her heart had also grown accustomed to seeing Tyler. But her father was correct. It wasn't feasible to keep on living at the cabin. She thought for a moment that maybe Tyler could finally move on if she wasn't hanging around the property. Her heart warmed to the idea of leaving.

"I will do it, but under one condition."

"Name it."

"I pay you back every dime after I get this certificate and get on with a dental office."

"Fine by me." Her dad was about to end the call, but she stopped him.

"Hey, Dad?"

"Yeah, Olive?"

"I love you. Thank you for caring about my daughter so much that you are willing to put her above what you know I so desperately want. I know it can't be easy for you to do that."

"You're welcome, and I love you too. Have a good night."

With a resolution in mind for not only the issue with Alex, but with her life moving forward, her stress decreased and she found herself hungry. On the way down to the dining room of the hotel for a bite to eat, she called Tyler to let him know she was safe and to tell him the plans for her life.

CHAPTER 35

TYLER KEPT SILENT AS HE listened to Olivia explain with great excitement her plan to move away. It cut deeper than the gash on his head, but he wouldn't dare tell her that. His bringing her to the cabin was to save her life first and foremost, not to keep her for his own. The thread of hope his heart grasped onto of the two of them being together slipped fully from his fingertips in that very moment. Suddenly, his house felt a whole lot bigger and emptier. As she came to the end of her speech of explanation and thankfulness, she waited on the other end of the line for him to speak.

"Tyler? You still there?"

He raked a hand through his hair and relaxed his head against the couch cushion. "Yes, I'm still here. That's great about the apartment and your parents. Sounds like things are working out for you, Olivia. I'm glad." His heartbroken state didn't keep him from truly being happy for her. His love would always want the best for her in life.

"I know. It's so amazing that they're coming around."

A smile curved his lips. "It's from the seeds of trust and respect you've sown with them. We reap what we sow."

"It's true." She breathed a relieved sigh, then her tone shifted. "You need to protect yourself from Alex out there. Keep both eyes open. Champ has him, and maybe others, looking for you."

"Oh, dang, I usually only keep one eye open, not both."

She laughed, and it sent a welcomed chill down the length of his spine. He loved her laugh. He loved her voice. He loved *everything* about her. She was going away now.

"You're going to be okay, right?" she asked, but he could tell in her tone that she already knew the answer was no. He couldn't be selfish about this no matter how much he wanted to be. He couldn't tell her how he really felt inside again. He'd already done so. He wouldn't try to sway her by explaining how things have gone downhill since their talk about their lack of a future together. He wouldn't bore her with details like how his food had become bland at meals and how time without her had become like slow-dripping faucets, drip by drip, with little to no purpose for its existence.

"I'll be okay, Olivia. I have to run, though. Ace needs fed."

"Okay, give him some loving from me."

"Will do. Enjoy your meal."

Tapping *End Call* on his cell phone, he tossed it to the cushion beside him and let his head relax, staring at the vaulted ceilings in his quiet living room. He began to talk himself into the idea of her not being out at the lake with him. *Without her a few steps away, maybe the heartache will lessen with time.* Tyler didn't like that she was moving, but he knew it was what she wanted so he would have to deal with it regardless. *Your will, Lord, not mine.*

Bowing his head a short while later, Tyler prayed before heading to Crosspoint for youth group that evening at seven thirty. *Lord, I need to have my head in the game tonight at church.*

I can't let this be a distraction from Your work. Please help me, recharge me, and restore me. It's only through Your grace and mercy that I am able to be who I am. You give and You take away, and I desire a heart within me that can humbly accept it and be content no matter what. Amen.

THE LORD PROVIDED a measure of relief in Tyler's soul, but Olivia was on the outer skirts of his thoughts that evening when he showed up to Crosspoint. Upon entering the youth building in the western lawn, he was greeted by Pastor Carson.

"How you doing?"

"Good. You?" Tyler forced a smile.

"I'm all right, but how are you *really* doing, Tyler?" Carson's hand came up and rested on his shoulder, his eyes fixed on Tyler.

Out of nerves, a light laugh escaped from his lips and he shook his head. "I feel like garbage. Olivia is moving out of the cabin and into her own place."

Carson studied Tyler for a moment. "I thought that would be a good thing for her."

"It is, but I had grown accustomed to her being around all the time. I'll miss her, that's all." Even as he said it out loud, Tyler knew how selfish he sounded.

"You worried she's going to fall into temptation?"

Tyler shrugged. "I don't know if it's as much that or just the fact that I love her and want to be with her. I feel bad for being discontented about it all."

Pastor Carson shook his head. "If you love this girl, you have to let her spread her wings and fly."

"I'm familiar with the cliché, Carson. If it's meant to be, she'll come back." Tyler smiled and turned as the door opened and youth started to file in one by one. It brought a great deal of joy to Tyler's heart to see his kids showing up. He hadn't expected their smiling faces to conjure such a relaxed state within him, but they did.

Parker walked over to him and asked to speak with him alone. Tyler obliged and joined him away from the other kids near a folding table with juice and treats.

"My dad's home."

"Wow!" Tyler raised his eyebrows. "That's great news. How are things going with that?"

He shrugged. "I think well. He told my mom he was sorry a whole lot and promised never to leave again."

"You don't seem too thrilled about it. You okay, Parker?"

Parker kicked at the carpet with one shoe, obviously nervous to speak the truth in his heart. Tyler lowered himself down and placed a hand on his shoulder.

"You can talk to me."

"I know I should be happy, but he really hurt me and my mom. I don't want to see her like that again, and I can't help but be scared he's going to just leave again. How do I know he won't?"

Tyler shook his head as his heart splintered. "Buddy, don't worry about it. Just focus on Jesus and the fact that He will never leave you nor forsake you. It's only through relying on God and His power that you were able to deal with it when your dad was gone, right?"

"Yes. I read a lot of the Bible to help with my anger and sadness."

"Good, and see? God sustained you. Just keep doing that. Keep giving yourself to Jesus, Parker. You're a good kid and things are going to work out for you."

"Thanks, Mr. D." He hugged Tyler. As Parker joined the other teens who were finding seats in the metal folding chairs, Tyler stood back and surveyed the crowd of young people.

Tyler's heart was suddenly overwhelmed with guilt for how much sadness he was enduring over Olivia. The work he was doing at Crosspoint with the teens was what was important in life, not a girl who didn't want to be with him anymore. He wouldn't deny feeling hurt by what was transpiring with Olivia, but he did resolve to stop letting it consume him. He made up his mind right there in the youth group building to start putting the past away and doing what he had just told Parker to do, to give himself to Jesus.

RISING THE NEXT MORNING, he showered, got dressed, and headed to the location in Otis Orchards where a small ceremony was taking place in honor of the new Children's Museum. The morning air held a bite to it, so Tyler put on his winter gloves, then exited his car. Approaching Jonathan and Mr. Chu, the client, Tyler shook their hands as they waited for the board of directors to show, along with the media reporters.

"I was just talking to Mr. Chu, and he said he came to know Jesus in North Korea over two decades ago." Jonathan directed his words to Tyler.

"Oh, wow! I bet you have an amazing testimony."

"Yes. Bible not allowed there. They ship in food crates from other countries. My dad read Bible at night. In day, he hide Bible."

"It's so hard to imagine life without the freedoms we have in America." Tyler turned to the plot of dirt, then back to Mr. Chu. "So, this is a real project of love for you?"

"Yes. I have large love for my Savior Jesus."

Within minutes, everyone expected had shown, and the wind started to pick up speed, adding to the already painful temperature. Tyler willed the ceremony to commence, but it seemed like everything was moving slowly.

"We can't find the shovel. Has anyone seen it?" A man asked as the crowd gathered. Nobody responded to the man and he continued searching around the area in a hurried panic.

Jonathan came over to Tyler.

"So Olivia is moving out of the cabin and into a place of her own."

"That's great." Jonathan looked happy for her, which hurt Tyler a fraction, even though he didn't want to admit it.

"Yep." Tyler glanced away.

"Remember, God has a plan, Brother. He *always* does. Don't give up hope."

Tyler turned and looked Jonathan in the eyes. "Honestly, I don't see us working out anymore, and I'm okay with that, or striving to be, anyway."

"I didn't mean don't give up hope on her. You might need to do that. What I meant is don't give up hope on God. There are plenty of other girls out there, Christian ones too. He will bring you a mate in His timing. You just have to wait."

Mr. Chu called Jonathan away a moment later, leaving Tyler with his own thoughts. His brother was correct in the fact that there were plenty of other women in the world, Christian ones too, but that didn't change how Tyler felt in the slightest. He loved Olivia, not those other women. He knew that even though Olivia was leaving physically, she'd be in his heart forever.

A cold gust of wind blew through the area and pressed against Tyler's already frosty cheeks, and he clenched his jaw in annoyance for the cold. Someone got in front of the gathered crowd and announced it was time for the ceremony to commence. Tyler was relieved and moved with the crowd to huddle near the mound of dirt where Mr. Chu was standing. With the shovel in hand, Mr. Chu tapped it into the cold ground and then jumped on it, shoveling up a large chunk. The crowd erupted in cheers and clapping.

ARRIVING HOME LATER THAT DAY, Tyler went inside his house and prepared a chicken salad. He sat down in the dining room and said a prayer over his food before diving in. Not long into eating, he heard a vehicle in the driveway and set his fork down to go investigate. Peering out the window in his living room, he saw Chet's truck and Olivia driving alone in it. Leaping at the chance to see her once more and offer a hand with her stuff, he put his coat on and headed out the front door. But upon stepping out onto the front porch, he saw another vehicle arriving in the driveway. It was her father, Dan, in his own car. Tyler stepped back into his house.

He shut the door and returned to his salad in the dining room after putting up his coat. Tyler's heart pounded at the reality before him. She'd be leaving for good and he'd not see her again after this, possibly forever. He fought every urge he had to go down to the cabin. He even stood up from the table several times to go but stopped himself each time. Unable to finish his food, he placed the salad bowl in the sink in the kitchen and took to the living room. He knew what he needed and dove into the Word. Tyler sat on the couch and turned straight to the book of Psalms, knowing it would soothe his soul to read of those who struggled like him.

God is our refuge and strength, an ever-present help in trouble.
Psalm 46:1

Tears in his eyes and a weariness in his heart, Tyler cried out in prayer. *You alone are my refuge and my strength, God. Oh, how I've failed to keep You in the rightful place in moments of weakness. I let my heart pull away.* He covered his moist eyes with his palms. With broken words, he uttered, "Let my heart rely on You alone, God!"

Returning to Psalm 46 a moment later, he continued reading. As Tyler continued, he pushed his heart and mind deeper into seeking God. Then, he came to Psalm 46:10 and he stopped.

Be still, and know that I am God . . .
Psalm 46:10

Stillness wasn't a part of Tyler's life in the slightest. He was always on the move, always doing something. The verse tore through layers of his being and confronted his core in a real way. He thought of the blue bird outside his window at the inn and how he had stopped to be still and listen at that time. He knew it was missing in his life then, and he knew it was still so. He stopped reading and relaxed himself on the couch. *Be still.* He controlled his breathing to short and controlled breaths and did his best to still himself fully. He was able to do it, but not for long, and not without his mind eventually tail-spinning out of control. Tyler kept trying, though. Eventually, he grabbed his cell phone and set a timer for five minutes. Not able to control his thoughts, he decided to focus on the Scripture as he was still. *'Be still, and know that I am God.'* He did this for the next thirty minutes, practicing in intervals of five minutes. By the end, he was more relaxed than he had been in a long time, and he felt a noticeable increase in peace. *Thank you, Lord.*

When he heard a vehicle outside driving by, he went over to the window and watched as Olivia and her father, with her father's packed car, drive past his house. The red glow of the taillights eventually vanished down the path and Tyler lowered his head.

"Goodbye, Olivia."

CHAPTER 36

SEVEN MONTHS FLEW BY FOR Olivia in the city. She had graduated with her certificate of dental assisting the same month she had moved into her apartment, then was able to get on with a dental office on the South Hill and had worked there ever since. A couple of months after starting that job, her parents dissolved the guardianship and returned Molly to her care as promised. Her mother still watched Molly. Olivia ended up not joining her parents' church, but instead attended a Calvary Chapel in the Spokane Valley. Her cousin Rachel had gone to rehab three months ago and had arrived back in Spokane just a couple of weeks ago. In rehab, she had mentioned on the phone that she wanted to go to church when she got back, so she finally did one Sunday. After service that Sunday, Rachel joined Olivia and Molly for lunch at *Zips*, a local fast-food joint in Spokane.

Olivia sat across from her cousin as they both ate burgers and fries. Rachel kept looking at Molly in her highchair and smiling, not saying much. Then, Olivia finally set her burger down on its wrapper and wiped her mouth with a napkin.

"Did you like Calvary Chapel?"

"Yeah, I enjoyed it. Did you know I believed in God before rehab?"

Olivia was surprised to hear it. While Rachel wasn't vocal like Olivia had been about her lack of faith, Rachel also didn't seem like one who had much faith in anything. "No idea. So, you've been a believer for a while?"

"Not like I am now, but I did pray. I asked God to kill me on many occasions. To let the next dose be the one that puts me over. I was in a *very* bad place toward the end."

"I'm so sorry, Rach. I wish I could've been there for you."

She shook her head, picking her burger back up. "No, that wouldn't have been good for you to be around. You did the right thing not coming around me. I think I was able to find my bottom that way."

"So, what's your plan now?" Olivia asked, then took a sip from the straw in her soda.

"I'm enrolled for business management at Spokane Community College and I'm living life."

"Where are you living?"

"The shelter."

Olivia furrowed her eyebrows. She didn't like the idea of her cousin being out on the streets and living in a shelter when she herself had an extra room going unused in her apartment. After saying a prayer and asking God, she felt convicted enough to know it was the right offer.

"Come live with me and Molly."

"Are you sure?"

"Yes, I am. I want to help. I'm also pleased with what you've been accomplishing in your life, and you are continuously moving forward. You can stay as long as you need."

Sliding out of the booth, she came around to Olivia and wrapped her arms around her.

"You're the best cousin and friend a girl could ask for!"

. . .

RACHEL WASTED no time in moving into the apartment. That evening, she showed up with a suitcase and a smile on Olivia's doorstep. As Olivia got ready for bed that night in the en-suite bathroom, she dabbed off her makeup with a wipe and paused as she peered at her reflection in the mirror. She thought of how thankful Rachel had been for the chance to come live with her and get a second chance at being in her life. Olivia couldn't help but think of Tyler and how he had handed her chance after chance when she didn't feel she deserved it.

Whenever he brushed across her mind, she missed him to the point it was almost painful. She'd pause whatever she was doing and let her thoughts, though painful, dwell on everything she had experienced with him. She hoped he was happy. She hoped he had moved on.

CHAPTER 37

*E*IGHT MONTHS AFTER THEY CELEBRATED the ground-breaking ceremony for the Children's Museum, *Willow Design* was invited to attend a pre-opening show of the exhibits a full two months before the official launch in August.

Tyler fell out of step with the rest of the crowd that evening and walked over toward a garbage can with his complimentary glass of champagne. He pitched the full glass in the black garbage receptacle and glanced up. There was no lighting for the exhibit before his eyes, and thus, it wasn't part of the tour that night. He came closer and saw two stuffed giraffes in the shadows. A little closer, and then his eyes fell on Noah's Ark. His heart raced as Molly and Olivia pressed against his heart and mind. He thought specifically of the mobile that hung above Molly's crib.

His heartache had lessened with time, but it still resided with him daily. He thought of the two of them often. He walked to the ark and rested a hand against the wood. Then he smoothed his hand against the soft grain. It was perfect.

For a moment, he thought of himself being in the position of Noah the day God had commanded him to build an ark. It didn't take long for Tyler to realize he knew he would question every aspect of the process and squirm the whole time. Questions came to his mind instantly that he knew would be present if he were Noah. *What if an animal gets sick and dies? How would they reproduce? How can I build this big boat by myself? Why's it going to flood when it's never rained? What is rain anyway?* And the questions kept going.

Pinching the bridge of his nose, he thought of Olivia's sea-blue eyes. He missed her so much it hurt, and all he wanted was for her to come back to him. If only she would come back. As his desires and thoughts of her spun out of control, he grabbed hold of them and prayed. *Lord, Your will, not mine.*

A pat of a hand on his back startled him in the dimly lit exhibit. He turned and saw it was Jonathan. He had his warm smile and black bowtie on.

"What are you doing, Tyler? You're going to miss all the exhibits that are ready to view."

"Just hanging out." Smirking, Tyler shrugged a shoulder and tried to push his thoughts away, but his brother was quick to notice something was off.

"You've got her on your mind, don't you?"

"Is it that obvious?"

Jonathan frowned. "Let's go catch up with the group, Bro. There's a 'remove the thorn in Paul's side' game in the next room and a pretty girl who wants to meet you."

Tyler laughed. "That sounds bizarre."

"I know, but she insisted she wants to meet you."

They both laughed as they went to catch up with the others.

CHAPTER 38

ONE DAY IN AUGUST WHILE on her lunch break at the dental office, Olivia was reading the Spokesman Review newspaper while she ate her tuna fish and pickles she had brought from home in a Tupperware container. She finished reading a story about a new free water feature in a park opening next week on the fourteenth and then turned the page, not meaning to stop on the Art section. Her heart leapt into her throat as her eyes fell on a picture of Tyler standing with his brother Jonathan and an Oriental man. She began to read the article and discovered they were involved in helping with the design of a brand-new Christian Children's museum that was opening. Her heart raced more and more as she combed the article for any mentions of Tyler, but there were none other than the mention of his name beneath the picture in the caption.

She set the newspaper down with trembling fingers on the table in the break room and tried to process her emotions. She thought of him occasionally, but she had thought it was remnants of the past, nothing serious. They were just pleasant memories that floated up from time to time, nothing to make her want to reach out to him. That is, until now when she saw his face. Picking up the newspaper again, she read over the article more and figured out the opening date for the museum. It was today. As soon as she read it, she started thinking of who could watch Molly, but then it dawned on her that it was a children's museum. This worked to her advantage as she wouldn't have to tell anyone what she was up to by going. She could simply be taking Molly to the museum. If Tyler had moved on and was dating someone, she could easily pass off her reason for being there on her kid, pretending to not even know Tyler was a part of it. The plan was bulletproof in her mind. As her deception tactics became apparent to her, she questioned herself. *Why do you want to see him? You chose to leave him. You broke his heart.* She confronted herself blatantly in thought. Without hesitation, her thoughts answered back clearly. *I miss him.*

Olivia returned to work and thought more of Tyler the rest of her day. She felt in her heart that now was a perfect time in her life to pursue a relationship with him, which made her wonder if it was too late. Her thoughts began to toy with her emotions and worried her. *A man that gorgeous, generous, God-fearing, and perfect doesn't stay on the market forever, Olivia. You missed your chance with him.* She had caused a lot of pain in Tyler's life, and she doubted that he still held the affection he once had for her.

AFTER WORK, she went to her parents' house to pick up Molly. She resolved not to go to the museum, knowing in her heart that he had to have moved on and she didn't want to see that. As her mother filled her in on the happenings with Molly over the day, she paused and touched Olivia's arm.

"Hey, your dad said there is a new Christian children's

museum that opened today in Otis Orchards. His friends just told him about it. You should take Molly."

Olivia's heart jolted. "Yeah?"

"Yes! She would love it. They have a Noah's Ark exhibit that is *amazing* from what your father's friend said who took his family this morning. All the exhibits are Christian themed and there is a ton of history from the Bible. I think you might enjoy it also!"

She took it as a sign from God that she needed to go. There was too much push toward that direction to ignore it any longer.

"Okay. We'll go right now."

PUSHING Molly in the stroller through the parking lot at the museum, the hot August heat was zapping Olivia of the remaining energy she had after working all day. By the time she arrived at the ticket booth to get inside, she was ready to leave. Then, Tyler's face flashed through her thoughts and gave her a burst of energy. She had to see him. She bought the tickets at the booth.

"Thanks. Do you sell water, by chance?"

"Yes, inside, we do."

Olivia took the tickets and headed in through the double doors with the stroller. As she came inside, the swirling fans above her head pushed cool air down over top of her and Molly, refreshing her and chilling her body temperature instantly. Spotting a food court to the left, she pushed the stroller toward it. With each step she took, Olivia glanced around the museum looking for the one face she wanted to see. Tyler. But he wasn't anywhere to be found.

After getting a cup of water, she and Molly went through the exhibits and stopped at each one, interacting and learning. On Noah's Ark, Molly ran through the ark and up to the top with glee-filled sounds. Olivia inspected the stuffed animals inside and it reminded her of the mobile that hung above Molly's head when she was an infant. She smiled.

Joining Molly up on the topside of the ark, the two of them peered over the edge, Olivia holding Molly tightly out of fear she might fall. The people below in the long-stretched lobby looked small from so high up, and Olivia again searched for his face, though the chances of recognizing him from so far away were slim. As they exited the Ark exhibit, she started to wonder why she thought he'd be at the museum all day. Of course, he might've been there when they opened the doors, but not all day. Tyler was a busy guy. When they were leaving the museum, Olivia left with a sense of defeat. She hadn't seen Tyler like she had hoped, and the longing to see him only grew larger.

THAT EVENING, after dinner, at about eight o'clock, Rachel came home from school. As she walked in, she shut the door and tossed her purse on the couch.

"I'm beat." She plopped down on a cushion and let her head fall back against the couch cushions. "This adult stuff is such a drag at times."

Olivia grimaced. "You okay?"

She sat up on the couch and nodded. "Yes, sorry. I didn't mean to worry you. I just get tired all the time and I'm not fully used to it."

"I don't think anyone *ever* gets used to it." Laughing, Olivia walked over to the toy box and bent down, grabbing Molly's toys and tossing them into the box.

"Molly asleep already?"

"Yep. She only took a short nap today."

"It's amazing that kids can sleep when it's still daylight."

"It's eight though. It's getting late." Rising to her feet, Olivia came over to the couch and sat down.

Rachel turned to her on the couch and stared at her. "What's up? You seem . . . off today."

"I saw Tyler today."

She gasped. "Shut your mouth!"

Grabbing the newspaper she had bought from the gas station on the way home, she handed it to Rachel. "Well, I saw a picture. He and his brother designed a Christian kids' museum."

"Wow." She pored over the picture and article for a moment. "How'd he seem?"

The teapot on the stove whistled. Olivia stood and went into the kitchen. "That's why I'm kind of bummed out. We went to the museum and he wasn't there, so I didn't get a chance to actually see him."

As Olivia poured her cup of tea in the kitchen, Rachel came into the kitchen. "Well, did you really want to see him?"

Olivia's heart pounded. She couldn't hide the truth. "Yes, I did. I didn't know it until I saw his picture in the paper, but I really want to see him. I miss him so much, Rach. He was a part of my life when it was really scary, but he still stuck around and loved me. He loved me more than himself, I felt like, and he's the reason I believe and have the life I do now. It was because of God, most importantly, but God used Tyler, and I can't help but be thankful for that. I still have feelings for him."

Rachel grabbed her hand and stopped her from putting sugar in her tea.

"You have to go to him, Olivia."

"What? To his house? No way. I would look crazy. Casually running into him is way different from purposely going to his house, Rach!"

She shook her head. "Listen, yes, to his house. Go now."

"What if he's seeing someone? What if he's mad at me?" Doubt crept into her head. A part of her still felt that he deserved someone better.

"You can't let what-ifs dictate your life. You've learned that, and I've learned that. Now go see him!"

"Molly's asleep."

"Exactly!" Rachel shook her head with a laugh and dragged Olivia by the wrist into the living room. Grabbing her car keys from the coffee table, she planted them in Olivia's hand. "Go. I have Molly for you. It's the least I can do, girl."

HER HEART DIDN'T STOP POUNDING on her way out to Diamond Lake. Each mile she came closer to Tyler, she could feel every part of her being light up with a deep passion she had lost track of in her heart over the last nine months. These emotions had been but scattered fragments, and now they were all coming together inside her at once. She prayed and questioned whether this was really God's will. She had no way of knowing for sure, but she knew that picture in the newspaper didn't have to be there. She also knew her mother didn't need to mention the museum. God's will or not, it was happening. They were going to see each other. She turned off the road and onto Tyler's property.

She walked up to his front door and knocked three times and took a step back as she waited. Glancing over, she saw a wooden swing hanging at the corner of the porch. She thought, *wow, that looks really nice.* It only took a minute before she recalled their conversation the first time he had brought her out to the property. She had made mention of that exact location and swing. Her heart smiled, wondering if he remembered it, wondering if he thought of her as much as she did of him.

She waited a few minutes longer.

There was no answer.

He wasn't home. *This is all a mistake,* she thought to herself on the way back to her car in the driveway as disappointment crowded into her thoughts. He wasn't home. Obviously, this was a sign from God that they were not meant to be. Her pounding heart was settling as she walked. Then she heard Ace barking down the dirt road toward the cabin and around the bend of trees. All the excitement and heart-pounding adrenaline flowed through her veins once again, and she forgot to get in the car. Instead, she started to run.

Sprinting down the road, dirt flew up behind her as tears and an indescribable joy bloomed in her heart. Coming around the pine trees and the bend in the dirt road, she came to the cabin. It was different though. Now, it had a large garden with a white picket fence enclosing it, the garden bigger than even her old one in Colville.

Olivia was breathless as she slowly approached the cabin and garden. Upon arriving at the garden, she unlatched the gate and went inside. Tingles washed over her entire being as she beheld every plant. Tomatoes, peas, sunflowers, and plenty more filled the garden, even overflowing the small walkway. Her heart was overwhelmed in the moment and she walked with tear-filled eyes, inspecting every plant, touching every leaf. She stopped at the tomatoes and bent a knee, plucking one in her hand. It was large and a vibrant red. She bit into it, and instantly, she thought of her dream from long ago. It was just as juicy as the one in her dream. Olivia smiled and stood up. Tyler had created the garden he said he would, the one from her dreams. She knew in her heart right in that moment that he still loved her.

CHAPTER 39

FINALLY MAKING HIS WAY DOWN the burned rafters in the barn, Tyler went over to the workbench and wiped his hands and face with an old dirty rag. There was an electrical fire last month in the barn, and it had burned a large area to a crisp black. Luckily, it had been contained in the rafters and the upper loft, so Chet's belongings Tyler was still holding onto were left undamaged. Finally clean of the soot, Tyler headed to the barn doors to go find out whose car Ace went running after a few minutes ago. He figured it was Jonathan stopping in for a visit.

Tyler had been balancing not only work, but projects around his property at Diamond Lake, cultivating his appreciation for the little things in life. First, it started out small, a broken fence, a bird feeder out back on the porch, and then it grew into other things like building a dock on the lake behind his house and letting the church use the cabin for weekend retreats. Each new project taught Tyler something new and grew his appreciation for all that God had to offer in his life.

Exiting the barn, he saw Olivia standing in the garden

and he stopped his steps. He couldn't believe what his eyes were seeing. He didn't think he'd ever see her again. Though he had grown over the months to be okay with that fact, his heart still beat hard in his chest knowing she was right in front of him.

The garden, he thought. Indeed, Tyler had built the garden she wanted, but what started as a labor of love had become so much more in the process. When Tyler started to care and tend to the garden's needs, he learned not only about himself but also about his Creator. The careful pruning he had to do in the garden taught him God's attention to detail in our lives and how the Lord often has to prune the dead areas that exist in our lives. When Tyler pulled the weeds, he was reminded of God's constant digging in our lives to bring out only the best in us. And finally, as he sowed the seeds and harvested the bounty, he learned of how the Word of God works in each heart. It's the Lord's watering that brings the harvest, not our own efforts. He had learned so much by the act of gardening, and he was eternally thankful for the experience.

After a moment of watching the beautiful woman he still loved with all his heart strolling through the garden, he approached her. His heart beat faster with each step he took toward the garden, toward her. He could feel his yearnings and passion for Olivia ignite within him, an old flame easily forgotten in the day-to-day, but just as strong as if she'd only left yesterday. Tyler came the last few steps to the garden, and she turned around.

They stood in silence for a moment, each of them staring into the other's eyes.

He felt love when he peered into her sea-blue eyes. He'd spent months dreaming of those eyes and longed daily to look into them again, never imagining he'd ever get the chance. He prayed. *Thank you, God.*

Finally, she took a step toward him and closer to the white picket fence. As she raised her hands to both sides and tears welled in her eyes, she said, "You made me a garden!"

Though Olivia had hurt him multiple times before, he couldn't help but be swept away in the moment and not hold any of it against her. He told her the truth that was ever-present in his heart. "I told you I would make you a garden, and that's what I did."

She smiled and came through the gate, closing it behind her with a gentle touch. She took a step toward him and he toward her. Then she stared into his eyes, caressing the soot-ridden five o'clock shadow on his cheeks.

"Tyler, you never moved on."

"No, I didn't. I couldn't. I would've spent the rest of my life alone. I know you were it for me, Olivia, and I know no one could fill the void you left in my heart except you. I have spent so much time wondering how you are doing. Tell me, are you still in pain?"

She smiled warmly at him as she kept her eyes fixed on his. "My pain still comes and goes, but I've learned to live with it and pray through it. What I haven't learned to live with is life without you in it, Tyler. I thought I had, but then I saw your face in the newspaper and it jostled a part of me that never moved on. I love you more now, Tyler, than I ever loved you before."

Tyler's heart radiated a warmth that he hadn't known before. It covered his entire body with a sense of security and trust that this time, she was back in his life for good. He pulled his face away from her touch and glanced toward the lake.

Olivia took a step closer to him and his heart pounded. She placed her hand on his chest and then laid her head against his shoulder. He loved her touch. He loved the smell of her hair and her being so close to him once again. It had been so long that he could barely remember how it all felt. But here she was, back again, and this time, for good. He loved every moment that was happening and cherished it in his heart. He lifted his arm and placed it around her, holding her close.

"I love you, my Olivia. I learned to live without you, but I always hoped a day like this would eventually come. Now that it's here, everything makes sense. God didn't cause every heartache along this path we've been on, but He did use them to bring us to this very moment."

Tyler turned to Olivia and peered into her eyes. He could no longer see any hurt and sadness and the sense of being lost. Instead, he saw only love. God had healed her soul and brought her heart to the exact spot it needed to be in order to fully be Tyler's. He brought a hand up and brushed her cheek gently as he leaned in and kissed her deeply.

The End.

Continue reading "A Reason To Love" series... Book 3, "A Reason To Forgive"

BOOK PREVIEWS

LOVE'S RETURN PREVIEW

Prologue

THE FIRST TIME I LAID eyes on Kirk was back in our senior year of High School while I was walking the track with Chloe. He was beneath the bleachers lip-locked with Vicky Haggar from the cheerleading squad. This wouldn't have been an issue outside of the fact that he was dating my best-friend, Chloe. Not exactly a best first impression.

Two years later when I was twenty, I decided to relocate from Albany, New York, to Spokane, Washington. Kirk had found out about the big journey across country through mutual friends and approached me about road tripping together. I quickly rejected him. When he offered to pay for all the gas, I couldn't help but give in. With over 2,000 miles to reach Spokane and a strong desire not to rely on my parents anymore, I knew his gas money would help me in the long run. I was on my way to Spokane to stake a claim in my independence from my parents and to work at a software company as a receptionist. Kirk had been into hockey and hoped for a chance at the big leagues by trying out for the Spokane Chiefs.

Through the long journey across the country, somewhere between Buffalo and Cleveland, I suspect, Kirk and I became friends. During our time together on the road, we laughed about Mrs. Bovey, our ninth-grade English teacher who hated children far too much to be teaching them in a school. We also shared our hopes and desires for the future.

When we finally arrived in Spokane five days after we left our hometown, I not only had a handful of memories from our road trip but a longing for something more for *us*. The trip had given me a chance to see past the façade he had put on in high school and see the real Kirk. At one stop along the way, at a gas station out in the middle of nowhere, he opened my car door for me. Then another time, he grabbed me my favorite candy bar without my even having to ask. When I became tired of driving, he'd willingly take over even if he was tired. Beyond those sweet gestures, I learned of a man who held a lot of regret over his checkered past. He had high hopes to start afresh and make a new life for himself in Spokane. Beneath all the muscles, I found a man with a big heart.

I couldn't give into my desire to see him again, though, or to possibly have a relationship. He was, after all, Chloe's ex-boyfriend. I dropped him off at the bus stop where his friend was picking him up and said goodbye for what I thought was forever.

Chapter 1-Jessica

FIVE YEARS AND TWO JOBS later, I was on my way to work when I stopped in at a favorite local coffee shop of mine downtown, Milo's, for an extra boost of caffeine. I had already been running late for work as it was, sleeping through all three of my alarms. There was a reason to the madness. It was all due to my friend Isabella, who had kept me up half the night on the phone. She was like me, single and living on the hopes of someday being swept away by a gallant gentleman who would show us the love we needed. We talked last night about how miserable she was being single in a world full of married men, the only single ones being creeps. I understood the pain of loneliness, but only to a certain degree. My singleness was part of who I was. It had almost become a friend. Sure, I wanted someone to love and hold, but I had to trust the fact that God was in control and knew my heart. Plus, I had my work, which filled much of my time.

Standing in the coffee shop near the counter, I waited for my order. I had on my new white pea coat I had just picked up the other day at the mall. When I saw it hanging on the rack on my way through Macy's, I instantly fell in love with it. It went perfectly with my red bucket hat, which I was also wearing. Scrolling through emails on my phone as I waited for my coffee, I felt the pressure of the day catching up with me. Already several new messages. Two from Micah, my boss, one from the graphics department on a design mock-up, and a reply from a pastor I had interviewed a couple of months back. Working at a startup magazine was anything but easy, but I loved every second of it. Not only was I a writer and reporter, but my boss, Micah's, go-to person for whatever he needed. Sometimes, it meant donuts and coffee on my way into work, and sometimes, it meant writing ten articles in five days and spot-checking the print run at two o'clock in the morning, four hours before it went to print. It was hard work, but it carried purpose and I thrived on purpose.

"Kirk," the barista said behind the counter, setting a cup down.

It took a moment for the name to register in my mind,

but when it did, my heart leapt as I lifted my eyes to find the face that went with the name. I didn't think about him often, but when he did brush across my thoughts, it was always with fondness for the time we'd shared together on the car trip five years ago. Over the years, the man had stayed with me in the depths of my soul, along with regret. Regret over the fact I hadn't pursued him the day I dropped him off at the bus stop. We hadn't spent time together before our car ride, but the time we did share over the trip was something special and close to my heart still to this day.

Surveying the coffee shop, I held onto the short string of hope I had carried all these years. It was like a loose thread from a piece of clothing that I knew if I pulled, it would unravel the whole thing. I refused to part with it. There was no certainty that Kirk still lived in Spokane, but it didn't stop me from holding onto the possibility. My friend Chloe, back in Albany, hadn't spoken his name in years, understandably, and I'd never found his name on the Spokane Chiefs' roster (I checked every season), but still . . . I refused to part with the string.

"Thanks," a man said, his voice rugged, worn.

Did you enjoy this sample? Pick it up on Amazon today!

ONE THURSDAY MORNING PREVIEW

Prologue

To love and be loved—it was all I ever wanted. Nobody could ever convince me John was a bad man. He made me feel loved when I did not know what love was. I was his and he was mine. It was perfect . . . or at least, I thought it was.

I cannot pinpoint why everything changed in our lives, but it did—and for the worst. My protector, my savior, and my whole world came crashing down like a heavy spring downpour. The first time he struck me, I remember thinking it was just an accident. He had been drinking earlier in the day with his friends and came stumbling home late that night. The lights were low throughout the house because I had already gone to bed. I remember hearing the car pull up outside in the driveway. Leaping to my feet, I came rushing downstairs and through the kitchen to greet him. He swung, which I thought at the time was because I startled him, and the back side of his hand caught my cheek.

I should have known it wasn't an accident.

The second time was no accident at all, and I knew it. After a heavy night of drinking the night his father died, he came to the study where I was reading. Like a hunter looking for his prey, he came up behind me to the couch. Grabbing the back of my head and digging his fingers into my hair, he kinked my neck over the couch and asked me why I hadn't been faithful to him. I had no idea what he was talking about, so out of sheer fear, I began to cry. John took that as a sign of guilt and backhanded me across the face. It was hard enough to leave a bruise the following day. I stayed with him anyway. I'd put a little extra makeup on around my eyes or anywhere else when marks were left. I didn't stay because I was stupid, but because I loved him. I kept telling myself that our love could get us through this. The night of his father's death, I blamed his outburst on the loss of his father. It was too much for him to handle, and he was just letting out steam. I swore to love him through the good times and the bad. This was just one of the bad times.

Each time he'd hit me, I'd come up with a reason or excuse for the behavior. There was always a reason, at least in my mind, as to why John hit me. Then one time, after a really bad injury, I sought help from my mother before she passed away. The closest thing to a saint on earth, she dealt with my father's abuse for decades before he died. She was a devout Christian, but a warped idea of love plagued my mother her entire life. She told me, 'What therefore God hath joined together, let not man put asunder.' That one piece of advice she gave me months before passing made me suffer through a marriage with John for another five trying years.

Each day with John as a husband was a day full of prayer. I would pray for him not to drink, and sometimes, he didn't —those were the days I felt God had listened to my pleas. On the days he came home drunk and swinging, I felt alone, like God had left me to die by my husband's hands. Fear was a cornerstone of our relationship, in my eyes, and I hated it. As the years piled onto one another, I began to deal with two entirely different people when it came to John. There was the John who would give me everything I need in life and bring flowers home on the days he was sober, and then there was John, the drunk, who would bring insults and injury instead of flowers.

I knew something needed to desperately change in my life, but I didn't have the courage. Then one day, it all changed when two little pink lines told me to run and never look back.

Chapter 1

Fingers glided against the skin of my arm as I lay on my side looking into John's big, gorgeous brown eyes. It was morning, so I knew he was sober, and for a moment, I thought maybe, just maybe I could tell him about the baby growing inside me. Flashes of a shared excitement between us blinked through my mind. He'd love having a baby around the house. *He really would.* Behind those eyes, I saw the man I fell in love with years ago down in Town Square in New York City. Those eyes were the same ones that brought me into a world of love and security I had never known before. Moments like that made it hard to hate him. Peering over at his hand that was tracing the side of my body, I saw the cut on his knuckles from where he had smashed the coffee table a few nights ago. My heart retracted the notion of telling him about the baby. I knew John would be dangerous for a child.

Chills shivered up my spine as his fingers traced from my arm to the curve of my back. *Could I be strong enough to live without him?* I wondered as the fears sank back down into me. Even if he was a bit mean, he had a way of charming me like no other man I had ever met in my life. He knew how to touch gently, look deeply and make love passionately. It was only when he drank that his demons came out.

"Want me to make you some breakfast?" I asked, slipping out of his touch and from the bed to my feet. His touches were enjoyable, but I wanted to get used to not having them. My mind often jumped back and forth between leaving, not leaving, and something vaguely in between. It was hard.

John smiled up at me from the bed with what made me feel like love in his eyes. I suddenly began to feel bad about the plan to leave, but I knew he couldn't be trusted with a child. *Keep it together.*

"Sure, babe. That'd be great." He brought his muscular arms from out of the covers and put them behind his head. My eyes traced his biceps and face. Wavy brown hair and a jawline that was defined made him breathtakingly gorgeous. Flashes of last night's passion bombarded my mind. He didn't drink, and that meant one thing—we made love. It started in the main living room just off the foyer. I was enjoying my evening cup of tea while the fireplace was lit when suddenly, John came home early. I was worried at first, but when he leaned over the couch and pulled back my blonde hair, he planted a tender kiss on my neck. I knew right in that moment that it was going to be a good night. Hoisting me up from the couch with those arms and pressing me against the wall near the fireplace, John's passion fell from his lips and onto the skin of my neck as I wrapped my arms around him.

The heat between John and me was undeniable, and it made the thoughts of leaving him that much harder. It was during those moments of pure passion that I could still see the bits of the John I once knew—the part of John that didn't scare me and had the ability to make me feel safe, and the part of him that I never wanted to lose.

"All right," I replied with a smile as I broke away from my thoughts. Leaving down the hallway, I pushed last night out of my mind and focused on the tasks ahead.

Retrieving the carton of eggs from the fridge in the kitchen, I shut the door and was startled when John was standing on the other side. Jumping, I let out a squeak. "John!"

He tilted his head and slipped closer to me. With nothing on but his boxer briefs, he backed me against the counter and let his hand slide the corner of my shirt up my side. He leaned closer to me. I felt the warmth of his breath on my skin as my back arched against the counter top. He licked his lips instinctively to moisten them and then gently let them find their way to my neck. "Serenah . . ." he said in a smooth, seductive voice.

"Let me make you breakfast," I said as I set the carton down on the counter behind me and turned my neck into him to stop the kissing.

His eyebrows rose as he pulled away from my body and released. His eyes met mine. There it was—the change. *"Fine."*

"What?" I replied as I turned and pulled down a frying pan that hung above the island counter.

"Nothing. Nothing. I have to go shower." He left down the hallway without a word, but I could sense tension in his tone.

Waiting for the shower to turn on after he walked into the bathroom and slammed the door, I began to cook his eggs. When a few minutes had passed and I hadn't heard the water start running, I lifted my eyes and looked down the hallway.

There he was.

John stood at the end of hallway, watching me. Standing in the shifting shadows of the long hallway, he was more than creepy. He often did that type of thing, but it came later in the marriage, not early on and only at home. I never knew how long he was standing there before I caught him, but he'd always break away after being seen. He had a sick obsession of studying me like I was some sort of weird science project of his.

I didn't like it all, but it was part of who he had become. *Not much longer,* I reminded myself.

I smiled down the hallway at him, and he returned to the bathroom to finally take his shower. As I heard the water come on, I finished the eggs and set the frying pan off the burner. Dumping the eggs onto a plate, I set the pan in the sink and headed to the piano in the main living room. Pulling the bench out from under the piano, I got down on my hands and knees and lifted the flap of carpet that was squared off. Removing the plank of wood that concealed my secret area, I retrieved the metal box and opened it.

Freedom.

Ever since he hit me that second time, a part of me knew we'd never have the forever marriage I pictured, so in case I was right, I began saving money here and there. I had been able to save just over ten thousand dollars. A fibbed high-priced manicure here, a few non-existent shopping trips with friends there. It added up, and John had not the foggiest clue, since he was too much of an egomaniac to pay attention to anything that didn't directly affect him. Sure, it was his money, but money wasn't really 'a thing' to us. We were beyond that. My eyes looked at the money in the stash and then over at the bus ticket to Seattle dated for four days from now. I could hardly believe it. I was really going to finally leave him after all this time. Amongst the cash and bus ticket, there was a cheap pay-as-you go cellphone and a fake ID. I had to check that box at least once a day ever since I found out about my pregnancy to make sure he hadn't found it. I was scared to leave, but whenever I felt that way, I rubbed my pregnant thirteen-week belly, and I knew I had to do what was best for *us*. Putting the box back into the floor, I was straightening out the carpet when suddenly, John's breathing settled into my ears behind me.

"What are you doing?" he asked, towel draped around his waist behind me. *I should have just waited until he left for work . . . What were you thinking, Serenah?* My thoughts scolded me.

Slamming my head into the bottom of the piano, I grabbed my head and backed out as I let out a groan. "There was a crumb on the carpet."

"What? Underneath the piano?" he asked.

Anxiety rose within me like a storm at sea. Using the bench for leverage, I placed a hand on it and began to get up. When I didn't respond to his question quick enough, he shoved my arm that was propped on the piano bench, causing me to smash my eye into the corner of the bench. Pain radiated through my skull as I cupped my eye and began to cry.

"Oh, please. That barely hurt you."

I didn't respond. Falling the rest of the way to the floor, I cupped my eye and hoped he'd just leave. Letting out a heavy sigh, he got down, still in his towel, and put his hand on my shoulder. "I'm sorry, honey."

Jerking my shoulder away from him, I replied, "Go away!"

He stood up and left.

John hurt me sober? Rising to my feet, I headed into the half-bathroom across the living room and looked into the mirror. My eye was blood red—he had popped a blood vessel. Tears welled in my eyes as my eyebrows furrowed in disgust.

Four days wasn't soon enough to leave—I was leaving today.

Did you enjoy this free sample? Find it on Amazon

Cole has fought hundreds of fires in his lifetime, but he had never tasted fear until he came to fighting a fire in his own home. *Amongst The Flames* is a Christian firefighter fiction that tackles real-life situations and problems that exist in Christian marriages today. It brings with it passion, love and spiritual depth that will leave you feeling inspired. This Inspirational Christian romance novel is one book that you'll want to read over and over again.

ALSO BY T.K. CHAPIN

A Reason To Love Series

A Reason To Live

A Reason To Believe

A Reason To Forgive

Journey Of Love Series

Journey Of Grace

Journey Of Hope

Journey Of Faith

Protected By Love Series

Love's Return (Book 1)

Love's Promise (Book 2)

Love's Protection (Book 3)

Diamond Lake Series

One Thursday Morning (Book 1)

One Friday Afternoon (Book 2)

One Saturday Evening (Book 3)

One Sunday Drive (Book 4)

One Monday Prayer (Book 5)

One Tuesday Lunch (Book 6)

One Wednesday Dinner (Book 7)

Embers & Ashes Series

Amongst the Flames (Book 1)

Out of the Ashes (Book 2)

Up in Smoke (Book 3)

After the Fire (Book 4)

Love's Enduring Promise Series

The Perfect Cast (Book 1)

Finding Love (Book 2)

Claire's Hope (Book 3)

Dylan's Faith (Book 4)

Stand Alones

Love Interrupted

Love Again

A Chance at Love

The Broken Road

If Only

Because Of You

The Lies We Believe

In His Love

When It Rains

Gracefully Broken

ACKNOWLEDGMENTS

First and foremost, I want to thank God. God's salvation through the death, burial and resurrection of Jesus Christ gives us all the ability to have a personal relationship with the Creator of the Universe.

I also want to thank my wife. She's my muse and my inspiration. A wonderful wife, an amazing mother and the best person I have ever met. She's great and has always stood by me with every decision I have made along life's way.

I'd like to thank my editors and early readers for helping me along the way. I also want to thank all of my friends and extended family for the support. It's a true blessing to have every person I know in my life.

ABOUT THE AUTHOR

T.K. CHAPIN writes Christian Romance books designed to inspire and tug on your heart strings. He believes that telling stories of faith, love and family help build the faith of Christians and help non-believers see how God can work in the life of believers. He gives all credit for his writing and storytelling ability to God. The majority of the novels take place in and around Spokane, Washington, his hometown. Chapin makes his home in Idaho and has the pleasure of raising his daughter and two sons with his beautiful wife Crystal.

facebook.com/officialtkchapin

twitter.com/tkchapin

instagram.com/tkchapin

.

Made in the USA
Coppell, TX
27 March 2021